DEATH

BEYOND THE LIMIT

B.M. ALLSOPP

DEATH
BEYOND THE LIMIT

FIJI ISLANDS MYSTERIES 3

Coconut Press

First published in Australia in 2020
by Coconut Press
Copyright © B.M. Allsopp 2020
www.bmallsopp.com
Contact the author by email at bernadette@bmallsopp.com
Print book ISBN 978-0-6488911-0-9
E-book ISBN 978-0-6488911-1-6

A catalogue record for this work is available from the National Library of Australia

BONUS – DELETED SCENES

Would you like to know what went into the recycling bin?

I ended up cutting several chapters from the final draft. However, I do rather like these scenes so I've clipped them together in a bonus booklet for you. Get the link when you've read the book.

EXCLUSIVE TO *FIJI FAN CLUB* MEMBERS

One of the things I've learned about my readers is that they are just as fascinated by the lovely islands of Fiji as I am. If you enjoy this book, I invite you to join my *Fiji Fan Club*. I'll welcome you with something new to read that you won't find in any book store. I'll tell you more after you've finished this mystery.

THE PRINCIPAL ISLANDS OF FIJI

AUTHOR'S NOTE: The village of Tanoa is fictitious, as are Paradise and Delanarua islands. Other places on this map are real, but nearly 300 exquisite small islands are omitted.

1

Fireti Kaba hated returning home empty-handed. Whenever his boat chugged to the village landing stage, eager children came running. Their faces fell when they saw a box with hardly enough fish to feed his own family, let alone share or sell. A few snapper, a parrotfish and two coral trout—nice but not enough. He decided to motor further out and troll around the FAD. The bigger boats had been and gone before dawn. Fish would return now all was quiet. He would use a lot more diesel, but if he was lucky a school of tuna would swim beneath his boat.

He made the right decision. He and his cousin Osi hauled in four of the six lines. They tossed two skipjack tuna, a yellowfin and a large wahoo onto the deck. Their scales gleamed in the dull grey light. Wordlessly, the two men killed the fish with hammers and knives. Another line jerked and ran out fast. The two men worked the line together, pulling it in then easing it out to avoid it breaking as the fish made a bid for freedom. The water erupted and they glimpsed the dorsal fin in the seething foam. Fireti and Osi hung on to the line, as determined as the shark. Eventually, they landed the beautiful tiger shark, killing it immediately before it could injure them or jump back into the sea. When that job was done, Fireti got going, setting his course for the outer reef passage. Exhausted, he thanked God for his good fortune.

'Fireti, come now! Look at this!' Osi shouted from the deck where he was gutting the fish and packing them in boxes.

Fireti tied off the wheel and hurried astern. Osi squatted over the tiger shark's slit abdomen, his gaze riveted on its open stomach. Staring up at him were the sightless eyes of a human head. The stench made him gag, although he ought to be used to it.

'*Oi lei*! I thought it was a monster, but it's a man!' Osi spoke at last.

The head, marbled blue and purple, nestled among unidentifiable bits and pieces and brown-green juices. It was slick as if it had shrugged off its skin like a sea snake. Maybe the skin had been unable to contain its bloated contents. The swollen tissue hid the face's features. It didn't look like there was a bony skull inside, although he knew there must be.

'Or a woman. How could anyone tell?' Fireti said. 'Why did God send me this?'

'What will we do, Skipper?'

Good question. Fireti didn't need this. He was bone-weary. He wanted to continue on home, distribute his bounty generously and send the women to market with the rest. Only then would he sleep, which was what he most wanted to do. He should say a prayer and toss the head overboard with the rest of the guts. Dear God, that's what he wanted to do.

But the head was part of a human, indeed the most important part. Where were the other parts? If there were any remaining, the family of the dead man or woman would certainly find comfort in burying the head as well.

On the other hand, he did not want to get involved with the police procedures which could bring him unpredictable trouble, possibly for weeks ahead. He didn't have the time. He had to earn a living. Above all, he needed to sleep.

'Skipper?' Osi nudged him to decide.

'Put the shark's stomach and guts into a separate fish box. There might be other bits of this poor person in there. We can't go home yet. I'll change course for Levuka.'

Osi's head jerked up. He looked at Fireti as if he was mad.

'I know it's a long way and a lot more diesel, but the closest police station is in Levuka. We'll hand our find over to the constables. That's the right thing to do.'

Osi looked disappointed. '*Io*, yes.'

When the tiger shark's organs were packed to his satisfaction, Fireti said, 'You can finish gutting and cleaning before we get to Levuka. We can try selling the catch there before we go home.'

Glad to get away from the smell, he went back to the wheel and changed course. After he handed the head over, he would avoid further involvement.

2

'Sure your stomach's up to this, mate?' Dr Matthew Young, Fiji's senior pathologist, liked to be provocative sometimes.

'I'm sure it's not. What about you?' Detective Inspector Josefa Horseman sat beside Dr Young in the single-engine plane. It was only a twenty-minute flight from Suva to the island of Ovalau, ridiculous really, but it was vital. A box of shark's guts containing a human head should not sit in temperatures above thirty degrees Celsius for very long.

'I'm glad you could charter the flight, Joe. A six-hour return trip on the police launch is too long.'

'I told the constable to find some refrigeration. I hope he's done that. Can a tiger shark really bite off a human head?' Horseman asked.

'An adult sure could. Tigers and great whites too. As an Aussie, I know a bit about sharks. In the summer they're something of a national obsession, especially for surfers and divers. The idea of being eaten alive terrifies people, including me. It doesn't keep them away from the sea though.'

'Or was the head dumped at sea and swallowed by the shark later?' Horseman asked.

'That's possible, too.'

'If the shark decapitated the body, the death could be accidental. But if the shark swallowed a disembodied head, the victim was murdered first.'

'With luck, I'll find a bullet hole. Then it'll be murder for sure,' Dr Young joked.

The plane broke through the grey clouds and landed on the grass airstrip at the edge of the sea. An officer leaned against a police Land Cruiser, watching them. Beyond the road the lush green cut off any view.

'*Bula*, hello, you're very welcome, sirs. I'm Sergeant Sauli Rogoyawa.'

They all shook hands then got in the vehicle. 'We can't get rid of this horrible package soon enough. It's stinking the place out even though it's wrapped in a tarp. Still drawing a crowd of onlookers. Some people! Shut the doors and they poke their arms through the louvres! We only have a small fridge in the station and I didn't know if we should put ice directly in the box. I didn't want to introduce contamination to the evidence.' There was pride in his voice, pride that he'd remembered his training.

'Well done, Sergeant,' Horseman said.

'Then there's that big shark. Too big for the fisherman's plastic fish boxes. So, we squeezed it into a body bag and zipped it up. I phoned PAFCO, you know the tuna factory? Closed on Sunday, of course, but the security guard's there. So I asked if we could keep the lot in a cool room there. He agreed, but there's still a smell at the station.'

'*Vinaka*, thank you. You couldn't have done better,' Horseman said.

Dr Young patted the sergeant on the shoulder from the back seat. 'Yes, you did exactly the right thing.'

The sergeant visibly relaxed. 'Been to Ovalau before, sirs?'

Horseman was eager to answer. 'I lived here as a boy. My father used to work for Burns Philp in Levuka way back. I loved it. I guess I ran wild a lot. After Dad died, my mother moved away, so it's years since I was last here. What about you, Matt?'

'Never, although I've always wanted to. I'm sorry my first visit is on such a dreadful case,' Dr Young said.

'Sirs, do you want to go straight to the remains, that's at PAFCO, or call at the station first?'

Horseman glanced at his friend. 'The plane's waiting to take Dr Young and the remains back to Suva as soon as possible. So, let's go to PAFCO first, then you take him back to the plane. I can get a cab into Levuka.'

'No need, Detective Inspector. I'll radio for our probationer to come and pick you up. He can drive if not much else! We have two vehicles at the station now.' His pride touched Horseman. This was a simpler place, without Suva's ambition and pretensions.

The Pacific Fish Company was certainly unpretentious. The corrugated iron sheds jumbled around the waterfront, where a substantial wharf projected more than a hundred metres into the sea. There were no boats tied up. A few makeshift timbers supported a caved-in corner of one shed. A couple of men were hammering buckled sheets of corrugated iron, presumably to fix a gap in a roof. What had once been a grand sign at the entrance was battered and cracked.

'How is PAFCO doing these days?' Horseman asked, trying to be diplomatic. Officers at small stations identified closely with the communities they served.

'Who knows? Last year's cyclone hit the factory bad. Management's done temporary repairs to keep the place running while they wait for the insurance pay-out to come through. They say they've got plans to upgrade then. If they shut down, Ovalau will suffer. PAFCO's the biggest employer by far on the island. Six hundred people work here, most of them ladies.'

The air around the sheds was a bit fishy, but not rotten. The burly security guard came up and shook hands.

'Josefa Horseman, I'm Pauli Leluva. So pleased to meet you again. I remember you as a boy. We never dreamed you'd play for Fiji! The whole island boasts you grew up here.'

'*Vinaka vakalevu*, sir. I remember you were in the church choir.'

The guard nodded, pleased. 'My condolences on your father's death, even though that was years ago. And your mother was a wonderful nurse. I'll never forget her help when our youngest had chickenpox... How is she?'

'She's very well indeed. She'll be pleased to hear I met you. She's retired now and spends quite a bit of time in her home village. She pays extended visits to my older sisters, too.'

'Please give her my best wishes. But you're here on duty, a particularly nasty one at that. Who could imagine a shark swallowing a head? Just like Jona, eh?'

Horseman smiled. *'Io*, Mr Leluva. I'm sure that's what the papers and the radio will say when they hear about this.'

'I won't hold you up. Sauli, you can all go straight through to the cool room. You know where it is.' They all shook hands again.

'You've made his day, mate,' Dr Young said, smiling, as they followed the sergeant to one of the smaller sheds.

They unwrapped the blue tarpaulin to reveal the shark's guts enfolding a monster of a head. Even the inured pathologist reeled away. But only for a moment. Dr Young then put on a head magnifier, took a shiny tool from his bag and probed, carefully lifting bits of entrails from around the head. He took a full minute to examine the mess.

'Now let's see this tiger shark.' Together, Horseman and the constable unzipped the body bag. The sleek grey carcase was still elegant, built for speed and attack. Its midsection, striped with darker vertical lines, gave the species its name. It looked like the shark was wearing a jacket with a subtle chalk-line. No more than two metres long, Horseman estimated. He was surprised its belly could accommodate the head. He glanced at the pathologist, questioning.

'D'you think it's not big enough, Joe?' Dr Young asked.

'I was expecting it to be bigger,' Horseman admitted, shrugging.

'Me too. No problems swallowing the head, though. Look at that jaw!'

The pathologist probed the cleaned belly, checking with the magnifying glass as he did so. 'This fisherman's a good surgeon— got a sharp knife too. I've got everything we need in the box of innards. He can have the shark back—it should fetch a good price, or feed his extended family. I'll take some shots first.'

Horseman waited, thinking about how the head got inside the shark.

Dr Young looked up. 'Now you can help me slide the innards into my plastic bag here. Sauli, can you return the box to the honest fisherman? Not everyone would've brought the head into the police, you know.'

'True, true. Fireti seems a good man. He's from the Viti Levu mainland but Levuka was the nearest police station. He caught the shark far, far out beyond the reef.'

'Where's Fireti now?' Horseman asked.

'Around the town, selling his catch. There are only two streets, so we'll find him as soon as you're ready, sir.'

They packed the plastic bag into Dr Young's large insulated cool box. '*Vinaka,* guys. Sergeant, I'm ready to go.'

'I'll be in touch the minute I get back to Suva, Matt.'

'You've got Susie on board this one, I hope?'

'Yep, all approved. Detective Sergeant Singh should be on the bus back to Suva soon. Thanks for your confidence in my abilities!' He grinned.

*

Horseman leaned against the weatherboard front wall of the two-room police station, taking the weight off his protesting right knee. The constable had gone to find Fireti Kaba. The station fronted Beach Street, the main road skirting the foreshore. Horseman strolled across the road to the grass strip behind the beach and looked back. Most of the single row of businesses had stood for a hundred years: one-story weatherboard and iron sheds in rainbow colours. Some facades boasted pediments and fancy mouldings.

But the ambitions of the foreign traders of the 1870s were puny specks on nature's melodrama. Emerald walls rose not far from Beach Street to the broken crater rim of the dormant volcano. When he lowered his gaze to street level, he spotted the constable walking towards him. A tall thin man pushing a trolley loaded with fish boxes followed him.

The constable rushed up. 'Sai Tuwai, sir. This is Fireti Kaba.'

Horseman held out his hand to the weather-beaten fisherman. 'Fireti Kaba, *vinaka* for staying here to talk to me. You must be tired and want to go home. I'm very grateful that an honest man found this head.'

Fireti's hand felt like knobbly tree bark. He kept holding Horseman's hand while he spoke, pumping it now and then. 'It's an honour to meet you, Josefa Horseman. I'm a big fan. I'm sad you're not playing anymore.'

'*Vinaka*, Fireti.' He tapped his knee. 'My leg's improving, so you never know. You might not have seen my last game yet.'

The fisherman released Horseman's hand. 'That's good news, sir.' He looked unconvinced.

'You know, God has already rewarded me for making the right decision. I just sold most of my catch to the Marist school for a good price, and now I've met the great Joe Horseman in person.'

'I'm glad to hear it. And there's more good news for you. Dr Young has examined the shark and doesn't need it now. So, you've still got a tiger shark waiting for you in the PAFCO cool store, along with your tarp and fish box.'

Fireti's leathery face furrowed in a broad smile. 'Sister Filomina at the school will probably want it. She told me it's hard to feed two hundred boarders with good food. They would be glad of it in my village, too. Sir, when can I go home?'

'I'd like to hear about your find this morning first, please. Sergeant Rogoyawa has given me your statement already. Just a few questions I'd like to ask you.' He withdrew the succinct document from his satchel.

'It's half past two, now. Have you had lunch? I could do with some,' he added.

The constable butted in, flushing with embarrassment. 'Excuse me, sir. Let's go across to the station and I'll get some takeaway. Fish and chips, roti or hamburgers?'

Horseman handed some cash to Constable Tuwai. 'Lunch is on me. The fish should be fresh, eh Fireti? It's probably yours.'

Fireti opted for a hamburger and chips.

After they had eaten and Horseman had teased out the fisherman's story, he asked, 'Could you find your way to the exact location where you hauled in the shark?'

Fireti was eager. 'Oh, easy! It was around the FAD, miles north beyond the outer reef. I've got it saved on my GPS. There's an orange buoy marker. I don't usually go so far out, with diesel so expensive, but I worked all night for half a box of fish. So I was desperate.'

'You'll have to explain what a FAD is, I'm afraid,'

Confidence straightened Fireti's back and brightened his eyes. 'Fish Aggregation Device. The Fisheries people have installed them all over. I went to a workshop and learned how to make one myself. You need some sort of raft—can be bamboo, oil drums, anything that floats and lasts a while. You anchor that out in deep water with a good current. You attach material that small fish like to hide in— old ropes or netting, even strings of palm fronds. Small fish appear out of nowhere and make it their home. And small fish bring big fish, including sharks. The FADs that Fisheries put in are bigger and better, but the home-made ones work like a charm too.'

Horseman thought, not for the first time, how his years of dedication to rugby had deprived him of so much other knowledge. 'Brilliant. Why is this FAD so far out to sea?'

'Ah, the Fisheries men are clever, sir.' He tapped his grizzled head. 'True, true. You'll only find tuna schooling in deep water, and that spot has an upwelling current which fish like. But the main reason is that the inner and outer reefs are overfished. Get it?'

Horseman nodded. 'I guess it's a way to stop you fishing the reef.'

'*Io*, so our natural coral reefs can recover. Fisheries put a FAD in the deep water so fish swarm around one point. Anyone who fishes there will get a good haul.'

'Sounds good.' Horseman wanted to get back to his questions

now, but Fireti had found his stride. It was always a mistake to interrupt a witness on a roll.

'I'm lucky, I was able to fix up an abandoned boat with a small inboard engine. I'm a mechanic too. Even so, the cost of diesel means I only go to the FAD if I'm desperate. Most village fishermen only have small open boats. It's too dangerous for them to venture so far.'

Horseman nodded.

'You know another name for FAD? Fishermen Aggregating Device!' Fireti chuckled at his joke. 'Sometimes, so many boats converge there, you can come away with little. And some are foreign too—small purse-seiners. They break the law, they think they can fish inside the twelve-mile limit and no one will notice. And they're usually right.'

Horseman was well aware only Fiji-registered vessels were permitted to fish within the territorial limit.

'Have you reported these breaches to Fisheries?'

'I've never seen it myself, but everyone knows it goes on.'

'Please, Fireti, urge your colleagues to report any foreign vessels you see breaking the law like this. Either to Fisheries or the police. It's important.'

The fisherman looked away, evasive. Horseman wondered about the substance for his complaint. His grumbles might have been based on generalised resentment of foreigners when coastal fish stocks were in decline.

Fireti nodded slowly.

'*Vinaka*, Fireti. I've learned a lot. I've got a proposal for you. You don't have to agree, but I hope you do. You'll understand my top priority is to identify the victim you found.'

Fireti bowed his head. '*Io*, sir.'

'If we can find any other body parts, they could help us greatly. I want to hire you and your boat to go back to the FAD and troll around the area again. Maybe you'll hook a body part. If you catch a shark, do what you did this morning. Go in daylight, and I'll get a diver to search the submerged FAD material. You never know, some pieces of the victim might be caught there. You'll be paid at the going rates in Suva. Are you interested?'

Fireti was silent for a few seconds. 'That's a good idea, sir. My young deckhand is a licensed diver. He can do that.'

'We'll hire him but I'll bring in a police diver as well. Too late now, but I'll arrange it all for early tomorrow. You can pick up the diver here around nine o'clock. Why don't you move your boat to the PAFCO wharf? Constable Tuwai will help you retrieve your shark. Then go home and get some sleep. I'm very grateful.'

'*Vinaka*, sir. We'll sleep on our boat to save travelling time. I should tell you, the chances of finding more of this person are small. The sea-floor is so clean because countless small creatures eat the dead very quickly. The pieces left by big fish won't last more than a few days.'

Horseman nodded. 'We've got to try, Fireti.'

'*Io*, sir. I'll go and pick up my shark now.'

3

As the rattly old bus made its leisurely way on the four-hour journey from Lautoka to Suva, Detective Sergeant Susila Singh pondered the weekend she'd just spent with her parents. She loved them dearly, but they couldn't understand that she'd moved a long way from the world of tenant farmers in the west of Viti Levu. The last thing she wanted was to scratch a living from the earth with the son of a neighbour, at the mercy of the weather, global sugar prices, Fijian landlords and perhaps worst of all, her husband. Yet if she complied with this future, her parents would be content.

When she'd given up Teachers College to join the police force, her avowed ambition to become a detective, they felt betrayed, even ashamed. Her mother lamented that no boy would marry her now.

But they did what they could, with the help of a professional matchmaker. Singh estimated this morning's elaborate morning tea was the seventh such occasion the matchmaker had organised over the last two or three years. Even though most parents would reject a police officer as a bride for their sons, the clever matchmaker dredged up yet another prospect. Singh's parents had agreed that the field could be widened to include respectable Hindus, far more numerous than Sikhs in Fiji's Indian population. Singh had flatly refused to consider marriage to an unknown man in faraway India, never mind the miracle of Skype.

She had liked a few of the previous six suitors and even dated two of them for a while. They'd liked her too. The trouble was, she would not marry a man who expected her to give up her career when the first child came along. And that meant all Indian men. But this seventh suitor, *Ma* told her, had made no such stipulation. He was a Suva lawyer so could easily afford a good nanny. Singh hadn't believed her. And why would a lawyer be interested in a detective who insisted on her way? He was 38, so why wasn't he married already?

Singh had permitted her mother to dress her in a beautiful sari, to oil and style her hair. She greeted the guests with downcast eyes and a closed-lips smile, she was quiet and gracious to her prospective parents-in-law, the model of a well brought up daughter.

Their son Brij surprised her. He was quite handsome really, slim, intelligent-looking, but maybe that was just the stylish wire-framed glasses he wore. She wondered if his mother had brushed his hair too. It certainly shone, and not with hideous smelly oil. He played a courteous role, sipping tea, praising her mother's home-made sweets. At the end of the visit, the parents left the room and chatted at the front door, leaving their children alone for a few minutes.

Brij whipped out his mobile phone. 'May I have your number, Susila?'

'Sure.' She took her own phone from her handbag and they swapped numbers.

'How about dinner on Tuesday? I'll send you a text.' With a quick handshake, a grin and a cheeky wink, he joined his parents at the door. She had to admit she liked him. Was he perhaps a bit too glossy?

As the bus headed east, she smiled to herself. It wasn't because of the sunlit sea, or the lush gardens of the resorts. She was happy to be going back to work. DI Horseman, the best boss she'd ever known, had sent her a text. A fisherman had found a human head inside a shark. Horseman was Senior Investigation Officer and Superintendent Navala had approved his request for her to join the team. If she did well on this one, Horseman might support her promotion to Detective Inspector. She couldn't wait. Her mind sifted the possibilities for identifying a head without a body.

4

Bindi Chopra, news editor of the *Fiji Times*, was waiting for Horseman at the steps of the Suva Central Police Station. Bindi was a friend from university days and she never let him forget it. A blonde Afro frizz framed her round face. It suited her.

'*Bula* Bindi, are you lying in wait for me?' They shook hands.

'You know I never lie, Joe. How've you been? How's that gorgeous girlfriend in the States?'

'Melissa's fine, thanks.'

'I hope she'll visit Fiji again soon. Perhaps for good?'

Horseman tolerated Bindi's prying about Melissa. There was no stopping Bindi anyway.

'I need to go to the States for a check-up on the knee surgery in January. I'll see her then. No further plans, Bindi.'

Bindi rolled her eyes heavenwards. 'Hopeless, Joe. You do know you're hopeless with women, don't you?'

'Why have you come to see me?' Surely she hadn't heard already.

'Can you confirm a fisherman off Levuka hooked a human head yesterday?'

He smiled. 'No, I can't confirm that rumour. I'm investigating a fishing accident in the Lomaiviti district. The police will release the facts to the press when we've discovered exactly what happened.'

'You know my standards, Joe. I never publish unfounded rumours. The upshot is that rag *The Mirror* scoops the hot stories. If

I hold off now, can you give me the heads-up on the release?'

He could trust her. 'Sure, but nothing more till then.'

*

Horseman liked to work out plans for any investigation with his core team. The brainstorming and mashing of ideas were what he enjoyed most.

'All we've got so far is a deformed head. The first challenge for us is identification. I've seen it and I can tell you this person's own mother couldn't recognise him or her. Even if we wanted to publish a photo it wouldn't help. Dr Young's already sent tissue for DNA analysis which will reveal sex and race, but even with the urgent flag flying, that will take days.'

DC Tanielo Musudroka's perpetual smile vanished. 'Do you mean we can't even tell if the victim is Fijian?'

'Not yet, Tani. No skin, no hair. Dr Young completed the post mortem yesterday afternoon. He believes the shark probably inflicted the injuries. However, he's still considering his conclusions and consulting with colleagues overseas.'

'Have you got a photo, sir? I'd like to know what we're talking about here.'

Horseman smiled at his enthusiastic apprentice. 'I had intended to spare you this, but okay, in the interests of your scientific training…'

He turned to his computer and clicked open the pathologist's shot of the bloated head with its lurid marbling.

They stared, transfixed.

'Thank God you can't smell it,' Horseman said.

Singh was the first to recover. 'Is it possible the victim was decapitated before the shark got to it?'

'Dr Young hasn't ruled it out, but he reckons it's unlikely. You and I will go up to the morgue this afternoon and he'll explain the evidence.'

Ashwin Jayaraman, specialist search officer and Scene of Crime lab manager, spoke up. 'I've never had a stretch of deep-sea as a crime scene before. Can anything more be done out there?'

Horseman shook his head. 'Time's against us, Ash. Fireti the fisherman and Dr Young both say body parts will be gobbled up within a few days. I've chartered Fireti, his boat and crewman. They'll troll their lines over the same course this morning. Luckily, the focus is a FAD. A police diver and Fireti's deckhand will search through the FAD material.'

After the shouted questions had died down, he said, 'What a lot of landlubbers you are! I've known what a FAD is since yesterday afternoon.'

He enjoyed enlightening them.

Ash looked thoughtful. 'Let's hope for the best. Are you going to repeat the exercise? If so, I'd like to poke through the FAD myself. I'm a certified diver. I'll start researching underwater crime scenes right away. I might get a different focus.'

'Great idea, Ash. I'll put it to the super. Ideally, I'd like Fireti to fish around there for another two days. But a separate trip for a team in the dive boat, with you on board, should be more thorough. Let's see this morning's results first.'

Ash nodded and started writing notes.

'Singh, I'd like you to coordinate a Missing Persons search.'

'Do you want a media appeal, too?'

'Not yet. We can hardly release that photo, can we? In a few days I hope we'll get more clues from the head—at least whether it's male or female. Why don't you check through the Mispers records, then tell me how much help you'll need? You'll also need to talk to local police about anyone missing who hasn't made it onto the central records—Lomaiviti province first, then spread out.'

'Right, I'm on it.' Like a terrier, Horseman thought. She thrives on the chase.

5

The hills behind Suva's waterfront did not permit a grid layout of streets and buildings. From Horseman's point of view, this was all to the good. The route to Colonial War Memorial Hospital was like a meandering river, overhung by spreading trees. The cab drove around the back of the hospital and dropped them at a door with the discreet sign *Deliveries*.

'You two took your time! It's three o'clock.' Dr Young sounded cheerful rather than impatient.

'Why are you so happy, Matt? Solved the case for us already?'

'No, I'm happy to see Susie, you dolt.' He held out his hand to Singh. 'It's been a while, hasn't it? Great to welcome you to my domain again, Detective Sergeant Singh.'

'Pleased to see you, Matt. Can I meet our victim?'

'Atta girl! Over here, both of you.'

The head, now disentangled from shark innards and cleaned of digestive fluid and other stomach contents, lay on a green cloth on a stainless-steel dissecting table. It was like a head sculpted from heavily veined marble. A modern sculpture where the features were lightly carved, just suggestions. The colouring was even more lurid today. Singh leaned over the head, examining it closely. Horseman was content to step back.

'Have you finished the post mortem?' Singh asked.

Dr Young looked grim. 'Yep. It's quick when you've only got a head. I've fixed the top of the skull back in place.'

'What can you tell us?' Horseman asked.

The pathologist put on gloves. 'Let's go through what I didn't find first. No brain disease or abnormality, no dental decay. The size of the head suggests a male, but I can't be sure. The teeth indicate twenty-five to forty years of age. The obvious bloating is normal a day or two after death, as is the slippage of the epidermis, together with hair. I couldn't identify any skin or hair in the stomach contents, so I conclude that the shark's digestive fluids and enzymes completely consumed it.'

Singh straightened up. Horseman gulped. They stood in silence for several seconds. Horseman guessed Singh, like him, was imagining being digested by a shark.

'Can we know how long the head was in the shark's stomach?' he asked.

'Less than a day, I'd guess. I've been swotting up, and I've sent photos to a shark attack expert in South Australia. Watch this space.'

Singh recovered her poise and leaned over the head again. 'Any chance the shark swallowed the head after it was dropped in the water? I mean, can we be sure the shark bit the head off an intact body?'

Dr Young pointed to a large monitor on a side bench. 'Come and look through the microscope.'

The large screen sprang to life and he zoomed in to the back of the mangled neck. 'See here? No?' He zoomed more, then indicated the neck edge with his cursor. 'See these punctures with serrated edges? A few centimetres below the right ear. They're the teeth marks, or rather, half of them. Obviously, the other half will be on the torso, which we don't have.'

As Dr Young's cursor danced from hole to hole, the marks seemed obvious.

'Rough, aren't they? Irregular.'

The pathologist flicked to some shots of a shark's teeth and jaws. 'The tiger shark's got serrated teeth. Technically, each tooth has a primary cusp with small cusplets kinda sprouting off it in different directions. The main point punctures and holds the prey, while the cusplets cut like a saw. There's nothing they can't eat. Tiger sharks easily tear through bone and cartilage, as you can see from this backbone.'

Horseman reeled as the vision of thrashing shark, bloody water and headless body flooded his mind. 'I'm still surprised that the shark we saw yesterday could do this. It wasn't all that big.'

'It measured 2.1 metres—a fair-sized young male. Joe, the tiger shark's the rugby player of the shark world: powerful, fast and aggressive. No offence, mate.'

Horseman hadn't thought of himself as a shark before.

Even unflappable Singh seemed appalled. 'Could the victim have been dead when the shark bit the head off?'

'You're hoping he was, Susie? I think we all are. Yeah, it's possible. But with just a head, I can't determine that, short of a hammer blow or a bullet hole, which we don't have here.'

'If we tone down the melodrama, Matt, the most likely scenario is that someone fell off a boat accidentally, probably at night. He drowned and was decapitated by the shark, we hope in that order.'

Singh looked dubious. 'The crew would have reported that, surely? Tried to get help?'

Horseman nodded, 'If it was an accident, yes. Maybe if there was a fight... The FAD's a long way out for someone to fish alone in a small boat, but it's possible. In that case he'd be missed, but relatives mightn't be too worried for a few days. If this happened on Friday or Saturday night the police may not have heard someone's missing yet.'

'I've already checked the most recent Mispers reports—there've only been a few. None fit this, sir.'

'I'll leave the detective work to you two,' Dr Young said, as he left the lab.

'Could I have a DC to start calling coastal police posts as soon as we get back?' Singh asked.

'Sure. Let's hope the only culprit here is the shark. But in the unlikely event the victim was murdered, the police won't get a report. Was our victim killed out at sea on a moment's impulse and dropped there?'

Singh's eagerness returned. 'Or was he murdered elsewhere, maybe on land, and the body taken way out there to be dumped. But why would the murderer do that? A deep burial in the bush would be easier and safer, wouldn't it?'

'Ordinarily, yes. But if the killer had a boat and could leave quickly, it makes sense to head straight to the FAD. He would know sharks cruise round there.'

'Yes! He would rely on the body being ripped apart immediately and the pieces not lasting more than a few days.'

Dr Young reappeared carrying three mugs on a shiny steel hospital tray. He served them with a flourish.

Horseman glanced up. '*Vinaka*, Matt.' He turned back to Singh. 'So, if we've got murder, we're looking for someone from the province who has access to a boat. I still think an accident's more likely and you'll get a report that fits soon.'

Singh sipped her tea. 'I always try to remember what you've taught me about wishful thinking, sir.'

'So you should,' he smiled. 'But I take your point, Singh. None of this speculation helps us identify the victim. Have you any tricks up your sleeve, Matt?'

'No tricks, Joe, but I've contacted a forensic anthropologist in New Zealand. She's got a great reputation, especially with identifying Polynesian and Melanesian remains. Whenever the condition doesn't allow identification, an anthropologist can help. They always prefer working with dry bones, but our victim is as we see. I think Professor Ferguson is the best expert to help us.'

'What about DNA?' Singh asked.

'DNA analysis will tell us the sex, and ethnicity, but we need the anthropologist too. I spoke to Dr Ferguson this morning and sent her photos and a video of our head. She's going to see what she can do at a distance and get back to me. She'll let me know if there's any point in her flying up to make a personal examination. Would you have the budget for that?'

'I'll ask the super. I'm not sure if he'll be keen. I've never heard him say a good word about anthropologists.'

Horseman glanced at his watch. 'I'll be late for Shiners training again. Thanks for the tea, Matt. See you at home. Are you coming, Singh?'

'Yes, I'd better get started on calling the Lomaiviti police posts.'

'Let's get a cab and I'll drop you at the station first.'

6

Junior Shiners training gave Horseman a lift. Now the motley crew of shoe-shine boys and ragtag street kids was an officially registered rugby team, their confidence and discipline had improved. Even though it was tricky to get to training, he could hardly preach commitment to them if he didn't show it himself.

He managed an even jog onto the field from the road. The boys clustered near the grandstand. As he got closer Musudroka pushed his way in and hauled two boys out of the huddle. He pulled them apart. A fight?

'What's up here, DC Musudroka?' Boys peeled away from the huddle.

'Sir, sir! Look, sir!'

Tevita, the boy who had begged Horseman to start the team back in January, was on the ground. He sprang up, devoted eyes on Horseman.

'Joe. Joe! Vili, he tried take my boots.'

So that was the problem. From the beginning, Tevita's ambition was for the Shiners to play in proper rugby boots. Most other junior teams played in bare feet too, but that fact didn't lessen Tevita's obsession. In a weak moment, Horseman promised he'd get them boots, but so far he'd failed to entice sponsors. Sure, Sonny Khan of Khan Sports Emporium had generously come up with smart team jerseys, but boots—not yet.

'Tevita, you've got yourself some boots? Good on you!'

The boy beamed. 'Found these in Clearance City. Ten dollars, but good, you see?'

It was a challenge to find shoes large enough for Fijian feet in the warehouses of second-hand clothes imported from Australia. Tevita's boots were well worn but his cleaning could not be faulted.

'Congratulations, Tevita. You'll kick a goal with those. But what are you fighting about?'

Vili muttered, 'Tevita's a bighead. He bought these old boots and thinks he's better than us. You say we don't need boots, sir.'

'Quite right, Vili. When you're young, going barefoot toughens up your feet, makes them flexible and strong. But Tevita really wanted boots. He worked to buy them himself and he can wear them at training if he likes. I don't see the problem.'

Mosese shouted, 'He's a show-off. Tevita can't kick for nuts, boots or no boots. He won't kick no goal!'

'Enough! Back to training. DC Musudroka, have they practised passing?'

'Not yet sir.'

Musudroka shouted. 'Boys, spread out in rows of five at the goal post. Start running as soon as I pass you a ball.'

The shambles soon resolved itself into rows spread out the width of the field.

Musudroka gave him the thumbs-up. 'Good idea for separating them, sir. I'll remember that trick.'

'You're doing fine, Tani. Off you go now. Let them take it slow on this first length. We'll get them to pick up the pace on the way back.'

Horseman strode along the sideline, observing gradual progress masked by fumbling, missed catches and poor passes. After reaching the opposite goal post, he and Musudroka demonstrated how to pass the ball more accurately before the squad set off again. The boys calmed as they kept their distance from each other and focused on their task.

As they ran back, Dr Pillai's car pulled up close to the grandstand.

The diminutive doctor waved and Horseman went to meet him. Together, they unloaded the boxes of food for the boys' dinner. Knowing that nutrition was one of the keys to fitness, Dr Pillai provided a healthy meal for every boy who turned up on time for training. No boy was ever late.

'It's chicken and dalo today, Joe. As usual, a bunch of bananas and milk afterwards. Oh, and my neighbour gave me a bag of oranges from her tree. Should be enough for each boy to take three.' Dr Pillai smiled up at Horseman.

The hungry youths cheered as the two men carried the boxes over to a trestle table set up near the grandstand. At first wary, even suspicious, the boys had warmed to the doctor who supported them with medical expertise and food without fail, twice a week.

'I hope you know how much the boys really appreciate you,' Horseman said.

Dr Pillai dismissed the heartfelt remark with a flick of his hand.

'Cupboard love,' he said. He ducked his head, embarrassed. His black crown of hair was so dense it looked impenetrable.

'There was a scuffle when I arrived at training today.' Horseman told Dr Pillai what had happened.

'Joe, if I may speak plainly, I don't think you realise how much the boys idolise you. Tevita more than anyone. He sees himself as your partner in setting up the team. The others resent his special claim on your friendship. There's nothing you can do about that. Not a thing, except treat all the boys equally and you do that, I know.'

'Do you think a word to Tevita might help? I could suggest he lay off boasting about being my friend. He was a real help in the Tanoa case so I don't want to seem unappreciative.'

'You could try. I doubt Tevita's mature enough to follow through. The others are jealous. Perhaps they think you bought the boots for him. Perhaps he told them you did. We can't know.'

Horseman was baffled. 'I'd better talk to him. But not now.'

'No, don't let the others see you singling him out.'

He didn't feel so certain about the boys' growing discipline anymore. Underneath the fragile surface, he feared they were as uncontrolled as ever. The only discipline many had known was a stick or a fist. And they were so young. He would try again to find a sponsor for rugby boots. New boots.

7

At seven o'clock in the morning, Dr Young stumbled into his kitchen, yawning. Horseman was already there, peeling fruit.

'Morning, Matt. Want some fruit?'

His landlord rubbed his hands through his sandy hair. 'Sure. I feel so bleary, don't mind me.' He slumped onto a chair.

'Get this inside you.' Horseman ladled chopped pawpaw, pineapple and guava into a bowl and set it in front of Dr Young.

'Thanks, mate. Taken Tina out yet?'

'That's why I'm up. She resorted to whining and scratching my door.'

The mongrel who was the subject of their conversation lolled in her basket, ears twitching at the mention of her name. Four months earlier, when Melissa was visiting him, she rescued an emaciated, diseased dog and her pups foraging in Ratu Sukuna Park. When Melissa returned home, she entrusted the mother to a reluctant Horseman.

Dr Young reached out his foot and rubbed Tina's black and grey stippled coat. 'Time for a nap now, Tina? Where did Joe take you today?'

'Just our usual route along the waterfront then back up the hill home. She loves hurling herself off the sea wall onto the sand when the tide's out. Today she chased crabs, sorted through piles of seaweed and ate a beche-de-mer for breakfast.'

Tina stepped out of her bed so Dr Young could rub her head and ears. 'You're a gorgeous girl now, aren't you?' he said. Tina's tail thumped.

'Toast?' Horseman asked.

The pathologist nodded. 'Please.'

Horseman filled the toaster and continued. 'I've been thinking, what exactly can we expect from this forensic anthropologist? I mean, can she produce a likeness? Like an Identikit?'

'At best, yes. I'm worried in this case that the bloating may conceal the head's bone structure too much. Let's see if she's got back to me yet.' He got up and came back with his laptop. Horseman put toast, peanut butter and marmalade on the table and sat down.

'Let's see, no, nothing yet.' The pathologist scrolled down his emails. 'Not that I expected anything so soon. As usual, we must wait.'

'I woke up in the middle of the night, thinking more about how our victim could have been killed on land. Want to run it past you.'

'Go ahead.' Dr Young spread a slice of toast with both peanut butter and marmalade.

'What if our victim was strangled or hanged, then dumped in the sea with the ligature intact? Is it possible that the corpse's swelling tightened the ligature and severed the neck right through? Then the shark simply swallowed it?'

Dr Young looked thoughtful as he munched. 'Might happen with a strong chain or zip ties. Hmm. Good idea. I'll take another look at those partial teeth marks when I get to work. But I reckon we wouldn't have those marks unless the shark was biting through the neck, tearing off a nice mouthful from something bigger. I'll take another look, though.'

'Just a thought. Eating at home tonight?'

'No, I've got a Hospital Board meeting. It'll probably be interminable, but the catering will be generous. I really wonder why they produce a huge feast for about twenty people. They must know more than half will be wasted.'

'Ah, but it won't go to waste, Matt. The staff will divide it up and take it home to their families.'

'Yeah, you're right. Well, I hope something turns up for you today.'

'I'm hoping Fireti and the divers will find more of the body.'

'I'm afraid there's not much chance of that. But then, what are the chances of catching a shark with a human head in its guts?'

'Exactly. Be in touch.'

*

Horseman shut the door to the super's office and returned to the CID room. Superintendent Navala would not approve funds to fly Dr Ferguson to Suva until he had a good idea what the result of her visit was likely to be. Fair enough. His own eagerness to race ahead on all fronts had only raised suspicion in the super.

He made two mugs of tea and found Singh. She was talking on the phone. He raised the mugs and went to his desk in the corner.

She joined him a few minutes later. This morning she had scraped her hair back into a gleaming ponytail. Her orange blouse and royal blue pants were just as immaculate. How did she do it?

'How's it going, Susie? Anything to report yet?'

'No possible matches for our head from any official Mispers reports. Musudroka and I are contacting all the police stations and posts in Lomaiviti. We'll get through those by the end of today and if we don't find our victim, we'll spread out to the adjoining provinces.'

'I'm pinning my hopes on Fireti and the divers who should be out at the scene now. Matt doesn't think they'll find anything, but...'

Singh's sea-green eyes were sympathetic. 'I know, it'd make this case—not easier, but possible.'

They sipped their tea. A new thought occurred to him. 'What if our victim was a diver?'

'I hadn't thought of that.' She looked out the louvres, frowning. 'That could fit.'

'No trace of the face mask or any bits of equipment in the shark.

But think—what if our victim is diving, has problems with his mask, removes it to adjust it and the shark zooms in.'

'Yep, or there's another problem only worse and the diver drowns. After all, that happens from time to time, both with tourists and locals. Shark bait, as they say.' The cheerful triumph in her voice made Horseman wince.

'Both Fijian and Indian fisherman dive for lobsters and eels even though they're not properly trained or equipped. Maybe we're onto a lead here.'

He gulped the rest of his tea. 'I'm going to consult our head diver. If he rates the idea, Musudroka and I will check on all the dive shops.'

'Shall I ask the local police stations about divers in their areas?' Singh asked.

'Yes, you can start that right away. Add questions about fishermen who dive on the job—they'll either know already or be able to find out easily enough. Get the constables to check where those men are if they can. The rural cops always boast how well they know their communities, unlike us in the big smoke. Let them demonstrate that now when we need them.'

'Let's hope they can. If we're going to double the time spent on each call, I'll need another constable.'

'Sure. Have you got anyone in mind?' he asked.

'Someone patient who won't need much training or supervising.'

'There's a new rugby volunteer who's got potential—Apolosi Kau. He's a good kid. I'll clear it with the super and you can try him out. He's conscientious about Shiners training. That's a good start.'

Singh made a note. Her notes were things of wonder to Horseman; so organised, hierarchical, neat. She used a colour code with underlining and highlighters known only to herself, which enabled her to retrieve information, dates and names almost instantly. One day he would ask her to share her system.

'Looking ahead a bit, if our checks and the forensics don't give us our victim's ID, the super will go public. I've made an appointment to see public relations at four o'clock to plan a media release kit. Time you got some experience with that, so I'd like you to come with me.'

Horseman wondered why she hesitated. 'Sure,' Singh replied.

The phone rang. Horseman grabbed the handset.

It was Ash bearing mixed news. Fireti had caught another tiger shark, but after sifting through its guts they couldn't find any human remains. Ash and the police diver had found some small pieces of fleshy tissue caught in the artificial reef and would bring them back to the lab. They would wind up their search tomorrow.

Singh made more notes as Horseman relayed the news. She looked up. 'D'you think this one was an accident?'

'I don't know, Singh. But we're going to find out, one way or another.'

8

Singh entered The Great Wok precisely on time at half past seven. She'd been on edge all day and not in a good way. Dread, rather than anticipation, was what she felt. She would far prefer to inspect severed heads or work the phones at the station than step inside a restaurant to eat a good Chinese meal with a matchmaker's choice bridegroom.

Brij sprang from his chair, smiling while Singh took her seat. Could he be nervous too? He didn't look it, unruffled in his string-coloured linen suit, striped tie knotted just a little below his collar. Quite the urban sophisticate. Singh was outclassed. She'd caught a cab straight from the station, first dashing into the Ladies to release her ponytail and smear lipstick on her mouth.

He offered his hand. It was strong and dry. That was something.

'I was beginning to worry you'd changed your mind, Susila. It was such a relief when I saw you talking to the receptionist.' Singh glanced at her watch.

'No, no, you're not late. It's just that I arrived absurdly early.' He gestured to his almost empty beer glass. 'What would you like to drink?'

'I'll have a beer too. Fiji Bitter, please.' She detected a flicker of surprise at her choice of drink.

He'd addressed her in Hindi. She hardly used her mother tongue in her life in Suva. English was the norm in the busy open-plan CID office where it was considered rude to speak a language not everyone understood, whether Fijian or Hindi or anything else. These days, she only spoke Hindi with her family and a few old friends.

'Do you speak Hindi at work, Brij?'

'Why, would you prefer English?'

She shrugged. 'It doesn't matter, I was just wondering.'

'Everyone in the firm is Indian, so we do speak Hindi a lot. With non-Indian clients and so on, we speak English, of course.'

'Does it seem strange that all your documents are written in English, but you discuss them in Hindi?'

He smiled. 'No, I've never thought about it. There's no policy. It's just what happens naturally, habits we've fallen into without even noticing. Oh, here comes our Peking duck.'

Singh was very hungry and demolished the delicate dish with indelicate speed. 'No time for lunch today, I'm afraid.'

Brij waved her apology aside. 'No plodding in Suva CID, then?'

'Sometimes. But we're racing more often. As each hour ticks over after someone commits a crime, the chances of catching the criminal decrease. After a week, another case will come along and we'll have less time to pursue the older one. There's a lot of pressure to crack a case in the first week. Mm, this looks good.'

A waiter served them stir-fried dishes and rice, then left them to it. Singh's mood improved as she tucked in.

'Your pace sounds the opposite of mine. No doubt you've heard the expression *the wheels of the law grind slowly.*'

Singh nodded while she chewed. Wasn't he being a bit condescending? No, she should stop being so picky and give him a chance.

Brij continued. 'I admit it's true. The law's not always to blame. Sometimes it's in a client's interest to drag out the process.'

'Yes, the wheel turns so slowly that criminals can jump off without getting hurt. That's what makes the police mad.'

Brij raised his eyebrows. 'Really, I didn't think they cared.'

'We care, of course we do. It's our purpose, to find out the truth

and to arrest criminals. If they're not punished, what's the point?'
She stopped herself before she said more. It was obvious, wasn't it?
What sort of a lawyer was he?

'Well, our practice is purely commercial law. I don't run across
criminals often.'

Singh doubted that—not that his practice was commercial, but
that he didn't encounter criminals.

'Who do you run across?' She hoped the question didn't sound
like a challenge.

Brij looked amused as he offered her the last of the prawns,
which she accepted.

'Business owners, of all kinds: farmers, traders, manufacturers,
importers. Government agencies, too. Anyone who needs help with
their contracts with other businesses. We aim to negotiate the most
favourable terms for our clients.'

The waiter cleared their dishes and brought steaming soup.

'Here's our comfort food. We can relax now.'

Brij slurped his soup in authentic Chinese style; Singh couldn't
bring herself to follow suit. He was right, the soup was relaxing.

'Are you only doing this to please your parents, Susila?' He didn't
seem to be offended, just mildly interested.

'They won't be happy until I'm married. It's not so much that
they're ashamed of me. I think they feel that they've failed as parents
unless they secure marriages for all of us. They believe they know
what's best for our lives.'

'Don't you think marriage is best?'

'When husband and wife are happy, contented—yes I do.'

'But not for you?'

'I wasn't going to say this, as we've just met. I don't know what
your parents and the matchmaker have said to you. But I don't want
to mislead anyone. My job is very important to me. I love going to
work. I've worked hard to be a detective, and for my sergeant's
promotion. I want to keep at it, go for Detective Inspector when I
can. If I was married to the right man, I could still do that. My

husband would be pleased with my success. Proud, even.'

'Wow, you're ambitious. I hadn't realised that. I understand—I'm ambitious too.'

'What's your ambition, Brij?'

'Win my cases, make a lot of money, put my feet up.'

He was making fun of her, but not unkindly. She'd let herself in for that. How could she have been so unguarded as to let him see her heart?

'Oh, I forgot! While my feet are resting on that cushion, I want to watch my wife and children chasing higher goals so that I can be proud of them.'

Singh laughed. He did have nice twinkly eyes. She glanced at her watch.

He took the hint. 'Susila, I'd like to do this again, get to know you better. Let's forget about the plans of our parents and the matchmaker. From now, let's meet because we want to.'

Singh suddenly felt shy, felt her face blushing. For heaven's sake, she was thirty-two!

'Yes, I've enjoyed myself, Brij. Thank you for dinner. I'd like to meet again.'

'You do know you have the most beautiful eyes, don't you?'

She said nothing, embarrassed. As a child, she hated her light green eyes, longing to be brown-eyed like everyone else. Now, she liked being different.

'How about Thursday night?'

'Oh, so soon? We have to go to the next meeting with the matchmaker on Saturday, don't we? I wasn't expecting to see you before then.' She hesitated. 'Well, why not? If I can. I'll call you.'

Brij wasn't put off. He still looked amused. 'Let me drive you home.'

'I live at the sergeants' barracks, but I need to go back to the station for a bit. You can drop me there if you like.'

THURSDAY 14th September

9

It was four days since Fireti Kaba released the human head from the shark's belly, and Horseman was disappointed. Still, a fresh direction might emerge from the review meeting. The super wanted to attend, which was unusual. Maybe he was disappointed, too.

Knowing the super's preferences after all these years, he ordered Musudroka and the new constable, Kau, to make tea in the big aluminium teapot using loose tea leaves. The big man had never taken to teabags, dismissing the product as expensive sweepings from the factory floor. Horseman inspected the white cups and saucers the two DCs had washed. He opened the packet of Monte Carlo cream biscuits he'd bought and arranged them on a plate.

'Where's the milk and sugar?' he asked. Musudroka hurried out. 'Bring some teaspoons, too,' he told Kau. When all was ready in the meeting room, Detective Superintendent Navala entered as if on cue. He wore a long-sleeved business shirt and a *sulu*, the wrap-around skirt worn by Fijian men. The big man, due to retire in just a few months, never departed from the standards of more formal times.

He glanced approvingly at the tea things. Musudroka dashed to pour him a cup, but the boss waved him away. '*Vinaka, vinaka,* Detective Constable, but I'll wait. I like my tea strong, I'll wait until last. Please serve yourselves and we'll begin.'

Horseman summarised. 'Let's review progress on our lines of enquiry. First, the hunt for more body parts. Fireti the fisherman finished his trolling near the FAD yesterday. His cooperation has been rewarded by good catches for himself, including another two tiger sharks, but no more human parts. Ash and the two divers have sifted through the bits and pieces clinging to the FAD material. Ash thought some might be human flesh, but they turned out to be crustacean.

'Second, forensics. As far as Dr Young can determine from the head, the individual was healthy, probably a man aged between the late twenties and forty. Petechial haemorrhaging in the eyes could indicate drowning but doesn't exclude several other causes of death.

'We can't know whether death was accidental or murder. Dr Young sent photos and X-rays to Dr Ferguson, a Kiwi forensic anthropologist. She thinks our victim is probably a Melanesian or Polynesian man. We're waiting on the DNA analysis. Dr Young is applying all the pressure he can.

'Our third line has been to cross-check our victim with reports of missing persons. DS Singh, can you brief us, please.'

Singh uncovered the whiteboard she'd prepared earlier and rolled it close to the table. 'Sir, you can see in the table columns the number of file checks and phone calls. There's a separate row for each command area. None of the official reports could match, due to the narrow window of the estimated time of death for our victim, that's last Friday or Saturday. One man we initially thought was possible has since turned up alive and well.

'Knowing that relatives may be slow to notify police of overdue fishermen, we've telephoned every police post in the area, not only for reports from the last few days. We've also asked officers to visit villages and businesses in their area and check with the village headmen whether anyone's whereabouts is unknown.'

Singh smiled a regretful smile. 'I really thought we'd turn up our victim's identity this way, but we haven't.'

The super clapped once in appreciation. 'Thorough work, DS Singh. Well done. I think it's safe to dismiss this sensible theory that our victim's a local fisherman. Do you recommend extending the telephone appeal to all police posts in the country?'

'It could certainly be done within a few days, given extra personnel, sir.'

'Do you support that extension, Detective Inspector?'

Horseman hesitated. He hadn't been presented with a crystal ball when he was promoted to inspector. But he trusted Singh to leave no stone nor stick unturned.

'I'm happy to. If you can release the resources, sir, we can start today.'

The super nodded. 'I'll arrange it.'

'Sir, as I flagged to you yesterday, I want to propose a public appeal through the media. It could start today and run simultaneously with the national police post callout.'

'Inspector, you know I don't like public media appeals. We get swamped with useless calls, the lines and the networks jam. People needing immediate police help can't get through. Thieves and burglars have a field day during every public appeal.'

'True, sir. On the other hand, they often lead to results, especially in cases of unidentified corpses.'

The super emitted a low growl which sounded noncommittal. A good start.

'Sergeant Singh and I met with Sergeant Taufa Smith in public relations. She's prepared press release mock-ups and a conference and interview schedule for your consideration. We briefed her fully and she's willing to handle radio and TV interviews. I hope you'll consider chairing the media conference. For maximum reach, Sergeant Smith suggests the conference be held at half past four so television channels can put together decent coverage for the six o'clock news.'

The super considered this for a few seconds. 'I don't think that's enough time for us to prepare. Not enough time. We can't be ruled by what's good for television. However, let me look at the material in detail. Knock on my door in an hour, Horseman. We'll discuss it then.'

'*Vinaka*, sir.'

'It was good to sit in, Inspector. Good work, everyone. Keep up your best efforts. I can't see how you could have bettered what you've done so far.'

Superintendent Navala pressed his hands on the table to push himself up and left the room.

'The super ate five biscuits, did you see?' Musudroka spoke softly.

'It doesn't hurt to know what your superior likes, Tani,' Horseman said. 'Back to calling the police posts. That's all we can do until the super decides about the public appeal. Start turning those stones over. Your next call may give us the answer.'

*

'I need coffee,' Horseman said to Singh after he told her the super's decision. 'How about Arabica?'

They dived into the midday crowds on the narrow streets. Tucked away in a quieter back lane was Arabica, an ideal refuge for a coffee fiend like himself. The business bought and processed beans grown in Fiji's highlands, packaged and sold them to American specialist outlets whose customers were seeking single-source organic coffee that their friends hadn't yet discovered. But in a tiny café in one corner of the former spice warehouse, locals could taste the best coffee in the world. He was patriotic but would never admit to prejudice.

The roasters were on. He inhaled the heavenly scent like a desperate addict, waved to the waiter and made a beeline for his usual table in the corner.

'This place always cheers me up. I feel let down, I must say,' Singh said.

'Well, you know how cautious the super is. Rightly so, there's not really enough time to prepare for a four-thirty media gig. He wants the force to appear as a well-oiled machine the public can trust.'

Singh widened her eyes in mock horror. 'I thought we *were* a well-oiled machine the public can trust!'

'Of course, but in the super's opinion we'll be even more convincing tomorrow morning. Another thing, he wants to delay the deluge of calls until the day shift is set up and trained. He's right there. Before the midday news will do,' he said.

'Good for radio and TV, I guess. The papers won't like it.'

The waiter served their standard order of a latte and espresso, together with water. They nodded their thanks.

'They'll go bananas whenever it's released. What's the bet they'll dub our victim Jona?'

'Safe bet, I'd say. Who's in front of the cameras?' she asked.

'Our super hates being on TV, so he's entrusting the gig to the Deputy Commissioner, which will be fine as long as he keeps to the script. Taufa from PR will introduce him. I'll be there so he can pass questions about operational details to me.'

Singh sipped her latte and smiled. 'I'm sure you'll draw the crowds, sir.'

Horseman was taken aback. Singh never referred to his rugby stature—one of the things he liked about her.

'You'd do a better job, Susie. Would you like to be on TV? Useful experience for you. I'll toss a couple of questions to you.'

This time, her horror was sincere. 'No, I didn't mean that.'

He downed his coffee and grinned. 'Okay, drink up, let's get operational!'

10

After Shiners training Horseman plodded up the steep road behind Albert Park with Tina. He was determined not to limp, willed his tired body into a balanced posture, concentrated on equalising his stride as Melissa had taught him. Tina looked up at him, as if curious about his odd gait. Walking the streets, like when he'd first started as a constable on the beat, helped him think.

He'd almost forgotten to give Bindi Chopra the heads-up about tomorrow's media conference as he promised. Lucky he remembered before he left the station. Bindi was happy to get the press release even just a few hours before her rivals. Just as she had earned his trust, he needed to justify her trust in him. A friend in the media could sometimes help.

As he'd failed to get either of the two big Suva sports stores to stump up the price of rugby boots for his tearaways, on Tuesday he approached Prince's, a department store with a prominent sports section. He invited the manager, Larry Tung, to this afternoon's training session. Tung was friendly and interested and both Horseman's assistant coaches and the boys rose to the occasion.

Tung said afterwards, 'I congratulate you on your work with these boys, Joe. Most laudable. You're making a difference here. I'll think about your invitation to sponsor rugby boots for the boys. I hope we can do it, but I should warn you that some on the board will oppose the idea.'

Horseman knew Tung was trying to let him down gently. 'Why?'

Tung counted on his fingers. 'One—cost. Two— the boys have Sonny Khan's logo loud and clear on their jerseys. Three—rugby boots aren't big enough for retail branding, so what's the advantage to Prince's? Four—we want to match Prince's with top-class winning teams, even at junior level.'

'Don't you agree that a reputation for helping needy kids could be an advantage to Prince's?'

'Indeed, community giving is a priority with us. Let's wait and see.' Tung smiled warmly and pumped Horseman's hand. 'It was wonderful to meet you, Joe. Many thanks for the opportunity. I'll be in touch.'

Horseman wondered how he might have succeeded with Tung. It couldn't be true that the man turned up only to shake his hand, could it?

As he cut around the corner by the Anglican cathedral, Tina whined, looking into the old fig tree that shaded an area the size of a house lot. A tall figure emerged from the shadows—a woman wearing a striking crimson *sulu* and matching tunic.

'*Bula*, oh, it's you, Joe.'

Tina tensed. Horseman reassured her with a pat. '*Bula*, Salome. How are you?'

Salome was unique among Suva's street prostitutes in wearing respectable Fijian dress to ply her trade. Not for her the sad, skimpy tops and barely-there shorts of her younger sisters. Or were they her competitors, perhaps?

'*Vinaka*, I'm well. Have you come to arrest me, officer?' She was teasing, but she couldn't keep a professional flirtatiousness from her voice.

'And how's your daughter?'

Salome gave him a sharp look, wary. 'She's very well. She'll be going to secondary school next year.'

'Already? Then it won't be too long before she finds out about her mother's occupation, will it?'

She looked disappointed in him. 'Oh, Joe, don't say it.'

'I must, Salome. You know I respect you. You're better than this. You should stop, earn your living in a legal and safe way.'

'You're one of the good guys, Joe. When I cleaned the dormitories, you were polite and respected me as if I was a fellow student. But boys like you were a minority. It was hard.' Her face softened at her memories.

He remembered a skinny maid with scared eyes, no more than fifteen or sixteen, who kept glancing over her shoulder as she mopped and scrubbed. By the time he left university, she'd disappeared. A few years later he met her in what was now her regular spot near Holy Trinity. He was in uniform, as was she, he supposed. She told him how her family had cast her out when she returned to her village with her baby daughter. That was when she took to the streets.

'But I might surprise you, Inspector Joe.' She was being provocative again.

'In a good way, I hope,' he replied.

'*Io*, I have a pal. He's a rough diamond, I know. He's away a lot. We both make good money and we're fair savers. I plan to settle down soon, start a little dressmaking business. Maybe. As you say, before my daughter gets much older.'

She always intended to give up her work but somehow she never did.

'That sounds like a wonderful plan, Salome. Please put it into action, and soon. You don't realise how you risk your life every time you come here.'

'I understand that better than you, Joe.' Her face softened again; her eyes weary beneath their kohl. 'I've got scars to prove it.'

Tina nudged his leg with her head, wanting to go home.

'*Moce*, goodnight, Salome.'

She returned his goodnight politely and turned away. As he walked off, he heard her greet another passer-by and the man's guttural reply.

11

Because the Deputy Commissioner was heading the media conference, Telecom acted with uncharacteristic speed. Half an hour before the gig was to begin, Horseman surveyed the bank of telephones dedicated to the new hotline number set up for the case. Singh had prepared a sheet of scripted prompts for the uniformed constables handling the calls. She'd spent an hour with them, rehearsing and role-playing so they'd be confident to make a basic value assessment themselves and not transfer every single call to a detective. Nothing was more predictable than that most of the expected flood from the helpful public would be useless. On the other hand, they could not afford a tip of substance to be dismissed. Some of the team would fumble or drop the ball, but he couldn't do everything any more than a captain could play a game of rugby by himself.

His own phone rang. 'Horseman.'

'*Bula*, sir. Constable Tuwai from Levuka station, sir. Something's turned up on the beach—another body part. Definitely human—a hand.'

'Have you got it?'

'*Io*. Children found it, playing with washed-up seaweed. It's tangled in some other tissue, too, but I'm not sure if that's human or not. Maybe a shark vomited it up? I put the whole lot in a bag. I have it here with me at the station, sir.'

'Lock it up and keep the key in your pocket, constable. Dr Young will leave immediately to collect it. Depending on available transport, he may not reach you for a few hours. Our press conference about the head will start in half an hour. If I can get out of that I'll come, too. If not, I'll send another detective with the SOCOs.'

'*Io*, sir.'

'Have you cordoned off the area of the beach?'

Silence for a few moments. 'No, sir. Sorry—I didn't think.'

The whole beach had probably been dug over by ghoulish kids already. 'Set up a crime scene now and post a guard. Keep tabs on the children who found it. The main thing is the physical evidence but we need their stories too. The detective who comes with Dr Young will need to speak to them.'

'*Io*, sir. Do you think the hand belongs to the head, sir?'

'Dr Young can tell us that. I'll be in touch. Good work.'

He alerted the pathologist.

'I'll drop everything and be ready to go pronto, Joe.'

'Thanks, Matt. Any word on the DNA yet?'

'Not yet, sorry. I'll call them again before I leave. Gotta keep the DNA guys onside, though.'

Twenty minutes to go. Singh's ponytail bobbed above the sound partitions Telecom had installed.

'What is it, sir?' She could tell from his face there was news.

'Can you stand in for me at the conference?'

She was shocked. 'In twenty minutes? No way, sir. I mean...'

'Sure, it's my responsibility, I just thought you might like to.'

He told her the news as fast as he could. 'You'll have to go with Matt. Fast transport is the priority. Unless there's a scheduled flight, try to get one of our speedboats. Get Ash to bring a small team. You'll have to take your own photos.'

She grinned excitedly. 'Leave it to me. Tani Musudroka will look after the hotline.'

'I'm on-air in fifteen minutes. Sorry, but I have to leave for the media centre two minutes ago. Good luck!'

'Don't worry, we'll manage. I'll keep in touch.'

12

Singh was glad the team expanded beyond the capacity of the police speedboat. so they travelled in the launch instead. Even though it was bigger and more comfortable, the launch tested her stomach. The squall they ran into a few kilometres off Ovalau nearly finished her—the sideways tossing and the up-and-down pitching. She wished she was in the TV studio instead. She wished she could die.

A few minutes on dry land and the balance of her mind and body was restored. The rain had eased to a light downpour. A sergeant in uniform was waiting on the jetty. He looked to SOCO Ash. Singh stepped forward, shook hands and introduced herself. Sergeant Rogoyawa failed to hide his surprise that she was the team's senior officer.

'*Bula*, welcome, Detective Sergeant Singh! I wasn't expecting Inspector Horseman—we saw him on TV this morning, but—'

She interrupted. 'You'll know Dr Young from last Sunday and—'

'Yes. Welcome again, Doctor.'

Introductions completed, Singh asked, 'Can you arrange transport for the search team to the scene, Sergeant? Dr Young and I will take a look at the evidence at the station.'

'All organised, sir—I mean, ma'am. The vehicle is parked back on the road. It's only a few kilometres to the beach. We can walk to the station. It's on Beach Street.' He pointed with his chin to the long strip of colourful buildings opposite what would be a pleasant waterfront park in sunshine.

Singh pulled up the hood of her raincoat, Dr Young put up his big black umbrella and they set off, trailing a retinue of children with undampened spirits. Clustered around the police station were more spectators of all ages, agog.

Dr Young greeted Constable Tuwai as a friend. He attracted liking with his easy manners and simple friendliness. It wasn't so straightforward for a woman to do this. She was always on guard to prove her authority.

'What ingenious storage have you organised this time, Sai?'

Constable Tuwai relaxed at the compliment. 'Oh, not so ingenious, Doctor. I double-bagged it, took out the bottom shelf of our fridge and it fitted in nicely without squashing. I've boiled the kettle. You could do with a cup of tea after that rough boat trip, I'm sure. I worried about you when the squall came up.'

'Let's look at the evidence first. All I need is a clear table.'

Dr Young spread a plastic sheet over the office table and the constable placed the black plastic bundle from the fridge in the centre. Dr Young and Singh put on gloves and masks and opened up the bag with care. The salty, rotting tang of sandy seaweed was not unpleasant. The dark green coils tangled lighter stalks of sea grapes, sand, bits of shell, sponge and jelly. A tiny crab crawled to the surface, breaking the tension. Dr Young's eyes smiled at her above his mask.

'I don't want to disturb the integrity of the bundle until I get it to my lab. But I'll pry gently to confirm there is a hand here. Let's hope the crab hasn't gobbled it all yet. This spongy tissue could be human lung, but I can't be certain.' He took photos.

Singh was taken aback. 'Lung?'

'Yeah, shark attacks are savage and messy. Smaller fish get in on the act too, breaking up the sharks' leftovers.' He must have detected the horror of her imaginings. 'Don't picture exactly how it happened too much. That's my job.'

He lifted the strands with his probe tool, to reveal bigger lumps of the tissue he thought could be lung. 'Ah, here we are.' He pointed at the middle of the mass.

Singh leaned closer. Through the translucent wrinkles of tissue, she made out fingers, curled as if relaxed in sleep. The pathologist handed her his magnifying glass. The little finger was uppermost, exposing the third and fourth fingers below. Seaweed and bits she couldn't name obscured the rest. But, round the base of the third finger, something protruded.

'Is that a ring, Matt?'

'Crikey! It may bloody well be a ring. Well spotted!' He took more photos. 'I'll pack this up in my cool-box now. I need to rush DNA samples through the moment we get back.'

'I'll radio the boss,' she said. 'We should be in time for the afternoon flight.'

The sergeant overheard them. 'I'll get on to the Air Fiji ground staff here. We'll fix it if the flight's not full.'

'*Vinaka*, Sergeant. Good luck! It's important.' To Singh's surprise, Sergeant Rogoyawa raced out the door. She soon realised the Air Fiji office was probably just a few doors further down Beach Street.

The constable turned on the kettle. 'You'll have time for that cup of tea now, sirs.'

By the time Dr Young packed the cool box to his satisfaction and helped with the tea things, Singh had radioed both Horseman and Ash's search team on the beach.

They all sipped the piping tea.

'The boss is excited. Wishes he'd been able to come. Calls to the hotline are flooding in, as expected. Ash needs longer to search the beach, which isn't exactly fun in this rain. If we can get on the plane, he'll take as long as he needs. The launch can wait. Five minutes, then I need to speak to the kids who found this. You said you were keeping tabs on them, Constable?'

'*Io*, I took them to their school, here in Levuka. They were hoping for the day off—you know kids. We can go there when you're ready, ma'am.'

The door opened. Sergeant Rogoyawa came in looking pleased

with himself and handed Singh an envelope. 'Your tickets, ma'am. I'll get you to the airstrip by two-thirty. That gives you an hour to talk to the children if you need that long.' He poured himself a cup of tea.

Singh took the tickets and checked them briefly. 'I'm very grateful, Sergeant. This will make a big difference. Dr Young must get the tissue samples to the DNA lab without delay.' And she was desperate to escape another boat trip.

The sergeant took a long swill of tea and smacked his lips. 'D'you think the head and the hand belong to the same person?'

'We can't know that yet. Fortunately we have our own DNA lab in Fiji now, so science will give us the answer,' Singh said.

Dr Young smiled. 'How many times have body parts turned up at your station before?'

'Never before, sir.'

'Exactly, Sauli. I can't prove it yet, but the chance of two individuals' remains turning up here within a few days is next to none.'

*

The children, three boys and a girl, were dishevelled. Understandable, after kicking around seaweed on a beach before school. They sat quietly, looking apprehensive yet interested in this new experience.

'You've done very well, children. You found something you knew was not right, and you brought it to the police. I wish all children were sensible like you. First, tell me why you were playing on the beach this morning, on a school day.'

The girl glared at the boys. 'We were ready for school. We waited at the bus stop—that's beside the beach. But the bus didn't come. Joeli here ran off to play with the seaweed on the beach. Masses and masses of it washed in overnight. Enoki and Sirilo followed him. They're all naughty boys!'

She rolled her eyes upwards in despair.

'Is she right, boys?' Singh tried hard not to smile.

The boys hung their heads and kicked the floor with their bare feet. The eldest said, '*Oi lei*! It's her fault. If she hadn't come yelling after us, we would have gone back sooner.'

'Eh! Not true! You threw armfuls of seaweed at each other, then you threw it at me!' She appealed to Singh. 'It was all over my head and neck. I tried to pull it off, like this.' She thrust both arms behind her neck and swept them forward over her face. 'And my hand felt another hand, inside all this jelly stuff. Yuck!'

Singh reflected that the masks, gloves and careful probing had hardly been necessary.

The boys giggled. 'You should have seen her, ma'am. Screaming and jumping around! We all had a look, then Ani wrapped everything up in the seaweed, with the hand in the middle.'

'I knew it was from a dead body. I said we must take it to the police.'

'I reckon a fisherman lost his hand in a winch or something. He probably just threw it in the sea.'

'You don't know. He might want it back!' The girl was shouting with self-righteous anger now.

'D'you reckon he chucked his head in the sea after that or before?' young Sirilo looked quite serious.

'Children, calm down now and let's be friendly. Ani was brave and did the right thing. I'm proud of you, Ani. What did you do next?'

Joeli put his hand up. Singh nodded her permission to speak. 'It was the bus driver's fault. We raced back when the bus came along but the driver wouldn't let us take the seaweed on the bus. He said we were lying about the hand.'

Ani cut in. 'I told the boys to tell the police, and I waited with Enoki. He's my little brother.'

'And you told the police,' smiled Singh. 'Sensible boys.'

'I didn't want to.' Joeli protested. 'The driver teased us all the way to Levuka. He stopped outside the station and made us get out and waited till we went inside. All the kids cheered and shouted. I didn't like it.'

'I hated it too. They just wanted to see us get in trouble with the police,' Sirilo added. 'But the constable believed us. He told us to go to school and he would drive the Land Cruiser to look for himself.'

Ani's eyes widened. 'It seemed like hours. I couldn't believe it when the Land Cruiser came along and stopped. Constable Sauli was kind. He drove us all the way to school. He explained to the headmistress why we were late.'

'The police are generally kind and helpful, especially with children. I've got the picture now. I'm grateful to all of you. We must find out who this hand belongs to.'

'He must be dead. He'd bleed to death, wouldn't he? Unless he was in a hospital with doctors. But hospitals don't throw bits of bodies into the sea, do they?' Singh hoped not. But anything was possible.

'*Vinaka vakalevu*, you can go back to class now. You have been good citizens today. I'll ask the Commissioner of Police to send you a letter thanking you for your service to the public.'

13

Dr Young teased out the wrinkled pink-grey tissue. He took it in his gloved fingers and stretched it, then pressed on the surface. A little fluid oozed out. Singh detected a faint crackling.

The pathologist pointed at the tissue. 'See, isn't this amazing? Definitely lung tissue and I'll bet it's human, even though I need cellular analysis to say so in my post mortem report.'

They'd got to the pathology lab twenty minutes earlier. Singh had expected him to zero in on the hand. She was impatient to know if what she'd glimpsed was a ring or a strand of seaweed encircling that third finger. But Dr Young had started at the top of the bundled-up stuff, removing each component one by one, examining it and placing it either in the bin or on one of three trays on the table.

'The lung's made of remarkable stuff, Susie. Gotta be my favourite tissue. Here, put this on.' He handed her a head magnifier and stretched the sample out more. 'It's light, soft, elastic and spongy. And it explains the mystery of our hand on the beach.'

'It does?' Singh prized Dr Young's compulsive teaching. She'd learned a lot from him in only a few cases. But she wished he'd tell her the answer straight rather than insisting she work it out herself.

She focused the magnifier. 'It's lots of globules joined together like fabric.'

He smiled. 'Exactly. I'll put it under the microscope and you can see them even better on the monitor.'

He pointed at the misshapen circles that separated on the screen.

'These are alveoli, tiny air sacs. This tissue has been in the sea for days—you saw the water that ran out when I pressed it. Yet there's still some air in the alveoli and there're thousands of them in this piece alone.'

He turned away from the microscope and looked at her, his eyes wide with excitement. 'How d'you think it behaves in water?'

Her mind went blank. He must think her stupid. Then it hit her. 'Oh, it floats in water?'

He looked at her as if she was the star student. 'Isn't it wonderful? Part of a hand has floated ashore thanks to pieces of lung tangled up with it! I don't know when the human parts met the seaweed, but that would have protected it too.'

'They must all belong to the same person, surely?'

'Almost certain, but let me get the lung sample tubes ready for the DNA crew, then we'll look at the hand. You're being very patient, Susie.'

'Not at all, I can't wait. Will we get fingerprints?'

'Highly unlikely after days of sea immersion, but we'll soon know.' He continued his separating and sorting, swifter now but just as careful.

'Excuse me, Susie, but you don't seem quite your usual self. Anything on your mind?'

Susie startled. What had he noticed? 'I'm fine. The only thing wrong today was that launch trip. Thank goodness we could fly back.'

'Hmm, I wonder if Ash has finished yet. The launch mightn't get back before dark if he hasn't.' He paused. 'Susie, I'm happy to listen if you want. About anything.'

Desire to share her dilemma seized her. Matt was so passionate and dedicated to his work, he would understand. Completely. But she didn't know what he would advise her to do, if anything. Why did that matter? Deep inside, might she already know what she wanted?

'Thanks. I appreciate that.'

Dr Young's sandy eyebrows lifted. 'Any time. Now, here's what you're waiting for.'

He removed the last material obscuring the hand, or what was left of it. The thumb and part of the palm were missing, bitten or slashed away. But Singh only had eyes for the ring. Solid, about a centimetre wide. She couldn't say what it was made from unless she cleaned it up. Dr Young flipped his head magnifier down and examined the torn edges of flesh and bone.

'Something's bitten this piece off. The teeth marks conform to those on the neck I showed you on Monday. So probably a tiger shark. But now, I need to rush these DNA samples off and the only way is to take them myself. I'll start on a full post mortem on my return. Is Joe dropping in?'

'I spoke to him the minute we arrived back. He's pretty excited. Said he'd come as soon as he could.'

'I'll only be ten minutes. Sorry, Susie, but I'd rather you didn't remove the ring yet. Take photos, by all means.'

She was disappointed but wouldn't dream of disobeying Matt. He must have a good reason. She took some shots. She was glad about one thing: she'd resisted the temptation to share her confusion over her brokered suitor.

Ten minutes later, as he'd promised, Dr Young returned with Horseman in tow. Both men looked alert, excited.

'Great job, Singh,' Horseman said, clapping her on the back awkwardly.

'What a day you've had. Between this hand and the hotline, we'll home in on our victim's identity soon. Seen the afternoon papers? As we predicted, the head's been dubbed Jona.' He handed her the *Fiji Times, The Mirror* and *The Sun*. Each front page shouted at the reader in huge block headlines.

WHERE IS JONA'S BODY?
WHO IS JONA?
JONA AND THE SHARK!

Horseman handed Singh a bulky envelope. 'We've all got packs of flyers to distribute. Don't make any extra trips—just carry them with you to hand out when you're walking along the street. Give them to any shops you pass to put up in their windows. We're going for saturation coverage. Every single person in Fiji needs to know about this.'

'Okay, we're in business, guys.' Dr Young had placed the hand on his table and was swabbing it down carefully. 'The hand's condition supports our theory that it belongs to the same individual as the head retrieved last Sunday, which means the hand must have been in the sea for six to eight days. That fits because the skin has slipped off, so no fingerprints for you, I'm afraid. The surface is white and waxy due to saponification. Small marine predators like crustaceans inflicted these little wounds. All these features are consistent with sea immersion for around a week.'

Good, good, but Singh wanted to see that ring. 'Could there be skin under the ring?'

'Possibly, Susie, I hope so. Let's take a look now. The finger's swollen so the ring may not come off.' Grasping the ring with shiny pliers, he gently twisted and pulled. 'I need to cut the ring. If there *is* skin underneath, I don't want to destroy it by too much agitation.'

He turned over the hand and severed the ring with a tool that resembled her father's fencing wire cutters. He stretched it a little with the pliers and lifted it over the finger easily. After removing the tissue adhering to the ring, he dropped it into a kidney dish and handed it to her.

'You can scrub at it all you like now. I'm going to put my microscope to work and hunt for skin cells.'

The boss followed her to the sink, watched closely while she rinsed and scrubbed. The black ring emerged from its bath transformed. She must look as excited as she felt because when she glanced up, his brown eyes held a trace of amusement.

14

'D'you think it's silver?' Horseman asked.

'Could be, I'm no expert on jewellery. It looks distinctive. Could be a good lead.'

'Yep, looks hand-made to me.' He picked it up, weighed it in his hand. 'Solid, quite heavy. Let's get some photos. We'll plaster posters of the ring around the place too.'

'D'you think we should organise another press conference?'

He pondered for a few moments. 'I think it's too soon after the show this morning. But we need to use the media to our advantage. Can you get onto Taufa Smith? We need a media release and posters. You two can decide on the text and pick the best photo. I won't be too far behind you. I know a jeweller in the Jubilee Arcade. I'd like his opinion on this. He'll give me an accurate description for the draft of the release. I'll give you a lift to the station and walk on from there.'

*

He rang the bell beside Regency Jewellery's door. He could see Hari through the glass, bent over his counter looking at something through a head magnifier exactly like the one Dr Young used. He looked up, flipped back his eye-piece and hurried to open the door.

'Aha, the great Joe Horseman has condescended to visit me after all this time! I saw you on TV at lunchtime. What a horrible case, this Jona business. What can I do for you on this occasion?'

Hari was even leaner than Horseman remembered, the bones of his face stretching the smooth brown skin. His shoulders were more stooped. 'Sorry we haven't run into each other lately, Hari. Are you well?'

'Never better, Joe, never better. Don't look so worried! No one has good posture in my trade. Hunching and bending all day to peer at tiny things isn't good for the bones.' His voice was cheerful. He didn't sound sick.

He pulled the evidence bag out of his pocket, putting it in front of Hari.

'Can I take it out?' the jeweller asked.

At Horseman's nod, Hari took out the ring and flipped down his magnifier. Horseman waited, noting the display of Chinese watches and Indian-style gold bangles and necklaces in glass cabinets beside the counter. Nothing valuable on show.

'It's hand-made, sterling silver, blue cold-enamelling. It's well made, isn't it? Probably a man's ring, from the size. Did you find it cut like this?'

'No,' Horseman replied.

Hari shook his head slowly from side to side. 'Aha, I get the picture. The pathologist cut it, perhaps?'

An impish grin took years off. 'I know you won't tell me, but I'm getting the picture. I've never seen a ring like this. Nice design, nice. There's a maker's mark that I don't recognise. I could give it a proper clean for you. You could see the fine detail then.'

'That'd be great, Hari. We've done our best but...'

'You did a terrible job! Just wait a moment.' He ducked behind the curtain to his tiny workshop. In no time he was back, smiling. 'Silver does reward a good clean and polish, isn't it?'

The ring gleamed bright, the sky-blue swirl of enamel sparkled.

'It's beautiful,' Horseman replied.

'I checked the maker's mark on my list while I was at it—I couldn't find it but that doesn't mean a lot. Many small jewellers don't register their marks. Unless someone recognises it you're unlikely to trace the maker, if that's what you want.'

'That would certainly be a help, but I'm more interested in tracing the owner.'

'Stolen, eh? Well, it's of no great value, but people are often happy to pay a fair sum for hand-crafted pieces like this. Sorry I can't be of more help.'

'You've helped a great deal, Hari.' He fished a flyer out of his bag. 'If you could put this up in your window, I'll be even more grateful.'

'Ah, yes, of course. What a horrible business. The ring's not connected with the Jona case?'

'We don't know. *Vinaka*, Hari. Look after yourself. Eat a little more, perhaps.'

They shook hands. 'Call in and we'll go and eat a curry together, watch the rugby,' smiled the jeweller, sceptical.

As Horseman closed the jeweller's door, he heard a rapping from the other end of the arcade. The distinctive sound of a shoe-shine boy drumming up business.

'Aunty, uncle, shoe-siiine, shoe-siiine.' Rap, rap, rap.

'Like a mirror, like a mirror, shoe-siiine.' Rap, rap, rap.

The insistent cry rang out as he neared the Victoria Street entrance. It was not just any shoe-shine boy—it was Tevita. Horseman suspected Tevita's eagerness to drum up business could come across as aggression to potential customers. Once or twice he'd suggested he could try softening his approach but the boy didn't get it. What would a policeman know about business?

He stepped out from behind Tevita and planted one foot firmly on the boy's box. He'd worn leather shoes today in honour of the media conference, which made no sense as the camera frame would never take in his feet. But dressing more formally helped his confidence.

'*Bula*, Joe! You got proper shoes today!' Tevita's face was all smiles.

'*Bula vinaka*. Just for you Tevita. I don't wear these often. They need a good polish.' He rolled up the hem of his best grey trousers, well away from Tevita's wild brushing.

Tevita evaluated his shoes in a glance. 'Sure do, Joe, sure do. You wear them for TV, eh.' He wiped the shoes off with his dirty rag before skimming his brush lightly over the black Kiwi-brand tin of polish. As he worked the polish in, he asked, 'I wanna help on Jona case. Terrible when tiger shark bite your head off, eh. You got job for me, Joe?'

How could he let him down lightly?

'I was a big help with the war club back in May, eh?'

'You certainly were, Tevita. You did well.'

Tevita now took his cleaner rag and set to work, bringing the leather to an even gleam. His loud rap on the side of the box startled Horseman, who obediently changed feet. His right knee protested at the increased weight as Tevita set to work on his left shoe.

'As a matter of fact, there is a job you can do for me,' he said. The boy grinned up at him but continued to work.

Horseman gave Tevita a five-dollar note—five times what customers usually paid, but he should give the boy something for his time. He pulled a wad of flyers from his bag.

'Tevita, your job is to give these out to your customers, or passers-by on the street. Don't shove the posters at them—be polite. You could say "Can you help the police find who Jona is?" Something like that.'

Tevita beamed. He gazed at him with the same adoring light in his eyes as Tina the dog. 'Count on me, Joe. This is easy job for me.' He took the bundle. 'You got any more? I can do more, Joe.'

'I'm very grateful, Tevita. *Vinaka vakalevu.*' They shook hands.

As he walked back to the station, passing out flyers himself, he thought how he should do more for Tevita. Despite his urgings, the boy had not made any moves to choosing a trade he would like to take up. His short-lived enrolment in the carpentry course run by Father Francis in Tailevu made Horseman reluctant to take over again. Tevita must decide. But the boy didn't see his life as disadvantaged and couldn't understand his future was pretty hopeless without some qualification. Before long he'd be tempted or coerced by those older and stronger into petty crime. Maybe he was already. Life in Suva was becoming more dangerous as the evil of the drug trade insinuated itself into the unsuspecting islands of Fiji. He must think of a way to use Tevita's hero worship for the boy's own good.

15

Horseman ordered his core detective team to take a break from the hotline phones. They were tired, thirsty and hungry. Their eyes lit up as he carried in a box wafting appetising smells in their direction. Singh followed him with a packed tea tray.

As they shared their phone experiences, from the hilarious to the horrifying, over warm salty food and scalding sweet tea, they relaxed. Horseman asked, 'Sergeant Singh, you've got a tall tale to beat these. Tell us about your day.'

They were agog at her news. Suddenly a hubbub erupted.

'Where's the ring?'

'Can we see it?'

'Is it a wedding ring?'

'Where's it made?'

'Is it gold?'

Singh extracted papers from her purple ring binder and passed them around. She'd already photocopied blow-ups of two ring shots. She was a gem of a sergeant. She closed her binder with a snap and passed a plastic sleeve to him.

'That's a draft of the press release text. It would be good to review it and get it approved this evening so it makes the late news and tomorrow's early editions.'

'Sure, we'll aim for that. Ash radioed from Levuka station before the SOCOs boarded the launch. They've got bags of bits and pieces that may or may not be human tissue. They're done in after searching a beach in the rain for most of the day. I urged Ash to store their collection at the lab, get a night's sleep and start on it tomorrow morning.'

Now he would surprise them. 'I've got something to show you all, but Sergeant Singh comes first.' He handed her the ring inside its evidence bag. 'See what a professional clean can do?'

Singh's eyes widened as she took the now-sparkling ring. 'It's really lovely,' she said. 'So bright, and the blue…' She passed the ring around the table.

'I consulted a professional jeweller who told me it's sterling silver and enamel, hand-made. Good quality. Unfortunately, he's never seen one like it before.'

'I think I have.' Everyone turned to Musudroka. 'I've seen some in different colours, too.'

They all froze, expectant. In the end, Horseman broke the silence. 'Where, Tani? You're a champ, but spit it out, man.'

Musudroka turned the ring so it caught the light. Then he grinned, punching the air. 'I've got it! It was at the ROC market!'

'What's the rock market?' Kau asked. 'Precious stones?'

'*Oi lei*, Apo! Where've you been? Okay, you're a newcomer to Suva. It's initials, ROC—Republic of Cappuccino. The ROC's a café on the corner of Victoria Parade and Loftus Street near the government buildings. Out of your league, man.' He nudged Kau's arm.

'The first Sunday of each month, they close Loftus Street and turn it into a craft market. Only quality local stuff—that's where I've seen rings like this.' Musudroka enjoyed prolonging his moment of glory.

'Since when have you hung out at quality craft markets?' Kau sounded offended.

'Mum's cousin has a garment stall there—*bula* shirts. She gets much higher prices than at the flea market. I often help out. I manage to have a look around while I'm there. Great stuff.'

'Please get back to the ring, Tani. Do you know who made it?'

Singh's patience was running out.

'Sorry, Sergeant. Well, I know him by sight, but I don't know his name. An expatriate—Aussie guy, I think.'

'Great, Tani,' Horseman said. 'Your knowledge of the ROC market has just pushed us ahead by days. With a bit more luck, we may not need the media release. Sergeant Singh, get Taufa to put a hold on that until further notice.'

'Right away, sir.' She went to the nearest phone and made a brief call.

Horseman thought aloud. 'It's possible this Australian jeweller sells his work in shops, too. Gift shops patronised by tourists, don't you think? Here's what we'll do. Musudroka and Kau, you do the rounds of Suva jewellers and gift shops with the photos. Find out if they know the maker and if they've ever sold this design. It's back to the hotline phones for the rest of you. It's off to the ROC café for Sergeant Singh and me. We'll get our coffee fix and just possibly solve the case in one blow.'

Things were moving; he could feel it. Singh inserted each photo into a plastic sleeve before sending the two young detectives on their mission. She was intent on her tasks, super-competent as ever, but something wasn't quite the same. The fire in her eyes when a case turned a corner—that irrepressible excitement was missing. Perhaps she was overtired. She'd had quite a day.

*

Horseman greeted the smiling barista. '*Bula,* Maura, I'll have an espresso, please. Susie, what about you?'

'Chai latte for a change, please.'

Horseman paid in advance. 'I have a question about your monthly market. Do you know an Australian jeweller who has a stall there?'

'Um, there are quite a few jewellery stalls. I've seen an expat, but I don't know his name. He has nice stuff. You'll need to ask Nicola—she looks after the market arrangements.'

'Great, can you give me Nicola's number?'

'Anything for you, Joe! Take a seat and I'll bring it over.'

'You must be tired,' he said as Singh propped her elbows on the table.

'A bit. It seems like forever since we got the news about the hand. And now, the ring and Tani's lead could save us a lot of time.'

Maura served their drinks and handed Horseman a ROC business card. 'I've written Nicola's number on the back.'

'*Vinaka*, Maura.' He took a sip of espresso, letting its smoothness bathe his mouth. The intense flavour was comforting and stimulating at the same time. He called himself an addict as a joke, but maybe coffee and he were becoming too close. He dialled Nicola's number. When it switched through to voicemail, he left a message.

He was disappointed, impatient. 'Doesn't anyone answer a phone call these days?'

Singh seemed lost in thought. Her chai was untouched. 'Sir, I put in a leave application yesterday. I wonder if you've approved it.'

'Oh, sorry, I haven't seen it yet. What's it for?'

'Oh, it's family business. My parents are expecting me to visit again this weekend. I'm rostered off duty on Sunday, but with this case, I imagine all leave will be cancelled. I'm not looking forward to telling them.'

'We'll manage something. I hope your parents aren't ill?'

'No, they're well. It's traditional religious matters they see as vital. I don't want to disappoint them.'

A solid middle-aged woman came up to their table and stretched her hand out to him. A wild curly mane of brown hair framed her face and hung over her shoulders. A smile lit up her face.

'*Bula*, so nice to meet you, Inspector Horseman. I'm Nicola. I was driving here when your call came so I couldn't answer it. I know you'll approve of me obeying the rules of the road.'

Horseman pushed himself up from the table and shook hands.

'*Bula*, Nicola. Indeed, I do approve,' he said with a smile. 'It's nice to meet you in person, too. This is Detective Sergeant Susila Singh.'

The two women shook hands and Nicola pulled up a chair to their table. 'I know you're on duty, but can I call you Joe? As I've been following your rugby career since the beginning, you're Joe to me. Just like the rest of the country. Inspector Horseman sounds totally weird, like a different person.'

'Joe is fine with me. But you're right, I am sort of a different person on duty.'

'Not too different, I hope.' Nicola's friendly smile included Singh too. 'I'm happy to help you if I possibly can.'

'Maura told me you manage the Sunday craft market.' He pulled the ring from his pocket and placed it in front of her.

'We'd like to know if this ring was sold by a stallholder.'

Maura picked up the ring and examined it.

'Well, I can't say if it was sold at our market, but it's certainly the work of a silversmith who regularly takes a stall. *Io*, it's definitely one of Bill Peterson's. Unless someone is copying his designs, I guess. Unlikely in a small pond like Suva.'

Singh opened her notebook and wrote.

'That's an idea I hadn't thought of. Let's hope it's the genuine article. Could you give me Mr Peterson's address and phone number, please?'

'Certainly. Excuse me a minute while I get it from the back room. Oh, I'll give you my card too.'

Singh took the card and copied the details into her notebook.

Nicola was soon back. 'Here, I've written it out for you. I've been wondering if the ring was stolen, or lost?'

'We're wondering too, Nicola. All we know is it's been found. It could well be a clue in an ongoing enquiry.'

'It must be important to warrant the attention of two senior detectives, I'm thinking.'

'Let's hope so. We're both grateful for your help.'

'Come to the market next Sunday week. You'll enjoy it.'

'*Vinaka*, I will if I can. *Moce*, Nicola.'

16

Today was one of those charmed days. Once an elusive piece of the jigsaw puzzle slotted into the right place, several others followed. The Australian silversmith, Bill Peterson, picked up Horseman's call on the second ring and agreed to see them at his home studio in Pacific Harbour, an hour's drive from Suva. They bought some of the ROC's legendary coconut chocolate brownies for the return trip. Horseman tuned in to the radio news.

The children's discovery of the hand near Levuka got top billing. He was glad they'd paused the release about the ring. If Peterson came good, the public need not know about that at all. If Jona's terrible death was murder, he did not want the killer to know the police were closing in on the identity of the victim.

It was completely dark when they arrived. The lawns and gardens of the hotel resort on the beach side of the highway were softly lit, romantic. But it was the odd mixed residential and commercial development on the other side that they were headed to. Horseman negotiated the streets of villas winding around the golf course while Singh shone her torch on the small number plaques planted in the lawns.

'Here it is, there's a sign—W. Peterson, Silversmith.'

The garden was sparse: the usual hibiscus hedges divided the single-storey house from its neighbours, and tree-fern trunks planted with orchids formed a guard of honour either side of the concrete driveway. As Horseman turned into the drive the front door opened and a man stepped into the pool of light on the veranda. He was short and muscly, dressed in a worn T-shirt and shorts.

'Hey there. I'm Bill Peterson. You must be the detectives, I suppose.' They shook hands and introduced themselves.

'Come through, come through into chaos.' He grinned broadly and ushered them into a big living room with a white-tiled floor littered with toys and cane sofas and chairs. A ceiling fan whirred gently. The presumed creators of the chaos, identical girls aged about three, were building a tower of blocks on a pandanus mat. In green spotted pyjamas, their wet hair combed, they gazed up at the visitors with enormous eyes.

A smiling Fijian woman rushed in, wiping her hands on her apron. '*Bula vinaka*, I'm Sala Peterson. Please excuse this mess.'

'*Bula vinaka*. Sala is my mother's name, so I've always liked it. Excuse our intrusion at this busy time.' He didn't want to prolong their visit, but extended pleasantries were compulsory in Fiji before getting down to business.

'Not at all. I don't see many new faces here. I'll make some tea.'

Horseman glanced at Singh. '*Vinaka* but nothing for us. We've already eaten and we had coffee just before we left Suva. Unfortunately, we have to get back there as soon as we can, too.'

A tremendous wail from behind startled them. They turned to see the tower reduced to a jumble of blocks. One small innocent was throwing them at her twin. Connecting, too.

'She knocked my tower down. She broke it.'

'Time for bed, you rascals. Come on.' Their mother grabbed them by their hands, smiling at the detectives.

'We'll leave you in peace. Say goodnight, girls.'

The reluctant pair, shy now, looked at their feet and mumbled their goodnights before their mother bustled them from the room.

Their father looked both amused and proud as he watched them go.

'What lovely little girls,' said Singh.

Peterson's fair skin flushed pink.

'The terrible twins are healthy and bright enough. That's all that matters, isn't it? Come and sit down. Let's see the ring you've brought.'

He looked at the inside of the ring. 'Yeah, definitely mine—here's my mark. It's not unique, though. This is my most popular design—customers like *Wave*. That's its name. The customer specifies the size and enamel colour. Still, they're hand-made, so each piece has small differences. This blue's the most popular.'

'Can you remember who bought this one?' Singh asked.

Peterson examined the ring closely and shook his head.

'No. It's a man's size, but that doesn't mean a man bought it. Most customers buy pieces as gifts. Whoever owns it, I'd say he wears it most of the time and does manual work. It's really bashed about: the enamel's scratched, there are nicks in the rim, here's a dent.'

'Can you tell how old it is?' Horseman asked.

'No. It looks old, but it's had a tough life. Because of the damage I can't tell. Could be quite recent. I wish people would look after their jewellery; it's not meant to be lived in.'

Did he resent those who liked his work so much they wore it constantly?

'How long have you been selling this design?' Singh asked.

'Three years. Just after the twins arrived. I retreated from their squalling to my workshop and came up with this. My inspiration was the famous woodblock print The Wave by the Japanese artist Hokusai. That and living here by the sea.'

'It's very attractive,' Singh said. 'I assume you keep records—a receipt book, for example?'

'Yeah, I do. Can I ask what this is for? You're going to a lot of trouble for a lost silver ring, even a stolen one.'

'It could be vital in identifying someone who has died,' Horseman replied.

Peterson's eyes widened. After a few moments he said, 'You

mean the hand they found today was wearing this? Really?'

'I can't say any more. I'd be very grateful if you didn't tell anyone.'

Peterson sprang up. 'Of course, you've got my word. Let me go and get my books from the workshop.'

He returned with two books, as well-worn as the ring. 'I sell a lot at outdoor markets, so old-fashioned paper works best for me. I hope you can read my writing.'

'Can you explain your system?' Singh asked.

'Yeah. This big one's my order book, and the little one's my receipts, carbon copies and all. See here. I number each order sequentially, describe the item, customer details and so on. The same number is repeated on the receipt, which has fewer details. Take a look.'

Singh leafed through a few pages of the order book, then checked the receipt book. 'Great, Mr Peterson. It'll be easy for us to find what we need in these.'

'I'm afraid we'll need to copy them,' Horseman added. 'I'll get them delivered back to you tomorrow afternoon. I hope that won't disrupt your work too much.'

'Not at all. Sala transfers the figures to her computer bookkeeping system. But I do need my books back. I work from my order book every day.'

'Of course, we'll look after them.'

Singh handed the books to Horseman. The deft sketches and neat notes impressed him. The word *Wave* appeared quite often. They might have a longer list to check through than he'd hoped. He flipped through the receipt book and a name popped out at him—Salome. A common name in Fiji, although he'd never understood why the betrayer of John the Baptist should be so popular.

*

Singh took the wheel for the return trip. Horseman offered her a brownie from the paper bag.

'Here, I'll take one for myself. You can have the paper bag to rest yours on while you drive.'

'Thanks. I'm ready for it now. Good result, don't you think?'

Horseman chewed his dense, sticky bite of brownie. 'Excellent. One of those orders will give us the name of our victim, or the name of the person who gave him the ring. Not only that, but their phone number and address too.'

'It's only eight o'clock. We can get the books photocopied as soon as we get back and I'll—'

'No, Susie. We both need a good sleep. Someone on night shift can do the photocopying. Tomorrow, I'll be in bright and early and start sifting through them. Tani or young Apo Kau can help. A good training exercise. We'll get a list of all the blue Wave ring buyers and work the phones. We'll find the right one well before the day's out. And you never know, the DNA results might arrive too.'

'But—'

'You'll be on leave, remember. There are times when family matters like yours must come first. You can take this vehicle. It's signed out to the case so you can return it Sunday afternoon. You'll get to the west in half the time the bus does. If the purchaser of the ring lives in the west, I could get you to go and see them. How about that?'

'I appreciate the leave, sir, but I won't take the vehicle. No one can understand it but I like the bus even though it's slow. I like stopping at the Coral Coast resorts and the villages. I don't have to pay attention to the road, I can just think.' Or daydream.

'And what will you be thinking about tomorrow?'

'The Jona case. See, I can't help calling it that name now.'

'We may as well adopt it. It's a good name, after all. Anything else?'

'Well, as both you and Matt have asked me what's bothering me today, I think you probably should know. The thing is…um…I mean.' She took a deep breath.

'My parents won't be happy until I'm married and they've tried several times to make a match for me over the years. Now they see me as an old maid and they're pinning their last hopes on a professional marriage broker. There's no way I can get out of lunch tomorrow in Lautoka with both sets of parents, the prospective suitor and the matchmaker.'

So that was it! None of his business, but the system of arranged marriages among the Indian population intrigued him. People said the marriages succeeded in about the same proportion as among those who married for love. What should he say to her? Probably nothing. She was the most dedicated detective he had ever met. He imagined the conflict she must be going through.

'Thanks for telling me, Susie. I'll keep this to myself.'

'I know I can trust you. But I don't mind if you tell Matt. He seems worried about me, too.'

'Have you met this suitor yet?'

'Yes, I met him last weekend at my parents' house. I've met him twice more this last week in Suva. He's a lawyer. He's like me in that he's managed to evade his parents' plans until now.'

'You might suit each other, you never know.' He brushed the brownie crumbs off his front.

'But none of my business! I won't say another word and I definitely won't advise you. I'm just as hopeless. Sorry, I didn't mean you were hopeless...um, forget I said that.'

They both laughed. 'It's alright. Brij and I are going to tell our parents and the matchmaker that we're happy to get to know each other at our own pace and we'll let them know what we decide. But tomorrow will be our last formal meeting with the families.'

'If you decide to marry this lucky man, you'll be missed, Susie. Greatly.'

Singh sputtered crumbs over herself and the dashboard. 'I thought you'd understand. I'd never marry anyone who wanted me to give up my job!'

She looked across at him. Even in the dimness, he could see the disappointment in her lovely eyes. He'd let her down.

'Of course not. Neither should you. Forget I said that. You're a born detective, Sergeant Singh.'

They drove back to the station in silence, but a comfortable one. At least he thought it was. He now knew what was troubling her, and it was nothing to do with him.

17

Bill Peterson had sold twenty-three blue-enamelled Wave rings, the majority made to the customer's specifications. Of these, nine customers gave overseas addresses, or Fiji hotel addresses. Horseman pictured visitors to Fiji going home wearing on a finger a striking souvenir of their holiday.

'Musudroka, we have fourteen people who bought a blue Wave ring to speak to today. After introducing yourself politely, you have just two questions to ask.'

'*Io*, sir.' If Musudroka had a tail it would have been wagging furiously.

'The first is: "Did you buy a sterling silver Wave ring with blue enamelling made in Fiji in"—and you state the month and year.'

'Got it, what's the second question?'

'What do you think it should be, Tani?'

'Have you still got the ring?'

'Exactly. If they have, note that and cross them off the list. However, if the purchaser gave it to someone, ask for the recipient's number and you'll need to phone them too. Can you take a break from the hotline and handle this job on your own?'

'Absolutely. *Vinaka*, sir.'

'When will you be finished, Tani?'

'Two hours. Tops. If not sooner.'

'Excellent. Here's your list, and your script prompts.'

'*Vinaka*.'

It meant the world to Musudroka that he'd identified the source of the ring. When he found the owner he'd be keener than ever.

After reading his own emails, Horseman checked all the incoming messages passed on from the station switchboard since yesterday afternoon, read the notes by the hotline staff and filled in his own diary. He dealt with the faxes, scrolled through the internal emails. Satisfied he'd missed nothing demanding action, he set about updating the case file. This was a task Singh attended to, but he didn't want her to return to an incomplete file. He flipped through it. It went without saying that Singh had already logged her actions in Levuka the previous day. Dr Young's post mortem report on the hand should arrive on Monday. He added the press conference material, the ring photo, the Bill Peterson interview and the resulting list of possible purchasers.

'Excuse me, sir.' It was Musudroka. He put a mug of tea on Horseman's desk. 'A fax just came in for you.'

'*Vinaka*, Tani.' The cover sheet showed the sender was the DNA lab. He ripped the page in his haste.

'The head and hand match, Tani! The lung pieces are definitely human but that DNA analysis isn't complete yet. What we wanted and expected. Now science confirms it.'

'*Oi lei*, boss! Great news. I'll tell the others.'

'Go ahead. Then come back and tell me who owned the ring. I'll call the super.'

He read the pages of details and diagrams. Jona was male, with Melanesian characteristics. Chances are he was Fijian. He was not on the police DNA database, which had only been in existence for two years. What with a population of under a million and a low crime rate, he knew that would be unlikely. So, no surprises, but they were edging closer.

He passed on the news to the relieved super, then sent a text to Singh who was on the Lautoka bus and possibly out of mobile range. But she'd check for texts when she arrived.

'I need your advice, sir.' Musudroka was back, holding out his list.

'Sit down, Tani. Let's have a look.'

'It's gone pretty well. I've eliminated eleven on the list. Seven still had their rings. Four gave them as gifts but I got onto the recipients and all of them still had their rings. I've called the remaining three purchasers a few times and left messages. They're not picking up. What should I do now?'

'Great work. I'll follow up with the three remaining buyers. One of them should have the answer we need. You'd better get back to the hotline. Give Kau a short break.'

'*Io*, sir.' The lad shifted from one foot to the other, clicking his biro, excitement lighting his eyes.

He thought the DNA result would be a breakthrough, but he felt a bit let down, to his surprise. The match didn't come close to identifying the victim, torn to pieces in the most savage way. But the CID investigation was getting closer now. This afternoon they could know the victim's name. All three elusive blue Wave ring buyers were women, so all three must have bought them as a gift for a man.

After he found out Jona's true name, the next question was whether that shark had killed Jona or preyed on a cadaver. He'd been pondering that from the beginning.

18

Horseman looked at the remaining three names on the list of ring purchasers. The first was Salome—no surname recorded. He hoped this Salome was not the girl who'd cleaned his university dormitory way back. He called the number. When the familiar low voice answered he felt nothing but sadness.

'*Bula*, Joe! My goodness, I don't see you in over a year and then you pop up twice in a week! I'm in town now, shopping.'

He couldn't do this on the phone. 'Can you come to the station, Salome? Something's come up that you might be able to help me with.'

She laughed briefly, an embarrassed, hesitant laugh. 'That sounds mysterious. Um—I'd rather meet you somewhere else.'

'No problem. I need an early lunch today. How about the Hare Krishna? I'll be there in five minutes.' He found Musudroka and told him he'd be back in half an hour.

Salome must have been close by the station when he called because she was waiting beside the café door when he crossed the road. She was clearly not working—her long cotton pants and loose *bula* blouse let her merge with the crowd of Saturday shoppers.

'*Bula*, Salome. How are you?'

An anxious frown wrinkled her brow. The midday glare lit fine lines around her eyes. She was getting older. Like everyone.

'I'm fine, Joe.'

He doubted she'd feel fine for very long, but he said, 'Let's get our lunch first, then we can talk.'

The vegetarian curry café was one of his favourites, not least because it was opposite the station. The cafeteria line was short so before long they unloaded their trays of curries, rice and sambals onto a table against the wall. The smell of the mingling spices made his mouth water. They didn't talk until half the food was gone.

'What have you been shopping for this morning?'

'Oh, I picked up some vegetables at the market and some specials at Hedstrom's. That's enough for me to carry on the bus. But the main reason I came to town was to check on Jimmy, the friend I mentioned to you. I'm worried about him now.'

'What's happened?'

'His boat berthed at Suva yesterday but I didn't hear from him and he didn't show up at my place. His mobile seems to be switched off, according to the message I get. This morning I went down to the boat and asked one of the crew. He said Jimmy had already left the boat. That Chinese seaman brushed me off, really. He didn't want to say any more, just disappeared below deck.'

'Your friend's name is Jimmy? Is he Fijian?'

'*Io*, Jimmy's just the nickname he uses because he works with foreigners so much. His real name is Semisi.'

He hadn't known her man worked on boats. That didn't augur well. It was entirely possible that Jimmy had changed his mind about Salome and wanted to avoid her. That would explain his mobile being switched off. However, he could not suggest that. No way.

'It's possible his phone's battery was flat and you'll get a call quite soon.' He smiled, trying to reassure her. But already he believed he had just discovered Jona's identity.

'This boat's a big tuna longliner—it has electricity. He usually charges his phone before he makes port.'

'Maybe something stopped him this time. Does he have a family? If there was some emergency, he might have gone to them as soon as the ship docked.'

'It's possible, but he would have let me know. His parents are in

Lautoka, staying with his sister's family.'

'How long has he been on this boat?'

'About a month. It's been a long voyage. Sometimes he might be away for a few days, sometimes a month or more. Often a longliner transfers the catch to other boats called carriers, so they don't waste time and diesel sailing to ports far away. Carriers bring supplies to the fishing boats at sea. Water, too. *Oi lei*, did you know that, Joe?'

'I didn't. Really?' His cases hadn't taken him into the world of large-scale fishing beyond Fiji's territorial limit.

'*Io*, Jimmy says it's another world out there on the high seas. Fancy that—I know something that a detective who went to university does not!' She raised her left hand and rubbed her forehead. Glinting on her third finger was a red Wave ring.

His heart thudded against his ribcage. He feared for her. 'I saw a blue ring just like that yesterday. I met the silversmith who made it, too—Bill Peterson.'

She held her hand out, proud. '*Io*, I bought it from him at the ROC Sunday market. I couldn't decide which colour I wanted, but this red one fitted my finger perfectly, so I took that as a sign it was the one for me. When Jimmy admired my ring I took him there and he wanted a blue one. His fingers are so big I had to order one and Bill made it specially for him. He made it wider and thicker, too. He said the proportions had to be right. That was about a year ago.' She gazed at her ring, far away in happy reminiscence.

He tried hard to summon his professional distance. His courage, too. He didn't succeed. He took the victim's ring from his pocket and showed her. 'This is the ring we found yesterday, Salome.'

She took it, rotating it on her little finger. '*Io*, this is just like Jimmy's, but it's broken. These blue rings are popular, Joe. This could belong to another man. It's too clean and shiny to be Jimmy's. And broken.'

'*Io*, you're right. It could belong to another man.'

'I suppose he could have polished it up because he was going to see me. But he's not much good at that sort of thing. How did it get broken? Did you find it in Suva? If it's Jimmy's, he must have lost it in the street yesterday, right after he left the boat.' She sounded doubtful.

'No, not in Suva. Some children found it on a beach near Levuka.' He waited.

'Levuka? Why have you got it in Suva, then?' She smiled, mystified.

Moments later the colour drained from her face, the ring dropped to the table. She looked at him, her mouth open.

'You don't mean—that hand? What I heard on the radio? Was this ring on that hand?'

'*Io*. And the scientists told us today that the hand, and the head that was found at sea a week ago… they match. The hand wearing this ring and the head belong to the same person.'

'*Oi lei*! No, this must be a coincidence!'

'It could be. For your sake, I hope so. For Jimmy's sake, too.'

Salome propped her arms on the table and held her head in her hands. Her own ring gleamed through her crinkly black hair.

He gave her time. A waiter came and cleared their plates. The proprietor followed and served them tea and home-made Indian sweets. 'Sweets are always complimentary for you, Josefa,' he said with an affectionate smile. Horseman nodded his thanks. The proprietor glanced at Salome and left them.

Eventually, Salome looked at him. 'I have to accept that Jimmy could have met with an accident while he was on deck alone. He might have fallen into the sea when there was nobody around. He always told me how dangerous his job was. But he would be missed! They would have searched for him! The captain would have reported it and asked for help!' Her hands trembled but colour started to return to her face, her lips.

'And if any of those things had happened, the police would know about it, right?'

He nodded. '*Io*, Salome, we would know.'

She took the dainty cup Horseman filled for her, added sugar and drank the tea. He poured her another.

'That's why I'm sure this unfortunate man is not Jimmy. But there's only one way to tell.' The teacup trembled in her hand. 'I need to see this head and this hand, even though the idea is horrible. Then I can tell you.'

She steadied now she had said the words. 'So, you never thought I'd be helping the cops, eh.' She managed a small smile.

'Salome, I'm so sorry, but I cannot allow you to see those remains. Believe me, even this man's mother could not recognise his head or hand. After some days in the sea, there's a lot of damage to a human body.'

'I'm no use to the cops after all.'

'Salome, what you've told me is vital. I'm grateful. The best way you can help even more is if you have something from Jimmy, like hair from a brush or a fingernail clipping. If we could get a good sample, the scientists can check if Jimmy's DNA is different from the DNA of the body parts. Then we can be certain, one way or the other.'

'Oh, DNA. *Io*, I know about that. I watch CSI on television. I don't know if I could find something. I'll have a look, though.'

'I can help you, too. The police can't work on finding Jimmy until you file a Missing Person report. Come across to the station with me now and we can fill it in together.'

Salome finished her tea, then looked down. 'I don't want to go inside the station, Joe. This is close enough for me. Can you do it for me?'

'What are you worried about? I'll be with you, Salome.'

'You don't want to be seen with me, Joe. Some of those cops may recognise me. One or two are not nice. I wouldn't do you any good.'

'*Vinaka*, you're a good woman, Salome. I don't respect any man who hasn't been nice to you. I don't care what they think.'

'Maybe you should. The bad will always strive to destroy the good.'

'Well, it's important we get these forms filled in. Prem won't mind if we do it here. I can go and bring back the forms in a minute. Do you have a photo of him? I'll need that too.'

'I haven't, I'm sorry.'

'Really?'

'We don't go in for things like that. We're both a bit different, you see.'

Horseman thought it odd that they went in for rings yet Salome didn't have one photo.

'When I get him officially logged as missing, I'll be able to start making enquiries. Police will be able to visit the ship and ask questions, for example.'

'*Io*, that's the best thing. Let's get it over with.'

19

Horseman had trouble following Salome's directions through the winding streets of the owner-builders development. Schemes like this gave town workers the chance to buy their own plot of land with utilities laid on. The proud landowners built what they could afford, adding and upgrading over the years. Citizens of different races saved, built and had no time or inclination to crime. They became a community through proximity, the borrowing and lending of tools, the sharing of food, the offers and acceptance of labour. The constables who staffed their small police posts grew attached to these communities.

After a few wrong turns he found Salome's cousin's house. It was a timber and corrugated iron rectangle raised on stumps, with a veranda across the front and glass louvres on opposite sides. It would be airy. Terraced food gardens took up all the space at the front. He followed a side path down the slope to the back yard.

Salome had described her lodgings as a garden flat. Horseman thought it a grandiose classification. The small corrugated iron shed would be the family's first dwelling, allowing space at the front for their dream house while they saved and amassed materials. Now it was almost hidden by banana clumps and orange trees. Certainly private. He knocked on the plywood door.

Salome opened it immediately. 'You found me at last,' she said.

'*Io*, it's a nice place, but hard to find.'

'It's my retreat.'

'No one visits you here?'

'Only my daughter during her holidays from boarding school. Jimmy too, when he's in Suva—not when my daughter's here, of course. Oh, you didn't think…did you? *Oi lei*, my cousin Elisa prides herself on her Christian charity, but I'd be out on my ear if I ever worked from here. No, I rent a small overpriced room in the heart of Suva. It's much better that way. Please come in, Joe.'

In one corner of the living room was a kitchen with a two-burner spirit stove on a lino-covered bench. It was quite dim until Salome propped open both iron shutters and lit a mosquito coil on the kitchen bench.

'I keep them closed because I can't stand the mosquitos. I once had dengue fever,' she explained. Pushed against one wall was a decent-sized table with a sewing machine, workbox, stacks of fabric pieces and garments under construction.

'Oh, you're already a dressmaker.'

'*Io*, I sew all my own clothes to save money. I make for my cousin and some of her friends. Neighbours and even people further afield ask me to make for them. Not just clothes—curtains and cushion covers too. I enjoy it and they're happy with my work. That's how I got the idea that I could make sewing my full-time business.'

'You should do that Salome.'

'Jimmy wants me to move with him to Vanua Levu to take up his clan rights to land there. Maybe buy a fishing boat. But now, I don't know what will happen.'

'Sit down, Salome. Can I make you some tea?'

She looked shocked. 'Oh no. But perhaps I will sit.' She sank onto a plastic chair, folding her arms on the table and laying her head on them.

'I'll get you some water,' he said. The kitchen boasted plumbing, so he filled a cup at the sink and brought it to her. She propped herself up and gulped from the cup.

'*Vinaka*, I'm better now.'

Horseman worried about her. 'Jimmy's now registered as a

missing person. As I explained before, it's possible he was the shark-attack victim last weekend. We know he was at sea then. The best way I can rule him out is by collecting a sample for DNA testing. Did Jimmy stay here between fishing trips, Salome?'

'*Io*, sometimes. He didn't have his own place. He had to be careful not to be seen by the neighbours—Elisa wouldn't like gossip. But he would stay with his parents in Vanua Levu, too. Or visit his sister in Lautoka.'

Horseman took out his notebook. 'Can you tell me their names and addresses, please. If they have telephone numbers, even better.'

Salome picked up a black diary from the table and supplied the information. She seemed well-organised. Perhaps she could make a go of a sewing business. He hoped so.

'The best way to find the DNA tissue is for our specialist team, the SOCOs, to come in and search your flat. I promise you, they won't damage anything or turn the place upside down. They know what they're looking for and where to find it.'

'No, Joe, absolutely not. I'd be out on the street. My cousin would be mortified by a police search, those suits, the van… no, sorry. This place isn't much, but I like it, it's my retreat.'

'I can see that. I'll have to find something then. Well, has Jimmy got a toothbrush here, a comb, nail clippers, any clothes?'

She bridled. 'I keep everything, clean, as I hope you can see, Joe. I don't leave old toothbrushes lying around. You can go in the bedroom—there's just a tiny shower cubicle there. Jimmy put that in for me so I didn't have to use the outside bathroom. I like privacy. I use the kitchen sink as a handbasin. The toilet is outside. I don't mind that.'

He put on gloves and stepped through to the bedroom. A metal bedstead was neatly made with a bright floral bedspread. When he opened the shutter, matching curtains billowed. The small shower was lined with glossy laminate. He fished around in the drain hole. No hairs, nothing at all. No men's clothes hanging on the rail. None on the open set of shelves either. Everything spotless.

Disappointing. He knew Ash could find something.

Salome appeared. He smiled. 'You're just too clean, Salome.'

She smiled back. 'I forgot about Jimmy's suitcase. It's the shock, I suppose. I keep it here for him. He doesn't take much on the boats.' She knelt on the floor and reached under the bed, pulled out a blue vinyl suitcase that had seen better days.

His knee protested as he knelt beside her. Damn the joint—it was high time it worked properly again. 'Is it okay with you if I open it now?'

Salome sprang up. There was nothing wrong with *her* knees. 'I don't think I want to look at his things right now. I know I can trust you with it, Joe. I'd rather you take it away.' Her voice cracked on her final words. Her hand stilled her trembling mouth.

'No problem, I'll do that and return it to you when we've finished with it. I think the SOCOs will find a hair or something.'

'If you don't, I've got this. I hope you don't need it.' She went back to the living-room table and opened a sewing box, lifted the top tray out and delved below. She withdrew a small envelope and handed it to him. Inside was a lock of frizzy black hair tied with a ribbon. It had been cut. There were no roots. This must be precious to her or else she surely would have revealed it before.

'Is this Jimmy's?'

'*Io*, I know it seems silly to keep his hair.'

'Not at all. I think I understand. Can I take it?'

She looked down and nodded. '*Io*, I have to know.'

'I'll give the SOCOs the suitcase. If they can't find anything there for DNA, I'll offer them this. How about that?'

Salome looked up at him, her eyes wet. She nodded.

'Has Jimmy been on the crew of this fishing boat for a long time?'

'The *Joy-13*? No, just this trip. He usually only does one trip on each boat.'

'Really? I'm surprised.'

'Oh, I should have explained, I suppose. He's not one of the crew. He's independent. He's a fishing observer.'

Horseman was taken aback. 'What's a fishing observer?'

Salome smiled at his bewilderment. '*Oi lei*, I don't know any details, Joe. He has to write down how many fish they catch, what sort of fish, that kind of thing. When he gets back the records go to the Fisheries Department. That's about all I know.'

'So, he's like an inspector?'

'He's called an observer. I don't know if that's the same or not.'

'Did, I mean does, sorry…does he like his work?'

'He does, especially the good pay. He always liked fishing as a boy. When he left school he worked for years on his uncle's small boat out of Savusavu. Later on, he did technical college certificates and moved on to tuna longliners. He got to know a fishing observer on a long trip once. That man befriended him and encouraged him to apply to be an observer. The pay is much better.'

'That's very interesting. You told me he's independent, not one of the boat's crew. Is he employed by the Fisheries Department?'

'I'm not sure. Jimmy doesn't talk a lot. All that time at sea, I guess. He's always gazing into the distance, as if he's at sea, looking for land. He does say it's lonely being an observer. But I doubt that's a big problem for him.'

'I'll do my best to find out what's happened to him, Salome.' They shook hands, said their goodbyes. He put the sad envelope in his pocket, picked up Jimmy's old suitcase, and made his way back up the path.

20

The lunch at the matchmaker's house was not elaborate but it would justify her fee. Singh felt she was an exhibit for Brij's parents. This time she had refused a sari. She and her mother had compromised on an embroidered *salwar kameez* pant-suit. She wore the matching shawl over one shoulder. She managed to remain demure and mostly silent while she wondered if Horseman had discovered the owner of that all-important ring, the ring she was the first to notice. She knew perfectly well that if she hadn't gone to Levuka yesterday, Matt Young would have brought the hand back to Suva, retrieved the ring and passed it over to Horseman. She hadn't done anything special. But still, it was a thrill to know she was the first to see it.

Young women drifted in to clear the table and serve tea and the colourful Indian sweets she loved. She smiled at her care-worn mother, whose anxious frown loosened the glittery tikka on her brow. Singh prayed it wouldn't fall off—her mother would feel humiliated in front of Brij's parents. She put her finger on her own tikka, pressing it in. Her mother noticed and did the same, flashing a grateful smile.

The stilted conversation died away as the families sipped tea. Brij's parents could not be faulted on their manners, but they were rather aloof. They thought her parents beneath them; they who had bred a lawyer.

Brij put his cup on its saucer, glancing round the table for attention.

'Mr and Mrs Singh, Mrs Biswas, *Ma* and *Baba*, I'd like to say a few words of thanks to all of you.' Instantly, he had their attention. Singh read on their faces their unspoken question: dare they hope?

'I'm grateful to all of you for the opportunity to meet Susila. Against tradition, she and I have met twice in Suva during the week and started getting to know each other as individuals, as well as possible marriage partners. It's good to know that we have our parents' approval if we decide to continue that process. But we are hardly sixteen-year-olds, in need of our parents' protection. Susila is a detective sergeant in the Fiji Police Force, trained in combat. She could see me off with a flick of her wrist, I suspect.' Singh's father beamed with pride, the others looked appalled.

'I assure you, she will never need to demonstrate her martial skills against me. As for me, I know my parents despair of me. I have evaded marriage again and again. Here I am, getting on for forty.'

His mother looked indulgent, his father annoyed. 'I can see I've made a bad start on my little speech. But the point is, Susila and I are adults and can look after this matter by ourselves from now on. We both would like to get to know the other better, and that takes time. We're career people, we're busy. We may lose interest in each other as time goes by, or we could become friends. It's even possible we might decide to marry. What would make us both happy now is that you forget about more formal family meetings. We want to do this in our own way, in our own time and in Suva where we both live and work. You can trust us to make the right decision about our lives.'

Mrs Biswas pressed her lips together in a thin line. Brij's mother rolled her eyes at her husband, who drummed his fingers on the table. Singh's parents' eyes widened in amazement. Singh herself looked around the table with what she hoped was a pleasant but neutral expression. Brij winked at her. He really was quite handsome. Bright, too. She couldn't understand why a lawyer would be interested in her.

Her mobile rang. Goodness, she'd forgotten to switch it to silent.

She fumbled it from her bag, saw it was the boss and dashed from the room.

'Susie, we've got a lead on Jona. The ring belongs to Semisi Inia, known as Jimmy. His parents are staying with his sister in Lautoka. I need a photo, and any comb or clothes he might keep there that might give us a DNA sample. I'll text you the details. Can you handle that?'

'Of course. I'd love to help.'

'Jimmy's a fishing observer. He was on a longliner a week ago. The boat docked in Suva yesterday but his girlfriend hasn't seen him. I helped her report him as a missing person this morning. Break the possibility that he's Jona to his family but stress that we just need to rule him out at this stage. Got it?'

'Sure, I'll do that.'

'I'll get a police car to pick you up and drive you there. Give me your address.'

Happiness surged through her. This was what she loved. She returned to the dining room and resumed her seat. Enquiring faces looked at her.

'I'm so sorry about that interruption. I'm afraid that's what my life as a detective is like. My senior officer in Suva has just asked me to interview a family in Lautoka.'

Mr Mishra straightened in protest. 'But we have police officers in Lautoka, CID too. Surely they can handle whatever it is.'

'They could, and the boss would have asked them to handle it except he knew that I was here today. But it's an ongoing enquiry and it would take some time to brief them. I know the case inside out. Lautoka station will send a car for me, so it's no bother.'

'Sounds like top-secret business to me, Susila,' Brij said, chuckling at his parents' frowns.

'Not at all. The driver will take me back to your place afterwards, too, *Baba*. So, there's no need for you to change your plans.'

Her father straightened his back, lifted his chin. He glanced at Mr Mishra. 'I didn't realise how important you were, Susila!'

She was amused but wouldn't let him get away with it. '*Baba*, every police officer is important.'

He wagged his head a bit. 'Yes, well, I suppose that's one way of looking at it.'

*

Jimmy's sister lived halfway up a hill in the old part of Lautoka, overlooking the port. She climbed the steep steps beside the uniformed constable, glad she wasn't managing a sari. As she knocked at the door the constable asked, 'Would you like me to come in with you, ma'am?'

'*Vinaka*, I can manage, Constable. If you'd like to observe, you're welcome to sit in. Otherwise, you can wait in the car.'

'I'll wait, ma'am.'

Horseman had rung ahead, so she was expected. A pretty woman in her late thirties answered the door. Her dark skin was set off by a calf-length dress patterned in yellow and white—much too old for her. Her Afro hairstyle was old-fashioned too. Three primary school-aged children clustered around her, the boy almost as tall as his mother.

'Come in, Sergeant Singh. I'm Kiti, Semesi's sister.' She cast a surprised glance at Singh's fancy clothes but made no comment.

'We were so delighted when the great Josefa Horseman telephoned us, weren't we, kids? Come in and meet my parents.'

Singh wondered what Horseman had told them since Kiti didn't seem at all apprehensive. Jimmy's parents stood to greet her, then sat down at a plastic table set with mugs. They were quite elderly, probably around seventy. She joined them while Kiti busied herself making the inevitable pot of tea.

'Did you know that Semisi's ship returned to Suva yesterday?' Singh asked.

Mr Inia chuckled. '*Oi lei*, we don't get that sort of detail from Semisi. Free as a bird, that one is. He works hard, mind you. But now he's a fishing observer, he's one week on one boat, a month on another, two days on a third. Not regular at all. We don't know when he's coming and going. He drops in to stay for a bit now and then, or sometimes just for a day, then he flies off again.' His hand mimed a looping flight before dropping to the table.

'Mind you, we live north of Savusavu, on Vanua Levu, most of the time. We like to visit Kiti and help with the grandchildren, but mostly we're at home. So, it's hard for Semisi to come to see us. The big longliners he works on don't bother with any other port but Suva.' He looked at his wife, who nodded her agreement.

Kiti put the teapot on the table, rolling her eyes at Singh in a sisterly way. 'Eh, Dad, you're always making excuses for Semisi!'

Kiti's mother joined in. 'He's alright. He earns good money nowadays. He brings us a fat envelope when he visits.'

'I'm pleased to hear that, Mum.' Kiti stirred sugar into the pot and set about pouring the tea through a strainer.

Singh waited until everyone had a mug in hand. She took a deep breath. If she wanted promotion, she must take difficult situations like this in her stride.

'Jimmy has a friend in Suva who has reported him missing. The ship he was working on docked yesterday morning. The friend says he always calls her before the ship docks and she goes to meet him. She's heard nothing from him this time. She visited the ship but the crew are avoiding her questions. She's worried.'

'Maybe he's gone off her,' Mr Inia smiled.

'Well, that's possible and that's what we hope. That's what his friend hopes too.'

'Eh? Why?'

Kiti answered his question. 'Because, Dad, another explanation is that Semisi has had an accident.'

'Surely not, he's experienced at sea.'

Singh continued. 'Last weekend the police recovered some remains of a Fijian man from a fisherman who found them. Semisi's ship was at sea at that time. We want to eliminate the possibility that the remains belong to him.'

There was silence. They all stared at Singh. Kiti was the first to speak. 'You don't mean Jona! You really think Jona is Semisi? No!'

The children were wide-eyed. Their grandparents looked blank.

Singh spoke directly to Jimmy's parents, trying to be gentle. 'It's possible, that's all. You've probably heard that more remains were found near Levuka yesterday morning. The DNA results have just come through, so we know all the remains belong to the same man. We found a ring on the corpse's hand, a distinctive silver ring hand-made in Fiji. The craftsman's records confirm that Semisi's friend ordered this ring. This lady has seen the ring and identifies it as the one she gave your son.'

'*Oi lei*, it can't be true!' Mrs Inia whispered. Tears sprang from her eyes.

'We need a photo of Semisi to circulate to all police posts as part of the missing person enquiry. Have you got one in the house here?'

Semisi's father seemed baffled. In a few heartbeats, he had aged into a confused old man. 'But we live in Vanua Levu. We have photos in our home. We don't have any here.'

'I might have one or two,' Kiti said. 'I'll fetch the album and check.'

Kiti returned with a fat album which she placed on the table and started to flip through. 'Here's one from a few years ago when he came to see us. Is it good enough?'

The photograph included Kiti, the three children and two men. 'This one's my husband, and this is Jimmy.' They were standing on the house porch, their faces in shadow. The focus wasn't sharp, but what the police photography specialists could do with photos was pretty impressive.

'Have you any others?'

Kiti searched right through the album. 'There are some others from many years ago, but they're not as clear as this one. I'm sorry.'

'Please don't apologise, Kiti. You've been very helpful. The police photographer will be able to enlarge the shot and crop the rest of you out. May I borrow this? I'll return it to you as soon as I can. In the meantime, may I take a photo with my phone and send it to Inspector Horseman?'

'*Io*, we'll do anything to help you and Inspector Horseman.'

'Does Jimmy store any of his possessions here with you? What we need for proof is a sample for DNA analysis, which we could get from a toothbrush, hair comb or even clothes.'

Kiti shook her head. 'No. As Dad says, Jimmy's the free-and-easy type. I don't think he has a lot of stuff. The things you mentioned would be in his cabin on the ship, wouldn't they?'

'We hope so, Kiti. Inspector Horseman will be checking the ship as soon as possible. But we always ask families in identification cases.'

'I know my son's hand, and his face. I can go to Suva and see these—remains.' Jimmy's father had recovered some of his strength. He was now resolute.

'I'm sorry Mr Inia, you wouldn't recognise what we've found. Because of the sea, and the shark—I'm afraid DNA is the only way.'

More silence. She hated bearing such shocking news. It would only get worse for them as they felt the full impact of their son's horrible death. For Singh was sure they had found Jona, DNA or no DNA. The evidence of the ring was conclusive. And she had found the ring.

21

Dr Young wandered into the kitchen. It was nine o'clock. Horseman had taken Tina for her usual waterfront walk, then made himself breakfast. Now he'd migrated to an armchair, propped his feet on a stool, his computer on his lap.

'Good morning, Matt. What do you know about fishing observers?'

His landlord yawned. 'Too early in the morning for brain teasers, mate.'

'Not a brain teaser. It's a real job. Hundreds of Fijians are fishing observers, working all over the Pacific, not just in our waters. And I need to know what they do because the man who owns that silver ring—Semesi aka Jimmy Inia—well, that's his job.'

'A fishing observer? Aren't they like inspectors, checking commercial fishing boats, that sort of thing?'

'That's what I assumed, too. Not that I ever gave it a thought before yesterday. But the internet is educating me. Some observers work onshore, reporting on the catches the commercial fishers off-load. Numbers, size, species—that sort of thing. Their reports go to the fisheries scientists in the region. If the evidence shows the stocks are in decline or even endangered, they recommend that fishery be restricted or even closed.'

'I'm a bit cynical, mate. Does that actually happen?'

'Apparently. The example I've just been reading about is the gemfish in Australia—used to be in huge schools and really cheap.

That species was declared endangered in 1994 with strict limits imposed on catch size. Naturally the price of gemfish soared. Stocks are now recovering and the limits may be relaxed down the track.'

The pathologist ran his hands through his hair. 'Come to mention it, that fits. I remember gemfish. It's what you used to get as the fish part of fish-and-chips when I was young. Well, I've always been Young, but you know, of tender years. Suddenly, there was no gemfish anymore, and I forgot it completely.' He yawned again. 'God, why can't I wake up this morning?'

'Late night?'

'Not too late, drank way too much beer with some guys from the medical faculty board. Can't seem to take it as I get older.' He rubbed his head again.

'Physician, heal thyself! Isn't that what they say?'

'Bang on. But I'm a surgeon to the dead. Not so good at healing. No practice. I'd better put the kettle on.'

'Sure. Fill it up. I'll make a plunger of coffee.'

'Tell me more about our tragic fishing observer while you do it. Did he work here in Suva?'

'Sometimes, but mostly he worked at sea. I gather these guys are employed by their own governments but they can be placed on fishing vessels from any country, just for one trip. Often they're sent on the tuna longliners you can see parked down at the wharves.'

'So, what does the captain do, when he sees the observer recording illegal catches?'

'Exactly. My question exactly. If I ever saw certain conflict, it's here.'

'Poor bloody guy. You reckon it was murder?'

'Don't know. But you wouldn't rule it out, would you?'

'Hell, no. If what you've told me is the case, and your rugby-damaged brain hasn't got it arse-about.'

'D'you want coffee or not?'

'I hope that's not a threat, mate!' Dr Young feigned moral outrage well.

'Not at all. I don't bother with threats. If I wanted revenge for your insult to my brain, you'd be on the floor now. It was merely a general enquiry.' But Horseman couldn't keep a straight face and burst out laughing.

He returned to the armchair with his coffee. 'I'm spending the rest of my Sunday morning finding out more about this conflicted occupation. After lunch I'll go to the station to do the file before Susie gets back.'

His landlord was already deep in the latest edition of *Forensic Pathology Case Studies* and didn't hear.

The more Horseman read, the more unanswered questions popped into his mind. He needed an expert he could talk to about this. He must know someone. Then he remembered Waisele, the young nephew who had convinced Ratu Tabualevu to initiate a marine reserve on Vula lagoon. At the time Waisele was a postgraduate biology student. He remembered someone mentioning the young man was now in the Fisheries Department after completing his master's degree. He should know all about fishing observers.

He looked up Waisele on the Department's website and sent him an email. Two hours later, he received a friendly reply agreeing to see Horseman at nine o'clock on Monday morning.

22

The last time Horseman met Waisele Tabualevu he was a postgrad student with dreadlocks, cut-off jeans and a Greenpeace T-shirt. Less than a year later he had his degree and an appointment as a project officer in the research section of Fisheries—fitting for the nephew of a maritime chief. His hair was short, he wore khaki cargo pants and a crisp blue-and-white *bula* shirt. His confidence and charm were just as Horseman remembered. His enthusiasm too.

'You know how I feel about conserving our reefs and lagoons, Inspector. I'm just as concerned about the bigger fishing picture— beyond the 12-mile limit and even beyond the 200-mile EEZ—our exclusive economic zone. It's all very well to have an international law of the sea and protocols, but how can it be enforced? Whatever nations might sign up to, the giant purse-seiners and longliners can flout the rules. Those vessels may have transferred their catch to carriers time and time again during their voyage of more than a year. Unless there's a fishing observer on board, there's no way breaches can be detected. Those brave guys are crucial.'

'How many vessels take on observers, Wes?'

The young scientist frowned. 'It used to be higher a decade ago, but the huge increase in the number and size of fishing vessels working on the high seas means that observer coverage has dropped. Our current goal is to achieve five per cent coverage for longliners, but it should be at least twenty per cent, just for statistical validity.'

'Tell me about a breach relevant to Fiji that I can latch onto.'

'Okay. You know that all commercial fishing vessels operating in Fiji's EEZ must be licensed and pay a hefty annual fee to the government. That license comes with a rule-book.'

'Sounds good to me. I guess there are quotas.'

'No, not quotas—they have a downside. You've got to remember there's intense pressure on the captains of the vessels to make a profit on each trip—they're paid a percentage. So are the engineer and crew. Now, a ton of tuna is not just a ton of tuna. The price the fish gets depends on the species, the size, the condition of each fish and so on. The captain wants to get the top price to maximise his share.'

'Sure, I can understand that.'

'So, if you can only catch a hundred tons, what are you going to do?'

'Make sure you catch the fish that get a higher price?'

'That would be ideal, but the captain doesn't often have that sort of control.'

'What can he do, then?'

'If he's desperate, he'll dump the small fish, and the unwanted species—they're called the bycatch.'

'What a waste—can't they be sold?'

'Not if they're prohibited—like turtles. Not if they're birds, like albatrosses. The rest can be sold, but if the vessel's quota is a hundred tons, the captain wants those hundred tons to be at the top price. Did you know tuna that die before the line is pulled in can have lower quality flesh than those that are landed onboard live?'

Horseman smiled at Waisele's intensity. 'No, but that makes sense. I guess that means a lower price too?'

'*Io*, so you'll understand why a captain might order all the dead fish dumped overboard. That's against the rule requiring fishers to use the whole catch: the tuna for sale and the bycatch for bait if it has no sale value.'

'I guess so. Do they often die before they're landed?'

'The longer the line, the more will die. It takes hours to haul in a line. Sometimes one in four or five fish can be dead. So you can see why Fiji doesn't have quotas, at least for now.'

'*Io*, makes sense to avoid those problems. But enforcing that rule-book seems almost impossible.'

Wes sighed. 'It is. I think the future is developing high-tech deterrents and making licenses dependent on their deployment.'

'Words of one syllable, please.'

Wes chuckled. 'Sure, I find myself slipping into the bureaucratic jargon already and I've only been here a few months! It could mean in future that if you want a license, you've got to have tamper-proof cameras fitted that record what happens at the business end of your fishing vessel.'

'Got it. So, what would that mean for fishing observers?'

'We still need more and more FOs. They're not meant to have a policing role at all. They have no power to enforce rules. Their role is to observe and record the catch, so people like me in research can get a handle on what's happening to our tuna fishery and keep the regional authority informed.'

'The regional authority?'

'That's the WCPFC—sorry, the Western and Central Pacific Fisheries Commission. Fiji is a member, along with what seems like half the world's countries whose vessels are fishing here. All our data goes to them, to the Scientific Committee.'

'What's their role?'

'Well, I don't want to bore you, but broadly, it's to manage highly migratory fish stocks—that means tuna here.'

Horseman had a vision of hordes of huge fish freewheeling around the vast ocean. How could they be managed? 'Is that possible?'

'Not without effective enforcement, no. But we've made a start. Now the members are obliged to do something about problems of illegal fishing by their own fleets. Speaking of high-tech, all vessels now have to install a device that allows fisheries managers ashore to track their whereabouts. But as I've been suggesting, the problems go a lot further than that.'

'What sort of scale are we talking about?'

'Nearly four thousand registered fishing vessels in the WCPFC area, which is twenty per cent of the planet's surface, by the way. The majority are longliners. Until we have better data, we can't say that number is sustainable or not. The FOs are essential for getting that data.'

'Has a fishing observer ever disappeared?'

'*Io*, it has happened. Working on a fishing vessel is dangerous—you're at the mercy of storms and lethal equipment. An FO's work should be safer than a fisherman's, but some accidents happen, including falling overboard. Rumours fly about violence among crews. Hard to know the facts.'

Horseman sighed. 'At last, that's a situation I can relate to. Semisi Inia, an observer on the *Joy-13*, was reported missing on Saturday. The ship docked in Suva on Friday. Has he checked in with a supervisor here?'

'Fisheries doesn't exactly employ observers. They're self-employed.'

'How come? Don't they collect data for you?'

'*Io*. I don't know why this system evolved, but that's how it is. We have a small section that coordinates the Fijian observers.'

'Have you got a name for me?'

'I'll do better than that. I'll let Marisa know you're coming.' He scribbled a name and number on a Post-it and handed it over. 'It's been great having a chat with you again, Joe.'

'I leave you a far wiser man. Thanks for the instruction. I can see a great career ahead of you in the WCPFC!'

'I prefer working for Fiji, I think. Talking about careers, when are you taking to the field again?'

Horseman was grateful. Wes was one of the few people who didn't assume his rugby career was finished.

As Horseman left, Wes said, 'I hope your FO turns up safe.'

*

As Marisa couldn't see him until eleven o'clock, Horseman returned to the station. Singh was briefing the hotline staff. He waved and went to his desk. He found some documents on the internet about the regional observer program and selected a few to print.

Singh joined him at the printer. 'Good morning, sir. I took the family photo of Jimmy down to Photography. Kelera says she'll do her best with it. What's all this?'

Her bright smile and perfect grooming, which he usually enjoyed, slightly irritated him for once. The hazardous lives of fishing observers bothered him. He summarised what he'd found out as the overworked old machine chugged along.

'I knew you'd want to read these papers so I ordered two copies. I think the old machine's confused. We can lay them out on my desk and collate them.'

As they worked, he shared his thoughts. 'The way these observers are sent to work all alone, without a colleague for weeks on end—it just seems careless to me, even reckless. Wes told me how common it was for the longliner captains to illegally dump fish of lesser value. If an observer does his duty and records that, what impact does that have on his relations with the crew, his position on the ship?'

'I imagine it would be difficult. Unavoidable conflict.'

'Precisely. He can't get off the ship. He eats and sleeps and works alongside hostile people. Yet Salome said Jimmy liked the work.'

After they stapled the bundles, Singh marked one set with her yellow highlighter, put it in a yellow wallet and handed it to Horseman. 'Your light reading, sir.'

'*Vinaka.* How's the hotline going?'

'The team are managing well. None of the potential victims matches our criteria. And since you found out about Jimmy Inia on Saturday…'

'Yep, time to close it down. I'll tell the super.' He had to admit he'd not taken a lot of interest in the hotline since Salome had told him about Jimmy Inia. He had no doubts that it was Jimmy's head the shark swallowed, Jimmy's hand and pieces of Jimmy's lung that washed ashore in a tangle of seaweed.

'Right, fifteen minutes to make what you can of the FO Program that Fisheries runs, and what the WCPFC means for the poor beggars, the FOs. Then you can come with me to meet Marisa who coordinates the FOP.'

'Will do, sir. Sounds like fun.' Her green eyes shone and his grumpiness disappeared. She seemed in a lighter mood today. He speculated about her weekend in the west. Not her interview in Lautoka—he knew about that. He was curious about the marriage broker and especially the mysterious suitor.

23

The coordinator of Fiji's FO Program looked tough. She was lean and well-muscled like an athlete—a long-distance runner. Perhaps she'd worked as a fishing observer herself. She skipped the customary leisurely formalities.

'Call me Marisa. What can I do for you, officers?'

'Semisi Inia, known as Jimmy, has been reported missing to the police, Marisa. We're obliged to investigate, and we owe it to his worried parents and friends. *Joy-13*, the boat he was working on, docked in Suva three days ago. Are you saying you didn't know that? You're his employer!' Horseman immediately regretted putting Marisa on the defensive. He wouldn't get much out of her now. She'd fall back on bureaucratic claptrap.

She looked at the open file in front of her and turned a page. 'As I said, Inspector Horseman, I can confirm that we offered Semisi Inia the *Joy-13* deployment, which he accepted. We liaised extensively with the fishing company, arranged his travel and visa to the Marshall Islands, where he joined the vessel. Both he and the captain were fully briefed about his role and duties as an observer. A complete Observer Kit was issued to him on deployment. Thus, all standard procedures were completed and recorded.

'However, I must stress that while it is FOP's aim to provide timely logistical support to our observers, they are definitely not our employees. They are independent contractors, as I explained.' She leaned forward, glaring at him.

'Who pays them? As a matter of interest.'

'We handle their payments, reimbursements and entitlements, but all these costs are recovered from the vessel owners. That's an article of the WCPFC Convention.'

Horseman glanced at Singh, who looked as surprised as he was.

'Does a FOP officer meet the ship when the observer disembarks?'

'Not usually. However, our observers' debriefing is essential to our goal of providing reliable data to the Scientific Committee. A placement officer checks the observer's reports are completed according to the correct procedures and verifies the accuracy and completeness of the data before entering it in the appropriate database.'

'Does the placement officer actually talk to the observer when they return?' Singh asked.

It was her turn for a scathing look from Marisa. 'Of course! Both the observer and the debriefer will have matters to discuss.'

'Forgive me, Marisa, but if the debriefing officer doesn't know when the vessel docks and the observer disembarks, how can they meet?' Horseman tried to sound polite.

'That's straightforward. The observer contacts his placement officer and arranges a meeting.'

Horseman felt like walking out, getting away from this bureaucratic circling. But he took three deep breaths to calm himself.

'Marisa, what would happen if the observer fails to contact his placement officer?'

For the first time Marisa was nonplussed. 'That's never happened.'

'It's possible in theory though, isn't it?' Singh's voice was friendly. She smiled.

'Well, the debriefer would probably get in touch with the vessel's port agent. They're the ones who know all the day-to-day details.'

'Great! Can you tell us the name of the port agent used by the *Joy-13*, please?'

The FOP coordinator was softening. She turned to her computer keyboard and clicked. 'Yes, I thought so. It's TTF: Tuna Traders of Formosa. Behind the port in Rodwell Road. Mr Toby Shaddock is probably the right person. I'll print out the details for you.'

Shaddock was a familiar name to Horseman. The Shaddocks of Lautoka were an old part-European family like his own, who passed the surname of their foreign ancestor from generation to generation. He remembered his father mentioning the name but had forgotten the context.

Another click or two and a tiny printer purred. Marisa handed Singh the sheet with a nod.

Singh smiled again. 'Many thanks for your help, Marisa.' They all shook hands.

They paused at the entrance, adjusting to the glare. 'How could you be so nice to the dragon?' Horseman asked.

'As you told me once, sir, dragons are just doing their job, guarding their treasure. I always remember that.'

Had he really said that? He must have been in a better mood than he was now. 'But no one takes responsibility for these fishing observers—I can't understand it. They're independent contractors, for heaven's sake. It seems to me they do an incredibly tough job in a hostile workplace with no protection at all. No one cares enough to check on their whereabouts. Salome said Jimmy considered himself well-paid. I damn well hope so. Let's see what the port agent has got to say.'

*

When he was told Toby Shaddock would not be able to see them until two o'clock, he was even more irritated. He stopped reading the papers he'd printed and turned to his computer. There was an email from Kelera with the processed photo Singh had got from Jimmy's family. The image showed a man in his thirties, a bit rough and weather-beaten, with a friendly smile. It was still a bit out of focus, but he knew Kelera would have achieved the best definition possible.

'Singh, look what Kelera's done with that poor family photo.'

He picked up the phone. '*Vinaka vakalevu*, Kelera. Can you email that shot to Missing Persons, please? They're waiting to slot it into their template. I want to get it out to all the stations nationwide as soon as possible. They'll print the posters for the small police posts, too.'

'*Io*, sir. I'm on it.'

Singh leaned over his shoulder to look at the image. 'Fantastic! You'd never know it wasn't an original headshot!'

'Yep, Kelera's magic.'

'While we're waiting to see Shaddock, why don't we go down to *Joy-13* and see if we can speak to someone?' Singh asked.

'We could be lucky I guess, but somehow I don't think so. These foreign fishing crews keep themselves to themselves. I can't see us being invited on board. I bet we'd be told to take our questions to their port agent. I deal with agents when I have to send or collect things from the wharves, but I always called them shipping agents. Do port agents have a different function?'

'Can't help you there, sir.'

'When we see Mr Shaddock I hope he'll arrange for us to visit the vessel. Fiji Police don't have a right to board foreign vessels unless they suspect criminal activity. I don't want to cause a diplomatic incident.'

'You could always say you had a tip-off there was heroin or cocaine on board,' she suggested, tongue in cheek.

'Detective Sergeant Singh, I'm shocked!' However, we could drop in on the Port of Suva Authority—POSA, yet another acronym. They should be able to fill in some blanks for us. Let's go now.'

*

As he climbed the steps of the squat tower, Horseman imagined the harbourmaster gazing out to sea through his telescope, alert for unauthorised ships entering the port. Of course, he should have known better. Although the lookout room at the top was glazed right around with a superb view of the whole bay, and there was indeed a telescope trained on the horizon, the officer on duty focused his attention on a bank of screens on his desk. The officer turned around at Horseman's knock on the open door.

'*Bula vinaka*, Detective Inspector Horseman, what an honour to meet you!' He gripped Horseman's hand and pumped it with vigour. 'I'm Manoa Naulu, one of the assistant harbourmasters. My goodness, I've followed your games since you were a newcomer playing for Police. You've given us moments of excitement over the years.'

'*Vinaka vakalevu*, Mr Naulu. In rugby the team is everything. The result depends on every player.'

'*Io*, but some players stand out and you are one of them, sir!'

'*Vinaka*. This is Detective Sergeant Singh.'

'Welcome, ma'am.'

'Mr Naulu, we have some questions about a fishing vessel, name of *Joy-13*,' Horseman said.

'*Io*, one of the Chinese longliners. We put the longliners on the Princess Wharf. Some people call it Fisherman's Wharf now, like in San Francisco. Let me see, come over here. I'll point her out to you.' They crossed the room, Mr Naulu brought the telescope and focused it. Princess Wharf and the row of white ships sprang to view in sharp detail. They all had low sterns and high bows, with a lot of elaborate-looking equipment protruding from the superstructure.

'Which one is *Joy-13*?' Singh asked as she took her turn at the eyepiece.

'You can't see her name, but *Joy-13* is the third along, right in the middle. These days, the longliners all look very much the same.'

'We've had a report of someone missing from this ship. Do you have a crew manifest or a list of everyone who was on board when *Joy-13* entered the port?' Horseman asked.

Mr Naulu consulted his computer. '*Oi lei*, I'm sorry. I wish I could help. However, we are yet to receive all the statutory entry documents for *Joy-13*.'

Horseman was confused. He believed ports, whether seaports or airports, were absolute sticklers for procedure and paperwork, even if it was now e-work.

'I understood a whole raft of paperwork was required of ships entering Fiji.'

'Quite correct. But we haven't received it from the agent yet.'

'You mean the port agent? Tuna Traders of Formosa?'

'*Io*, that's the one.' Naulu nodded cheerfully.

'Doesn't the ship have to have permission to enter, take a pilot on board and hand over the documents before it can berth?'

'*Io, io*, that was the old way. You're right, Inspector. Nowadays, the ship's agent informs us the ship will arrive and submits the Request to Enter online. We send out the pilot who navigates the vessel the five kilometres into the port. Because the *Joy-13*'s agent is a well-respected company which has never given us any problems whatsoever, her entry was facilitated to allow the fish to be unloaded promptly.'

'Surely the fish is deep-frozen?' Horseman asked.

'Most is. But this load was chilled tuna for the Tokyo sashimi market, you know. Top prices. The agent will lodge all the forms electronically in a day or two. With so many foreign fishing vessels in recent years, there may not be anybody onboard who speaks English.'

'Am I correct in concluding that the Port doesn't know who was on board when *Joy-13* docked?'

'Well, you are correct, technically. But all those details must be fixed up before she leaves again. We're very strict about that.' He nodded his reassurance.

'*Vinaka*, Mr Naulu. Your explanation has been very enlightening.'

'My pleasure, Inspector. Any further help I can give you, please get in touch. Here's my card.'

They said goodbye and Horseman followed Singh's bobbing ponytail down the narrow spiral stairs. Once outside, he threw up his hands.

'Hell's bells, Susie, what's the country coming to?'

'Sounds strange to me, too.'

'Something's definitely fishy here.' He couldn't resist the pun but Singh showed no sign of having heard it. Was she trying to tell him something?

At the wharf gates, a spicy aroma cut through the hot diesel fumes. The roti seller called out to them.

'I could murder a roti or two. Hungry, Singh?'

Horseman chose his usual pumpkin and pea combination while Singh settled for eggplant and tomato.

Across the road from King's Wharf, a stately two-storey colonial building put the encroaching steel sheds to shame. Turned timber posts supported a curved awning that provided shade for passers-by and balance to the flagship store of the old Steamships Trading Company.

Horseman lifted his chin. 'There's our destination, Singh. I don't know how our properly constituted authorities came to hand over their operations to a private shipping agent, but that seems to be what's happened. *Oi lei*! Tuna Traders of Formosa! This Mr Shaddock better be good.'

24

Toby Shaddock looked Fijian except for his light eyes, more amber than brown, and his thin, straight nose.

'I heard my father mention the name Shaddock sometimes when I was a kid, but I can't remember the connection,' Horseman remarked as they shook hands.

Shaddock smiled, courteous but cool. 'There's bound to be at least one, after a hundred and fifty years. I'll ask my parents.'

'Let me come straight to the point, Mr Shaddock. I'm enquiring about a fishing observer on a vessel you manage, if that's the right word. His friend reported him missing when he failed to contact her after the ship docked last Friday.'

'Understood. How can I help?' Toby Shaddock clasped his hands on the old mahogany desk. They were smooth and manicured hands. He looked more like a prosperous banker than someone in the fishing sector.

'You can help by giving me some details of the observer's voyage. But first, I hope you can dispel my confusion about what a port agent actually does. Is it the same as a shipping agent—that's the term I'm familiar with?'

'Yes, essentially. A port agent acts for ships, so the functions are specialised to ship's needs.'

'I see. This morning I went to two sections in our own Fisheries Department, then the Port of Suva Authority. I wanted to know if the observer in question was on board the vessel when it berthed in

Suva and whether he disembarked. I thought someone would be able to look up a file and tell me that. Yet they all say the port agent is the man with the answers.'

Shaddock smiled again. 'I can understand your frustration, Inspector Horseman. Welcome to the brave new world of global fishing enterprise. Exponential growth, just like population growth.' He unclasped his hands and spread them wide.

'Modern Pacific fleets need access to the EEZs or exclusive economic zones, of many island states like Fiji. For some tiny countries like Niue, licensing foreign fishing vessels is their only income. The owners of tuna longliners aren't skilled enough to comply with the regulations of different states. They need to be out at sea, hauling in tuna. When they come to port, they want to offload their catch, sell it, take on supplies, get repairs done and get out again quick, knowing everything is legal. A good port agent makes all that happen for them.'

'That makes sense. You don't talk in acronyms like some I met this morning.'

'I can if you like. But mostly I leave that to the public servants.'

'Touché. I admit the police suffer from creeping acronyms as much as anyone. I can see you provide an essential service to the fishing vessels. But what about the government authorities? How come they rely on you, too? An assistant harbourmaster just told me he's waiting on your agency to supply port entry forms for the longliner in question, including what I need, the list of people on board.'

'Ah, well, it's the same advantage for the authorities as for the fishing companies. Does Fiji's Fisheries Department have the capacity to attend to enquiries about license applications from hundreds of foreign vessel owners who can't speak English, don't understand the system, can't fill in the forms? Can Fisheries staff help them correct their mistakes? Can they do all this quickly so Fiji doesn't miss out on badly needed revenue?'

'Hmm, I suppose it could be a problem for them.'

'You're not wrong! We ensure the information about the vessels is accurate, we fill in the application, check all I's dotted and T's crossed, submit it in whatever format Fisheries prefer, pay the fees. We're Fisheries' best friend.'

'I can see you must make their life easier.' Horseman feared the Pacific island countries' preference for an easy life could well be their undoing.

Shaddock leaned forward. 'We make life *possible*, Inspector. We make the difference between coping and not coping, between capitalising on their EEZ or surrendering to the pirates because no one can stop them.'

'Thanks for clearing all that up, Mr Shaddock,' Horseman said.

Singh was taking notes. Time to get back to Jimmy Inia. He nodded for her to take over.

Singh flashed a winning smile at Shaddock. 'What we need is evidence that the observer Semesi Inia, aka Jimmy, was on board *Joy-13* when the vessel berthed in Suva last Friday, and that he disembarked.'

The port agent returned her smile. 'I want to help, but I'm not sure I can release that information. Until the documents are filed with the port authority, they're private. Commercial-in-confidence status.'

'I can't see any commercial secret connected with the presence of a fishing observer who joined the vessel in Majuro and expected to leave in Suva,' Singh's tone was pleasant.

Shaddock lifted his eyebrows. 'I guess you're correct, Sergeant Singh. However, my client is sensitive about all his ship's records. It's a cut-throat world, you know.'

'Cut-throat? Really?'

'Just a manner of speaking. Let's say intensely competitive.'

'When will you send the records to POSA? After all, they should have been handed over and checked before *Joy-13* berthed,' Horseman asked.

'Should be tomorrow. We were flat out servicing vessels all

weekend. You'll know how impossible it is to get anything done on a Sunday here. I'm afraid the compliance forms take a back seat to preparations to return to sea without delay.'

'I prefer to use your agency rather than visit the ship ourselves, Mr Shaddock.'

'Good choice, Inspector. The captain speaks hardly any English.'

'The police have interpreters, that's not a problem. But I expect he will say, like so many other people I've spoken to today, that it's Tuna Traders of Formosa that have all the information. By the way, how come your company is the agent for a Chinese ship? Isn't communist China the enemy of Taiwan?'

Shaddock smiled a condescending smile. 'This is trade, Inspector. We prefer to be known as TTF these days. Our origins in Taiwan are almost irrelevant now. We're global, we provide the best service and Chinese fishing companies appreciate that. To honour our client's trust, I'm afraid you'll need a warrant for me to provide the information you seek.'

The only way was to bluff it out, which he suspected was what Shaddock himself was doing. He kept calm, but it wasn't easy.

'Mr Shaddock, I am empowered to investigate the disappearance of a Fiji citizen who was on board the *Joy-13* at the direction of the Fiji Fisheries Department. The captain of the *Joy-13* is responsible for Semisi Inia while he was on board the vessel. I am not asking for permission to search your premises, or to search the *Joy-13*, for which I would certainly need a warrant. I am simply asking you for information that you must have access to. Unless that is, the *Joy-13* entered Suva illegally, with no intention of producing the mandatory records. If that was the case, the police would take steps to impound the vessel.'

Shaddock was silent. He stared from one to the other. Then he picked up the phone. 'Leo, could you get me the crew manifest for *Joy-13*, please?'

'Would an observer appear on the crew manifest?' Singh asked.

'Should do, yes.' Shaddock no longer seemed as certain of his domain as before.

Soon there was a knock and an eager young man entered. He smiled at the officers and handed a page to Shaddock, who skimmed it quickly before passing it over to Horseman. 'That will be all, Joni. The manifest includes the name of Semisi Inia. As I thought most likely, your missing observer probably just changed his mind about his girlfriend and ran away.'

'I very much hope so, Mr Shaddock. By the way, do ship's crew fill in the same Immigration cards on arrival that air travellers do?'

'Yes indeed. We make sure our captains have a supply.'

'What happens to those?'

'I don't handle those yet, I'm afraid.' Singh shot him a stern look. 'Just joking, Sergeant. Immigration should have them.'

*

They walked back to the station. Horseman couldn't tolerate being stuck in a cab inhaling diesel fumes while container trucks reversed in and out of warehouse yards. Quicker to walk, better for body and mind. And the latter certainly needed some help.

'I'm kicking myself for not thinking of those Immigration cards before. I've filled in enough of them myself, but always at airports.'

'Don't kick too hard, sir. I forgot about them too. Not that I've ever been overseas.'

'I've never thought about entry formalities for ship's crews. But why would they be any different from plane crews?'

'Now we know they're not, we're a step ahead.'

'True. I don't believe that manifest. I'm ninety-nine per cent certain Jimmy Inia disembarked at sea, out beyond the 12-mile limit. I'll call Ash again the moment we're back. We can't challenge the manifest without a DNA match between Jona's remains and Jimmy.'

Sweat trickled down his neck and between his shoulder blades. The air was thick and lifeless under the grey clouds. He was glad to turn off the main road and walk under the shop awnings. He pulled out his handkerchief and mopped his face.

'I'll buy you an ice cream, Singh.' He loved the home-made ice cream at Hare Krishna. He bought two cups: lime-coconut for Singh and ginger-pineapple for himself. They hurried across the road and into the station before the ice turned back into cream.

They sat at his desk, enjoying the cold treat.

'I'm going to put Musudroka, Kau and some constables in plain clothes watching *Joy-13* round the clock. They can photograph who comes and goes, ask casual questions of workers. I don't want to show our hand before the DNA evidence comes in. The super will clear it with wharf security so we can access their records too.'

'Good idea, sir. What do you want me to do?'

'Track down the *Joy-13* entry records at Immigration. If they've already made it to the database, get authorised access and download them. Persist if Immigration is obstructive. Their Records section will close for the day soon and knowing them, they won't want to work even a minute more. It's unlikely the cards have been entered yet, as the vessel arrived on Friday. If that's so, you'll have to charm or bludgeon your way into getting copies. That won't happen today, though.'

'No chance. I'll call right away and hope they're uploaded.'

25

Horseman enjoyed having sole charge of Shiners training this afternoon. Lately he'd encouraged Musudroka and Kau to take the lead. He would arrive part-way through. But today the two young DCs were at Princess Wharf, being shown the ropes by the wharf security police. He was glad of the assistance of Constable Tui from Traffic, another regular volunteer.

The boys were improving in all aspects of play. When he thought back to nine months ago when they started, their progress was impressive. He watched them jogging along in more-or-less straight lines now, passing the ball from one to the other; often fumbling but rarely missing the catch or dropping it.

'Okay, Shiners. We'll finish up with a practice game. Mosese, you're the Skins captain. Vili, you take the Shirts. Captains, pick your teams!'

Dr Pillai's car pulled up as if on cue. The team's honorary doctor enjoyed watching the practice match that ended training. It had become something of a ritual for the two men to share their hopes for the boys no one else cared about. He signalled to Tui to take over and jogged over to the doctor's car to help him carry the boxes of food he always brought for the squad.

'Six more boys turned up in second-hand rugby boots today. There's no more antagonism. No one makes a remark, but they all notice. What do you think's going on, Doctor?'

'Oh, my goodness, human nature is going on, Joe. Nothing more, nothing less.'

'What particular facet of human nature do you mean?'

'Tevita turns up with boots. The others are jealous and attack him because he's got something they want and he's a bit of an outsider, always boasting he's your friend. But there's nothing to resent when a few other boys, boys that claim no special status for themselves, manage to scrounge boots somewhere. A few more do it, and suddenly, second-hand rugby boots are a new trend. The boys who manage to get them for themselves are admired and copied rather than envied.' The doctor ducked his head. 'That's my reading of the situation, anyway.'

'Makes sense, as you always do.'

Horseman looked back onto the field. 'I'd better get back and start blowing my whistle.'

'No problems, I can set the meal up, Joe.'

After training finished, Tevita wanted to speak to Horseman. He stayed behind on the pretext of carrying Dr Pillai's boxes back to his car. When they waved the doctor off, Tevita said, 'Joe, you see Pita and Simeone, they copy me?'

'Oh, how's that, Tevita?'

Tevita grinned, delighted. 'You know, Joe, you teasing me!'

'Oh, you mean they copied the way you dodge a tackle?'

'No!' he insisted. The compliment pleased him all the same.

'They got boots, like me!'

'*Io*, Dr Pillai told me you've started a trend.'

'Eh, true, Joe?'

'That's what the doctor said.'

'Joe, I want report to you about my job. I gave out all flyers to customers. I did not waste one, Joe.'

'*Vinaka vakaleveu*. That was a big help to me.'

'That Jona head. You find out who he is yet?'

'Not quite yet. We've got some clues, though.'

'Horrible, that one, Joe! Horrible!' Tevita became a shark, running in a menacing circle around Horseman, scissoring his outstretched arms. He turned, rushing at his prey, snapping his hands at his neck. Horseman ducked and they both laughed.

'You think I can get work as paperboy, Joe? I liked handing out the flyers.'

'Maybe. You could try, Tevita. But I think you'll have a better future if you learn a trade. I can help you get training, like before. I know you didn't like carpentry much, but choose something you'd like to learn and I'll help you.'

'*Io*, Joe,' he said with a shrug.

'Tell me, do you ever go to Princess Wharf, where the big fishing boats dock?'

'I been there, but not much, Joe. Not much business there for me. Fishermen wear old trainers. They don't want to spend money. But big King's Wharf, that's better for me. Cruise ships very good business, Joe. Nice people.'

Horseman wondered. Tevita would be adept at sneaking around the wharf, keeping out of sight, eyes sharp. When discovered, he would be tolerated as a shoe-shine boy. And no one would suspect he was a police scout. Tempting.

He kicked himself for even entertaining the thought. If he put Tevita in danger, how could he ever forgive himself? The days of Sherlock Holmes were over. Anyway, Holmes was a private investigator, not a sworn police officer.

Tevita watched him, intense. 'You want me watch on Princess Wharf for you, Joe? No problem for me!'

'No, I don't. I've already got police officers watching there.'

Tevita's face turned to stone. Horseman hated stamping out his eagerness. 'If you happen to be at the wharves anyway, you can keep your eyes open, of course.'

Tevita brightened.

Horseman was anxious to divert him. 'Where are you staying now, Tevita?'

'Good place, Joe. You like it, I know. Pita, he staying with uncle near rubbish dump. Good place. I stay with Pita in room with other kids. They his cousins. But I like in town better, Joe.'

The first drops of rain fell, swollen with waiting. Tevita pranced, holding his arms out. 'Rain is here. Cool now, Joe.'

'*Io*, Tevita. It's getting dark too. Go home. Be good. *Moce.*'

'*Moce mada*, Joe.'

*

Horseman had one more thing to do at this end of Suva. He slogged up the hill to the Anglican cathedral, wondering if it was dark enough. But there she was, leaning against the trunk of the fig tree, tall and elegant in emerald green, scanning the passers-by with a practised eye. He always thought of her as vulnerable prey, but now he caught her on full alert, there was a hint of the predator, too. They met in the shadows; Salome understood he was embarrassed to be seen talking to her while she was working. The encounter was open to misinterpretation, to say the least. She had told him some of her clients were policemen. If accused, how could he prove he wasn't also a client?

'*Bula*, Joe. Any news?'

'*Bula* Salome. *Io*, the SOCOs checked everything in Jimmy's suitcase and found a few hairs with roots attached and a piece of torn fingernail. They're much better for extracting DNA than hair which has been cut. So, I'm giving this back to you. *Vinaka vakalevu.*' He took the envelope out of his pocket and gave it to her.

'Is there any hope for Jimmy?' Tears welled in her eyes. She patted them with a tissue. He supposed she didn't want to smudge her make-up.

'The only possibility I can see is that another Fijian man was wearing Jimmy's ring. I know Jimmy was the only Fijian aboard *Joy-13*. I don't think it's likely, do you?'

Salome shook her head and looked away.

'The DNA results will settle that question for sure. Perhaps tomorrow. *Moce*, Salome.'

He walked to the next streetlight, where a cab stopped for him. He asked to be driven to Princess Wharf, to help the inexperienced surveillance team.

26

Horseman was strung out on tenterhooks waiting for the DNA results. He checked both his physical and digital inboxes every other minute and didn't stray beyond reach of a phone. Singh was at Immigration, Musudroka and Kau were sleeping off their first night's surveillance at the wharf.

There was no point ringing the lab, they were doing all they could.

Telecom technicians dismantled the hotline set-up, rolling up cables and packing their boxes. Lacking a physical task, Horseman busied himself moving the detectives' furniture back to its usual places. The two technicians rushed to lend a hand. Nice helpful guys, efficient. Too bad the open office was restored completely in fifteen minutes.

He sat down at his desk and filled in search warrant applications for the TTF offices and *Joy-13*. They would be ready to go as soon as he got the call about Jimmy's DNA. He left the date blank, just in case the results didn't come through today. The section detailing the evidence that justified the search, he also left blank. He could have filled it in, but something held him back. He surprised himself; he who sneered at superstition.

Singh rushed in at half-past ten, bits of hair escaping her bun, one sleeve yanked down by a strap of her backpack so the edge of her top was almost off her shoulder. She still looked neat by normal standards but dishevelled by her own.

'Anything yet?' she asked.

Horseman shook his head. 'Good morning, Singh.'

She seemed distracted. 'Sorry, yes, good morning.' Her smile was worried.

'What happened at Immigration?'

'Well, I guess you got my text?'

'Yes, that's why I'm asking.'

'Okay, let me recap this frustrating business. I called yesterday afternoon, but the officious woman wouldn't even consider checking the computer for me because it was fifteen minutes before knock-off time. So, this morning I'm waiting on their doorstep, well, at reception, until a few data entry ladies stroll in late, chatting away. The effort of getting to work apparently exhausts them, because they spend half an hour making tea, using the toilet and goodness knows what else. After that, they deign to arrange themselves at their desks. I ended up knocking on the counter and announcing myself most politely. They were not impressed that a police detective wanted some vital information from them. You know, I'm so glad I don't work with a gaggle of women!'

He was amused. 'Singh, I've never seen you in such a mood. It's me who's the grumpy one, you're supposed to be a lesson in calm.'

'Not today.' She smoothed her hair and adjusted her top. 'Well, the grudging work of ten seconds established that the *Joy-13* info hasn't been entered yet. Then two of them searched through the cards waiting to be entered on four separate work stations. Hurray, someone found them, but—'

'Oh no, not a *but*. But what?' Horseman was relieved that the cards did actually exist.

'But the photocopier's broken down. I offered to check it myself, I'm not bad with criminal photocopiers, as you know. But they wouldn't let me. I suggested bringing the cards here to copy them but that was a no-no, too. I mean, how could they be safe in a police station!' She flung up her hands.

'Go on,' he said.

'So I offered to photograph them with my phone but they looked at me like I was proposing espionage.'

He laughed out loud, he couldn't help it. She looked reproachful at first, but after a bit she smiled. 'I suppose it's a bit funny,' she admitted.

'You're the funny one, Singh. Please don't leave me in suspense.'

'I threatened them with a search warrant to seize the cards. They couldn't believe it. Final upshot—Mrs Patel and Mrs Sikivou have taken the cards to copy on another machine in a different section. But they insisted I return in an hour to pick them up. I mean, there are no more than twenty cards!'

'Double-sided though! Well done, Singh. I've got the search warrants filled in and ready to go to the magistrate the moment we get the word from DNA.'

'I've got to update the case file unless you've another job for me. I intended to do it last night, but somehow I didn't get back.'

That was unusual for Singh. 'Fine, I hope you got some rest. Go ahead and do it now.'

'I'll call Toby Shaddock and apply a bit of pressure.'

Shaddock didn't pick up the call to his mobile, but when Horseman dialled the TTF general number he was switched through to Shaddock's office.

'As you know, Mr Shaddock, there are irregularities with *Joy-13*'s compliance with port entry protocols. We've found out this morning that there's a problem with the Immigration records too. I need to talk to the Captain about all of this today, so we can fix this situation up and avoid the possibility of police charges being laid.'

'I'd like to help, Inspector, but I have no idea of his whereabouts from one minute to the next. I'll certainly let him know you'd like to see him today.'

'It's more than *like* if we're to avoid holding *Joy-13* in port while the captain answers serious charges. I'm trying to be polite, but this is official, Mr Shaddock.'

'I'm not sure you can order the master of a foreign vessel to attend a Suva police station, Inspector. However, I'm sure the captain will be happy to talk to you when he finds out you're looking for him. By the way, Captain Shen doesn't speak English.'

'No problem for us. I'll arrange an interpreter. Which language would he prefer to use for the interview?'

There was silence for a few moments.

'I'll ask him and let you know. Probably Hakka or Mandarin.'

'How do you communicate with Captain Shen?'

'I use Mandarin. But that's the only Chinese language I'm fluent in. I'm a registered interpreter of Mandarin to English myself. I could translate for you.'

'That's interesting. How did you become fluent in Mandarin?'

'University in New Zealand, followed by working for TTF in Taiwan for some years.'

'Impressive. I expect to see the captain later today, then.'

'I can only do my best, Inspector.'

'I understand. But if he doesn't turn up, we'll push ahead with Plan B, which is to deploy uniformed officers to guard *Joy-13*, and control entry and exit.'

'We'll try to avoid that, Inspector. Goodbye.'

*

Singh returned smiling from her second visit to Immigration of the morning.

'Success?' Horseman asked.

She slid her backpack from her shoulders and extracted a buff government envelope. She handed it over. 'I don't think I'd have them yet if the section manager hadn't dropped in at the same time as me. He couldn't have been more helpful. I've got the copies of the cards, and I can confirm that there isn't one for Jimmy. In that envelope, you'll also find a memory stick with scans of the passport ID page for every crew member. I've got Jimmy's too. The manager said he'll email a digital file of their data when his staff have entered it in their database.'

'*Vinaka*, Singh. That's real progress.'

'I probably should have gone through the section head in the first place. Just thought I'd cut out the middleman. I never imagined Immigration staff would treat a police request so flippantly.'

'Don't worry about it. A lesson for next time, perhaps. Just in case Captain Shen does honour us with his presence, can you—'

He snatched up the phone at the first ring. When he heard who was calling, he switched to speakerphone.

'Inspector Horseman, we've got a match between the head and the DNA samples from Semesi Inia's clothing. The report isn't ready yet, but I know you're waiting on this. I'll email you the report as soon as it's done. Should be later this afternoon.'

'*Vinaka vakalevu.* Wonderful news. I really appreciate you moving this one to the top of the queue. A lot's hanging on this.'

'Happy to help. I'm glad it's the result you wanted.'

Horseman grabbed his search warrant applications. 'As I was saying when I was so rudely interrupted, let's get ready to interview the captain: photos, the lot. We want to scare him.'

'I'm on it!' She jumped up.

Horseman rushed away to tell the super and get the search warrants signed.

27

The spectacular sunset views drew diners to the Garden Grill, perched high above Suva on the western escarpment. Brij said there was no point arriving after it was dark. He wanted to pick her up at the station at quarter to six so he could drive her. Really, it was to make sure he wasn't sitting on his own waiting for her as usual. Fair enough, too.

Singh convinced him it would be impossible to park near the station and promised to call him if she was running late. She would try her best to be on time.

When she followed the waiter through the glass-walled dining room to the terrace, she understood what the fuss was about. The low sun silvered the deep green sea and blazed the serried hills with colour. The jumbled town of Suva was hidden.

'Aren't I clever?' Brij asked. 'From this table we can both watch the sun setting over the sea.'

'Very clever. I've heard about this place but never been here. Wow, I didn't imagine it would be so, well, beautiful.'

It was much too expensive for her and for anyone she knew. She was no stranger to the cheaper Chinese and Indian restaurants in central Suva—pizza places too, but Brij's favourites were a few notches above hers. At least. But he insisted on paying for her meal, saying that was non-negotiable. It would be easy to get used to a higher life.

'Don't expect too much of the food—it's not on a par with the view. The steak can be tough, I recommend the lobster.'

She laughed. 'Lobster! The only lobsters I've ever had were caught by a cousin who has some traps. They were heaven.'

'The lobsters here won't be as good as your cousin's, but I rate them. You only live once, you know!'

She was still high after the DNA result, which was indeed a cause for celebration. Suddenly she wanted to tell Brij about the success. But she couldn't.

'Okay, I'd love to have lobster. Are you celebrating something?'

He chuckled. 'What do you think I might be celebrating?'

'Let's see. A win in court?'

'Not today.'

'A new and very wealthy client?'

'I wish!'

'You've been promoted to chairman, or whatever your boss is called?'

'Really, Susila, can't you think about anything but work?' He frowned, quizzical. He looked amused rather than irritated, though.

'I give up.'

'It's my birthday.'

Singh was embarrassed. 'Brij, you should have said! I wish you a very happy birthday indeed.'

The waiter brought champagne. Drops of condensation already covered the bottle, less than a minute out of the refrigerator. The label was sodden. He popped the cork and poured the fizzing wine into chilled glasses.

'Here's to you, Brij. Many happy returns.' She raised her glass to touch his.

'This is good, isn't it? My birthday present to myself. Champagne and lobster.'

'It's an honour to share it with you. Thank you, Brij.'

She couldn't admit she'd never drunk champagne before. The bubbles somehow got themselves into the back of her nose. Brij finished his glass quickly. The waiter plucked the bottle from the silver ice bucket and poured him another.

'Do they celebrate birthdays at your office?' she asked.

Brij swigged half his glass. 'You do have a one-track mind, Susie.'

She smiled in apology.

'I'm interested in what you did on your birthday, Brij. I just assumed you were at work as it's Tuesday. Did you take the day off?'

'No, I was at work. The partners took us all to lunch. Nice of them, but it's on the expense account.' He shrugged.

'Then my parents called. Mum said it's high time I was married, now I'm thirty-nine.'

She finished her champagne so she wouldn't ask the wrong question again. This was not his usual easy-going mood. He seemed tense, resentful. Maybe they had too much alcohol at the work lunch. Maybe it was another year rolling over; next birthday he would be forty.

She must remember he was not a suspect in an interview room. Change the subject.

The arrival of the lobster saved her from putting her foot in it again. It was served in the shell, dressed with herb butter. As she savoured the delicate flavour, the melt-in-the-mouth texture, she saw the tension drain from Brij's shoulders and neck. She was glad he had something to eat with his third and fourth glasses of champagne. Her head was already fizzing and she'd only started her second.

Neither of them tackled their salads until the lobster was gone. The silence was no longer awkward, though. They gazed at the show-stopper sunset, entranced. At least, she hoped he was entranced.

As the sun dipped towards the horizon, he said, 'Don't take your eyes off it or you'll miss the green flash. Thump the table when you see it.'

'Right.'

They waited. It was a sliver of an instant, but she caught it. Brij thumped the table first. They smiled at each other.

'Gelato?'

'Yes, please,' she said.

'What do you expect from marriage, Susie?'

Suddenly, she could confide. Maybe it was the champagne.

'Love, companionship, babies, a home. Most of all love. To love and be loved.'

'It would be nice, wouldn't it?' His voice was wistful.

The lurid orange, red and gold intensified on the western horizon as they relished their dessert.

'Thank you, Brij. I enjoyed your birthday so much. This place is special.'

'Saturday night?'

'On condition that I choose the place this time.'

'Oh, alright. Where?'

'Pizza Perfecta, near the cinemas. We could catch a film afterwards if I can get the time off.'

'What? Don't the criminals go out on Saturday night?'

'They go out, but they're working. That's why the police have to work, too. I'm not rostered, but crime is unpredictable.'

28

Musudroka and Kau arrived mid-morning to find their shared desk covered with photo enlargements and sundry papers.

Horseman was glad to see them. '*Bula*, we've got good news. A DNA match for Jimmy and search warrants approved and on their way to the magistrate.' The two young detectives grinned, high-fived and gave him the thumbs up.

'Don't touch anything, guys.' Singh warned. 'I'm assembling all our evidence here. We're going to blow Captain Shen out of the water with this. How can he argue that Jimmy disembarked in Suva when we show him the photos and the DNA?'

'Why don't you explain your sequence of evidence to these kids while you're putting it in order, Sergeant Singh? Just think aloud. Part of their training. I'll check my email for that DNA report one more time.'

A uniform knocked and entered. Spotting Horseman, he said. 'Sir, excuse me. You've got two visitors waiting at the counter. Mr Toby Shaddock and Captain Shen. Mr Shaddock asked me to give you this.' It was a TTF business card with the message: *Captain Shen is ready to see you. I will translate.*

Singh was still marshalling the evidence.

'*Oi lei*! The captain's here already? Well, I'm not ready to see him quite yet. Put them both in a free interview room, will you? Offer them tea. Say that I'll speak to them as soon as I'm free.'

'Musudroka! Whistle up a Mandarin interpreter who can get here within fifteen minutes. Kau, help DS Singh with whatever she needs.'

*

Captain Shen was wiry, weather-beaten. The skin of his face was dry and pock-marked, his coarse hair bristling straight out of his skull like a brush. He gave a stiff little bow when Horseman introduced himself, Singh and the interpreter.

'Did you get my message, Inspector? I'm here as Captain Shen's agent and interpreter.'

'*Vinaka*, Mr Shaddock. You don't have the right to represent the captain in a police interview as you're not a solicitor, I understand.'

Shaddock shook his head.

Horseman continued. 'However, I appreciate your cooperation so I invite you to remain and listen to the interview on condition that you do not speak unless I ask you to. Your advice will be useful as your port agent role seems to be all-encompassing.'

'Sure, I understand.'

Singh switched on the recorder and led the introductions.

Horseman began. 'Captain Shen, you're aware that you need to submit documents at every port you visit during your fishing voyages.' Shen stared at him, frowning.

The interpreter translated. 'Yes, I know. My agent handles all that for me. I'm too busy.' The captain's voice was loud and rough, as if dried out by a lifetime of wind and salt spray.

'You supply the information, Captain. It's your responsibility.'

Shen shrugged. Singh placed the manifest on the table, pointing to the highlighted name of Semesi Inia. Beside it she placed the enlargement of Jimmy's passport photo.

This time he spoke directly to Horseman. 'Me no savvy.'

Interesting—he must have picked up some Pidgin in Papua New Guinea or the Solomons. He was willing to say something, at least.

'Captain, this highlighted name is Jimmy Inia, the fishing observer you took on board at Majuro in the Marshall Islands on

26th July. This is his passport photo. Do you recognise him?'

The captain nodded, grudging.

'But we know he was not on board when you entered Suva. You know this too. This information you supplied to the Fiji government is a lie.'

The captain continued to frown at Horseman as he listened to the interpreter. His face was expressionless. When he made no reply, Horseman said, 'Detective Sergeant Singh, explain why the observer did not enter Suva.'

Singh laid in front of the captain the horrific colour post mortem shot of the head which they now knew to be the head of Jimmy Inia.

'He entered the sea on Friday 8th or Saturday 9th September. His head was found in a tiger shark's stomach on Sunday 10th September. DNA analysis has now confirmed that this is the head of Jimmy Inia, your fishing observer. No doubt about it.'

Shaddock paled. He put his hand over his mouth and gulped. Horseman gestured to the door—he didn't want the man to interrupt the interview with vomiting.

Singh placed the enlargement of the hand in front of the captain. 'This hand and pieces of lung washed up on a beach near Levuka last Friday. DNA analysis shows that the hand is from the same person as the head, namely Jimmy Inia, your fishing observer.'

Next, she passed the evidence bag with the ring to the captain. 'Do you recognise this ring, sir?'

Shen examined the ring, his frowning expression unchanging. He shrugged.

'Would you speak for the recording, please sir?'

Shen spoke directly to the interpreter who translated. 'He says he doesn't. He's seen many silver rings.'

'This ring has been identified as the ring purchased by Jimmy Inia directly from the maker, who works here on Viti Levu,' Singh informed him.

'What happened to Jimmy Inia, Captain?' Horseman asked. Shen remained silent, expressionless.

'Let me remind you, Captain, that the safety of everyone onboard your vessel is your responsibility. You must account for the fact that your fishing observer is proven to have died at sea, five or six days before *Joy-13* entered Suva. What have you to say?'

Shen looked at the interpreter while he translated, then turned to Horseman and spoke. Again, his voice was loud and gruff. Perhaps his usual utterances were orders barked at his crew, above the noise of ship engines and the wind. He didn't look rattled or annoyed. Horseman couldn't read his frowning face at all.

The interpreter said, 'Captain Shen thanks you for giving him this information. He will consult his legal advisor and afterwards make a statement about this matter.'

*

Toby Shaddock called Horseman late on Wednesday afternoon. 'Captain Shen wishes to present you with his statement on board *Joy-13* tomorrow morning at eleven o'clock. How does that suit you?'

'If he can't do so before then, I suppose that's fine,' said Horseman. 'But why on the ship?'

'Despite his taciturn manner, I believe he wants to show you some hospitality. The ship is his domain and he's very proud of it. He's asked me to show you around.'

Taciturn? Shaddock was a master of diplomatic understatement.

'He wants to impress me?'

'I'm not sure. Perhaps he feels more comfortable there.' Shaddock replied. 'The truth is he initially refused to return to the police station. His solicitor suggested this compromise and between us, we persuaded him to agree.'

Really? Horseman would like to have been a gecko on the wall during that conversation.

'Tell him I accept his invitation with thanks. I need to speak to all the crew about Jimmy. Please make sure they're all present and we can interview them after we've spoken to the captain.'

29

'Have you ever been on a tuna longliner before?' Shaddock asked after greeting them on the wharf alongside *Joy-13*.

'Never,' he said. 'I'm looking forward to rectifying that today.'

Sleek and white, bristling with masts, antenna, radar dishes and cranes, the vessel was a different kettle of fish from the small Chinese fishing boats rusting away at anchor in the main harbour. Chinese characters were emblazoned on the bow beside the English name, *Joy-13*. He wondered if they meant *joy* or something completely different.

Captain Shen stood to attention at the top of the gangway. He looked more the part in his white epauletted shirt and his captain's hat with gold insignia catching the sun. He greeted them with his stiff bow again as they stepped aboard. He spoke to Shaddock in Mandarin. Outdoors, his voice didn't grate so much.

Shaddock was the tour guide. 'The captain wishes you to understand the way his vessel and crew work. The line is set to drift horizontally at a certain depth by attaching floats to it at regular intervals. Come along to the stern and I'll show you the fishing gear.'

As they squeezed along the narrow side deck, Shaddock pointed out the location of the freezing compartments below. They passed above the isolated fish hold, which could store chilled fish for a few weeks, the bait store and the powerful engines needed to speed their voyage to distant fishing grounds on the high seas.

'The longline is paid out fast through these plastic pipes, while the crew attach branch lines and buoy lines. *Joy-13* has a baiting machine which can bait ten thousand hooks a day. The crew take the bait out of the freezer and let it partially thaw. Then they spike each bait on a conveyor belt which feeds into the machine.'

'How long is the line?' Horseman asked.

'Usually a hundred kilometres. It takes seven crew five or six hours to set the line, even with the baiting machine. They set radio buoys at intervals so they can find the line at the start of the haul.' He demonstrated how all the gear was accessed. He flicked a switch and the line paid out. Flicked it again and it retracted.

'Now I know why they call this industrial fishing,' Horseman said.

Shaddock smiled, proud. 'This is where premium sashimi-grade tuna comes from. Vessels like this can process and freeze at minus 60 degrees Celsius. However, the market prizes large, fresh yellowfin or bigeye tuna above all else. You can multiply the average price for frozen, smaller fish by ten. At least. That's why *Joy-13* docked at Suva on Friday. Captain Shen had a chiller hold full of prime quality bigeye and yellowfin. We offloaded them and they flew to Tokyo that night, sold at Tsukiji market Saturday morning. He's a happy man.'

What would Shen look like when he wasn't happy?

'The crew take a break for several hours, then it's all hands on deck for the haul. At least eleven hours for fifteen men to land, gut and wash the fish, clean and stow the gear. It's hard, hard work. These guys are tough. They feed the world's billions, they do. And TTF enables them to do it.'

'*Vinaka vakalevu*, Mr Shaddock. This has been an eye-opener. Is Captain Shen ready to give us his statement now, do you know?'

Shaddock smiled. 'He'll be waiting for us on the bridge. Let's go now.'

As they returned to the vessel's midsection, Horseman looked up and asked, 'What are all these masts for?'

'All sorts of communications, radar and navigation systems. Finding fish is science now. It can't be left to luck.'

Captain Shen was waiting on the bridge beside an array of lifeless screens. Horseman noticed one was lit up and went over to look at it more closely.

'Why is this one blinking?' he asked.

The captain barked at Shaddock who nudged Horseman's elbow.

'Captain Shen prefers you not to lean over the equipment, Inspector. You could accidentally trigger controls and we might ram the next boat, or the wharf or something.' Shaddock was trying to make light of the captain's clear annoyance or fear. Which was it?

He smiled and stepped back. 'Of course, my apologies. Let's sit down and we can consider Captain Shen's statement.'

The captain indicated fixed benches either side of what Horseman supposed was the chart table. Did such vessels even have real charts? Was there any paper on the bridge at all? They sat and both detectives set their notebooks on the table in front of them.

A steward in a white shirt served everyone green tea in china bowls.

The captain handed a slim document in a plastic sleeve to Shaddock and barked at his agent some more. Shaddock smiled in apology to the detectives. 'Captain Shen makes this statement on the advice of his solicitor, who has translated his account of relevant events on *Joy-13* into English. He wishes me to read it to you word for word before giving you both hard copies.'

What was the point in dragging it out like this? 'Go ahead then. As the captain wishes.' Horseman nodded to Captain Shen. They all sipped tea.

Shaddock took a single page out of the envelope.

'We hauled in a line in the EEZ north-east of Viti Levu on 8th September. The fishing observer Semesi Inia, known as Jimmy, didn't appear in the mess room for the evening meal at 1730. His colleagues didn't worry at first as they assumed he was working in his cabin or sleeping. At about 1900 I was notified that Jimmy could not be found onboard. I ordered a thorough search of the vessel. Crewmen reported Jimmy's life vest and emergency beacon were in his cabin. By this time it was dark and there was no chance of finding a man in the sea who did not have this safety equipment. Nevertheless, I turned around and slowly retraced the course of the last several hours, sounding the horn and sweeping the lights over the water. At 2130 I concluded Jimmy had been lost overboard and resumed my previous course.

'I acknowledge that under the regulations I should have reported the Man Over-Board (MOB) incident by radio. However, I knew I would not be able to meet my catch target before I needed to dock in Suva to offload my fresh bigeye tuna. My priority was to minimise my turnaround time in port. I don't have the time to be detained in Suva for prolonged formalities for a MOB report. I now regret not complying with my legal obligations to report a MOB incident.'

Horseman's instinct was to shout just like the captain. No, his instinct was to explode. He took a deep breath instead.

'This is unbelievable, Captain. Unbelievable. If no one witnessed Jimmy fall overboard, I understand that your report may have been unavoidably delayed by some hours. But whenever your report was received, our coast guard and navy would have immediately mounted extensive searches. How could you write off a man's life like that? A man who has been a fellow voyager for an entire month!'

The noise produced by the captain was like the warning growl of a threatened dog. He then shouted at Shaddock in rapid Mandarin. Again, Shaddock looked apologetic.

'Captain Shen says there was no point searching. The observer must have been dead already.'

'You can't know that, Captain. There are amazing records of people surviving and being rescued after a much longer time in the sea than a few hours. You're looking at criminal charges that will detain you in port much longer than if you had reported the accident as the law requires.'

Another ear-splitting barrage from the captain, which Shaddock translated. '*Joy-13* was in the open sea, outside the 12-mile limit. Fiji has no jurisdiction over my vessel.'

For the first time, the captain cracked a smile. His right front tooth was missing. He gaped, throwing his head back. A sinister cackle erupted, chilling Horseman.

30

Horseman and Singh stood on the deck below the bridge, literally thinking on their feet.

Horseman simmered. 'What if he'd been a truck driver and left someone for dead on the road and failed to report it? His action was criminal.'

'I agree, but perhaps the maritime law is different.'

'Not really. It's still a criminal act. Not to mention perverting the course of justice by lying to us yesterday. That's a crime that was within our jurisdiction for sure. We can persuade him to come to the station for another interview or we can arrest him. Once he's off the ship, the crew will talk more freely. I bet they're intimidated, the way he barks all the time.'

'We're not quite ready to conduct the most effective interviews yet. I could go through the crew list with Shaddock and ask his advice about which interpreters the crew will need.'

'How about we work it out ourselves from the Immigration information? I prefer not to work too closely with Shaddock. I'm not sure he knows which side he's on.'

'Okay, let's try that,' Singh agreed.

'Or we could do it the other way around. Leave the captain here and take the crew to the station for interview. They'd be protected from his threats there.'

Singh thought about this. 'They could feel even more frightened, sir. Some of them come from countries where citizens avoid police stations at all costs.'

Considering the options, he moved to the gangway and looked down at the wharf. Musudroka and Kau were there, trying not to look like police, and four uniforms provided a visual presence, two near the bottom of the gangway, the others at either end of the vessel.

'Excuse me, please.'

The voice was smooth, educated, with a strong Chinese accent. He turned. This was no fisherman. His bulky build and pudgy face wouldn't survive the onslaught of long hours of physical labour and exposure to the elements. His body would have morphed to lean muscle and tough skin.

'*Bula*, sir. I'm Detective Inspector Horseman and this is Detective Sergeant Singh. Are you a crew member on this vessel?' Singh stepped forward with the crew list.

The man stared at them, unblinking. 'No, I'm visiting the vessel on business. Please excuse me.' He started to move past Horseman, leading with a shoulder as if to squeeze through the gap, but Horseman planted his feet apart so the man couldn't get off the ship without knocking him down.

Singh spoke up. 'We need to see your passport, sir. Unless your name is on this crew list, of course.' She brandished her clipboard, smiling.

'Why would it be on the crew list? I've said I'm visiting on business. I don't carry my passport on me. Too dangerous. You should do more about stolen passports, you know.' He flicked his head up, dismissing them.

Horseman enjoyed playing the plod at times. He smiled politely. 'Do you work for TTF, sir?'

'TTF? No, I don't.' He sounded a little irritated but his face was unperturbed. Expressionless, even.

'It's just that I understood TTF handles all the business in port for *Joy-13*.'

The man was silent.

'Well, Sergeant Singh will take your details down now, sir. You can bring your passport to Suva Central Police Station any time today before six o'clock for confirmation.'

'What? Why? I'm much too busy to do that.'

'Just procedure, sir. The *Joy-13* is now under police guard. Anyone boarding or disembarking must register with us. Sergeant Singh?'

'I comply under protest. Make a note of that. Be sure I will complain to the Chinese Embassy about this abuse.'

Singh smiled. 'That's your right, sir. Here's my card with the station address and numbers. Now, your name?'

'Mao Li.'

'Could you fill in your address, Mr Li?' Singh handed him the clipboard. He scribbled quickly.

Horseman didn't believe the details the man gave would prove genuine. He wouldn't turn up to the station with his passport, either. This message was for Captain Shen and Shaddock as much as for the mystery visitor. He stepped aside to allow the man to leave *Joy-13*. Kau took several photos of him as he descended to the wharf.

'I'd be happier with a formal crime scene set up here, but we'll have to make do with guards for now. I hate to do it, but we'll need to postpone interviewing the crew, even if just for a few hours.'

'I agree that's best, sir.'

'Okay, can you go through the passport and Immigration card info and figure out the languages of the crew? It won't be a hundred per cent accurate but it will be quick. Then organise the interpreters. Take Kau and use him for the grunt work.'

'Yes, sir.' Her mouth turned down. 'It'd be quicker if I did it myself.'

'I know, but we've got to bring the DCs up to speed.'

She grimaced again. 'Yes.'

'You're a great teacher, too.'

'Flattery, sir.' But her green eyes sparkled like sunlit water. She seemed to be getting back to her old self.

'I'll check if the search warrants are through yet. Until we've got them, I don't want to ask the captain's permission to search the ship— I wouldn't get anywhere, the mood he's in now. But he has no right to Jimmy's possessions. I think all I can do for Jimmy's family and Salome is to insist on retrieving those now. Ash and his SOCOs are standing by to pounce the moment we get those warrants. Pray that the magistrate signs them before he takes his lunch break.'

'I'll work out the interpreters we'll need.'

'Ask the super to snaffle another DC from somewhere and get him down here.'

*

'No, you take nothing. Ship belong me!' Captain Shen barked.

'Captain, search warrants for *Joy-13* are being processed as we speak. I remind you that you do not own Jimmy Inia's things. His professional kit and his records belong to Fisheries, who contracted him as an observer on *Joy-13* and supplied his equipment. I will take them to Jimmy's supervisor, who can tell me if anything is missing.'

He waited while Shaddock translated. The captain growled, staring at Horseman, who took this response as an admission of Horseman's claim.

'As for Jimmy's personal possessions, I promised to return them to his family, who must come to terms with the ghastly reality that he is dead and most of his body will never be recovered. Do you really want to haggle over his bits of clothes and his ukulele? These things mean so much to his family.'

Shaddock nodded his approval then translated. The captain folded his arms across his chest.

'No, you take nothing.'

Horseman got up and went out on the deck. He radioed Singh.

'Any news on the warrants?'

'The super's had a word with the magistrate, explaining the pressure. He sent a constable to sit outside the magistrate's door. I'll let you know.'

'I can't spin things out here much longer. The captain's getting angry and something more. Frightened, I think. I was relying on the search to intimidate him, but without the warrants…'

'I'm sure they won't be long, sir.'

'Bird in the hand, Singh. I can't rely on the captain, he's volatile. He could take off with the ship and all of us. I wouldn't put it past him. I'll drag it out for another ten minutes, but if we're still waiting for the warrants then, I'll arrest him and send him back to you with the uniforms.'

'Right, sir. I'm rustling up the interpreters we need. Three of the crew are from the Philippines, so they'll probably speak good English.'

'*Vinaka*. Keep in touch.'

When five minutes had elapsed, Horseman radioed Musudroka. 'Join me here on the deck, Tani. I'm going to arrest the captain. Bring two of the uniforms. They can drive him to the station.'

He contacted Singh. 'Any news?'

'Sorry, sir.'

'I'll arrest Shen now. Be prepared to receive him. Station a constable inside the room and outside the door.'

'Will do, sir.'

Ten minutes was up. He returned to the bridge. Shaddock was there alone. 'Where's the captain?'

'He said he was going to his cabin for a nap. That's what he said. It's hardly my role to stop him.'

'True. Please take me to his cabin,' Horseman said.

Shaddock sighed. 'This is difficult for me, but I don't suppose I have any choice. It's just through here.'

Horseman followed the agent down a narrow companionway. Shaddock knocked on the first door and spoke loudly in Mandarin. Musudroka and the uniforms were forced to press back against the walls. Shen's usual bark was muffled. Then the door opened and Shen emerged, rubbing his bristly hair.

'Captain Shen, I arrest you for failing to report a fatal accident at sea, while in command of *Joy-13*.'

After stating Shen's rights, he nodded to Shaddock to translate. The captain frowned but displayed none of his previous hostility.

'Who is second in command? I will inform him he is now responsible for the vessel until you return.'

The captain muttered. 'Engineer Santo.'

'The constables will escort you to Central Suva Police Station. I'll be along later to talk to you more about the disappearance of Jimmy Inia.'

'May I go with him?' Shaddock asked.

'You can visit him later. I need your help for a little while.'

Shaddock spoke quietly to Shen. To Horseman's surprise, the captain offered no resistance as the constables led him away.

'Mr Shaddock, is the engineer on board?'

'I'll check.'

Horseman returned to the deck in time to see Shen bundled into the police car and driven off.

Shaddock joined him soon enough with Alon Diego Santo in tow. Like most of the *Joy-13* crew, he was short, wiry, weathered and strong. His crew cut hair was greying and he wore a gold cross around his neck.

'I've explained things to Alon, Inspector. He'll help you.'

'Pleased to meet you, Mr Santo. I'm here to collect the possessions of Jimmy Inia and return them to his family. I'll take his professional equipment too and return it to Fisheries as soon as possible.'

'Thank you, Inspector. Jimmy was a good man.' He crossed himself. 'Come this way.'

'*Vinaka vakalevu*, Mr Shaddock. You've been helpful.'

Shaddock winced. 'I'll go to the station and see what I can do for Shen. His bark is worse than his bite, you know.'

'Let's hope so. Do you understand his appalling negligence as captain?'

'I don't, but I'll try to talk to him about it. I think it's as he said.

He sees his duty as running a successful voyage for the owners.'

'Then he misunderstands the duties of a ship's commander.'

Horseman followed Santo down companionways and along corridors to Jimmy's cabin.

Two narrow bunks, two steel lockers, two plywood desktops fixed to the wall.

'I put Jimmy's things in his bag. It's ready for you. Please take it to his family.'

The familiar Fiji Rugby sports bag, black with the white coconut palm logo, tugged his heart. He pulled gloves from his pocket and unzipped the bag, lifting items carefully. All seemed normal.

'If you packed his bag, you'll need to come to the station to be fingerprinted. Your prints will be on some of these items.'

'Yes, sir.'

'Where's Jimmy's computer?'

'Oh, maybe in his locker.' He reached to open the steel locker but Horseman intervened.

'Allow me, please.' He turned the handle. A bulky laptop bag lay on a shelf below the hanging space. 'Did you pack this, Mr Santo?'

'No, I guess that's the way Jimmy left it.'

'You packed everything else. Why didn't you pack this too?'

Santo shrugged. 'I don't know. Probably I thought it was safer in the locker. I can't remember.' His voice quavered.

Horseman checked under the mattresses, bunks and behind the locker.

'Did Jimmy share this cabin?'

'Not at first. There was a reshuffle, and he shared with another Filipino, my friend Filipo. He liked Jimmy. They could speak English to each other.'

'Are there any more of Jimmy's things on the ship?'

'I don't think so. I can't be sure.'

'I appreciate your cooperation, Mr Santo.'

'When will the captain return?'

'I don't know. You're the master of this vessel until then.'

'Mr Shaddock may find another captain to replace me.'

'Oh, does Mr Shaddock supply crew to the vessels he manages?'

Santo nodded. 'Him or someone else in TTF. Their Manila branch posted me to *Joy-13* three years ago.'

Tuna Traders of Formosa was like an octopus, its elastic tentacles reaching into every niche.

'Have you got a mobile phone, Mr Santo? I'll be in touch.'

He noted the number. Santo shouldered Jimmy's sports bag, Horseman grabbed the laptop case and followed the new master of *Joy-13* back to the gangway. The police car was waiting below on the wharf.

31

Singh calculated that if she booked all three available interview rooms, she would need two Mandarin interpreters. Eleven of the eighteen seamen spoke that language. She got a few blank interview room schedules from the duty sergeant downstairs and played around with the permutations. It was already half past three. They needed information from the crew who shouldn't be kept waiting for hours. Singh wanted them in a mood to cooperate.

She preferred the three-room plan, but who was to conduct the interviews? She agreed with the boss that Musudroka wasn't ready to lead, mainly because he had no experience working with interpreters. She explained the situation to the super.

'Sir, would you be able to allocate an experienced detective to help us? Perhaps yourself?' She smiled brightly, so he could choose to construe her second question as a joke if he wished.

'I can get you someone to assist, yes, but not to lead. Not even me. If an interviewer doesn't know the case in detail, the risk of missing something important is too great.'

Singh felt the wind behind her drop, her sails left flapping.

'Only you and Joe can lead these interviews, Detective Sergeant. So, two interview rooms and it takes as long as it takes. From the little I know of seamen in port, don't expect a hundred per cent attendance this afternoon. You may need to haul a few out of their bunks tomorrow morning.'

'Yes, sir. Thanks for the advice.'

'Musudroka and Kau will benefit from this experience. However, if you need them for other duties before you finish the interviews, I'll be happy to step in to assist.'

*

Singh reviewed her notes from the first four interviews. She wouldn't need to check the transcript from the interpreter service when it came through.

Language: Mandarin
Joy-13: 3 years, deckhand
Jimmy: denies that FO was on board, concedes may be mistaken
MOB: did not witness or hear about MOB

Language: Mandarin
Joy-13: 7 months, deckhand
Jimmy: knew FO was on board, never spoke to him
MOB: did not witness or hear about MOB

Language: Mandarin
Joy-13: 20 months, deckhand
Jimmy: denies that FO was on board, concedes may be mistaken
MOB: did not witness or hear about MOB

Language: Mandarin
Joy-13: 2.5 years, deckhand
Jimmy: knew FO slightly, played ukulele on deck occ. Can't remember last sighting
MOB: did not witness MOB, heard later, unaware of search effort

If the quality of information didn't improve, the interviews would be over before dinner-time. She conferred with the interpreter, a young Eurasian teacher of Mandarin at Suva International Grammar.

'Sam, it's inconceivable to me that in a crew of twenty men, some could be unaware of the presence of a fishing observer.'

'Yeah, they'd all know Jimmy was on board. For sure.'

'Do you think they've been instructed in what to say, maybe by the captain?'

Sam shrugged. 'I don't know. They might have decided among themselves.'

'Any cultural insights to help me read the situation?' Singh persisted.

'I dunno. The two who deny there was an observer onboard are from the People's Republic of China. Maybe they're more scared of authority. The two who admitted he was there are both from Taiwan. But I don't know. I'm straying into political opinion here, which I shouldn't do.'

'If it's relevant, I don't see why not. This is off the record.'

'Well, if I'm pushed I'd say that fishermen, or seamen generally, have a reputation for being reticent, a bit dour. I suppose it's always noisy: engines, wind and sea. But I'm straying into speculation again.'

'Any ideas, Tani?'

'No, ma'am. But these four have put me off going to sea if they were to be my companions. Maybe they're resentful or scared—I don't know any more than you two.'

'We'll take a short break and hope we strike a talkative witness afterwards,' Singh said.

*

After speaking to three more deckhands whose range of response was identical to those of the first four, Singh was impatient. The final Mandarin speaker could not be found so she let Sam go. Musudroka offered to get snacks for all of them. She wondered what he'd choose. She hoped it was chocolate.

Singh thought about the interviews. The necessary translating process distanced the witness from her. The pressure she generated by varying her voice and timing was out the window. Her questions were more formal and less effective. The witness could easily evade her pressure by looking at the interpreter and using the time gap to compose an answer. What could she do? There must be professional studies looking into these questions. She'd hunt them down as soon as she could. Not now.

Maybe the boss was having a more fruitful time next door. She hoped so. She checked the list at reception and saw Horseman had just signed in a Filipino deckhand, Filipo Moreno, to his interview room.

*

Filipo Moreno smiled at Horseman. His teeth were chipped and stained with brown-red streaks. Did he manage to chew betel nut with lime at sea? He must take a good supply with him, or else confine his habit to tropical ports.

A constable brought in a tray with biscuits, Moreno's coffee and mugs of tea for Kau and himself.

'Mr Moreno, take a few moments to start on your coffee and biscuits before we begin.'

'God bless you, sir. You are kind. Please call me Filipo.'

When Moreno began to relax, Kau started the recorder and identified the participants. Horseman signalled him to start.

'Mr Moreno, how long have you been a crew member of the *Joy-13*?'

'Sir, four years now. *Joy-13* is a new ship, I join her on her first voyage.'

'Tell me about your job onboard.'

'I'm senior deckhand. I oversee baiting and setting longline, hauling it in, sorting and processing fish, maintaining fishing gear.'

'Wow, that sounds like a big job.' Kau was impressed.

'It is a big job, sir, but I'm still only a deckhand. I work like a donkey but I get blame from captain when things go wrong. I'm in charge, so I should earn more. I want to complain about conditions on board that vessel.'

Kau looked at Horseman, his eyes pleading.

'How about telling your agent, Mr Shaddock at TTF?' Horseman suggested.

'It's very difficult for me.' He looked from one detective to the other.

'Why?' Horseman asked.

'I need my job. I grow up in a fishing village on a small Philippines island. Since primary school, I work on my father's boat. Hard work, but it is our own small business. Then Cyclone Horace destroy our boat and most of our village so we have nothing. I join longliners to save money and go home, help my father repair an old boat we can buy cheap. Already I'm thirty-five and I still can't afford to support a wife and children. I can't risk my job, even though my pay is miserable.'

He was only a few years older than Horseman, but he looked middle-aged.

'I sympathise, Filipo. Fiji gets destructive cyclones, too. They smash up people's livelihoods, not just buildings.'

'Jimmy is a good man. I talk to him about my worries. He say he will try to help me get more money.'

'How did he plan to do that?' Horseman asked.

'He say he will help me become a fishing observer. I tell him I don't have education, but he say there are ways for experienced fisherman. He say I can do training at a fishing school in Philippines. He say he can help me with money for that.'

'Really? He was a good friend, then.'

'Sure, because we can talk to each other in English. I share his cabin for some time, too.'

'Did Jimmy like his job as a fishing observer?'

'Yes, he likes his work. He likes sea, stars, nature. He likes helping scientists know about fish. He likes good money, too.' Moreno smiled, remembering.

Horseman nodded to Kau to take over.

'When did you last see Jimmy Inia?' Kau asked.

'I saw him Friday 8th September. We finish hauling and he stand there watching, counting the fish. When he finish writing in his clipboard, he wave to me and go away. I think he is going back to his cabin to do his paperwork and put the data in his computer. I never see him again.' He touched the pewter crucifix which hung from a leather thong around his neck.

'What time was it when Jimmy left the fishing deck?'

'I'm not sure. Maybe three o'clock. Weather is fine, sea is calm, little breeze. How can he fall overboard?' Tears flooded Moreno's eyes. Kau turned to Horseman again.

'When did you realise he wasn't on board?' Horseman asked.

'Not for a long time. After Jimmy leave, we work for several more hours gutting and cleaning, sorting tuna for chill hold and preparing rest for deep freeze hold. Tough work. Careful work, too—bruised tuna fetch lower price. Then we clean all gear, deck, everything. Captain came to look and make us clean some more. Everything got to be perfect.' He shook his head.

'How did Jimmy and the captain get on?' Horseman asked.

Moreno shrugged. 'I don't know. I hear them talk sometimes. Captain shouts but he always shouts. Other times I see Jimmy show him his records—all forms he fills in for scientist.'

'Can you estimate the time when the crew noticed Jimmy was missing?'

'Our meal is late because of the haul work, maybe six o'clock. It is light. Jimmy isn't there but that isn't strange. I think he probably eat earlier. Sometimes in calm weather he take his dinner out on deck and listen to music through his earplugs.'

'Did he wear his life jacket when he did that?' Horseman asked.

'Always. He obey all safety rules. Strict, he is. He isn't our boss, but he tell any crewmen to do the right thing if they forget. He mime his order—he is funny. "Make people laugh and they don't mind an order," he say to me.'

Horseman needed a time to compare with the captain's statement. He'd try another angle. 'Who raised the alarm, Filipo?'

'I suppose it is me. When it's dark I go back to our cabin. I am off shift and hoping to sleep for eight hours. Jimmy isn't there—unusual. I go around decks but he isn't there, even look into the mess room. When I return to cabin he still isn't there. I notice his life jacket and PLB in there so I tell Alon Santo, the engineer. Alon report to captain.'

This was more like it. 'What's a PLB?'

'Sorry, personal locator beacon.'

Another acronym. 'Of course. What happened next?'

'Nothing for a while. Alon call us to mess, split us up to search different sections of the ship, even the freezer holds. No one find Jimmy. Alon go to bridge to report to captain.'

'What did the captain do?'

'He turn ship around, put on spotlights, sound foghorn and all the crew look for Jimmy in water. For one hour, I think. No trace. Captain order to resume our course. He say no chance Jimmy is alive without safety equipment.'

'What do you think, Filipo?'

'How can I know? Captain may be right, but we should search back along our route for longer.' He shook his head, gazing into the distance.

A good place to end for now. Horseman was almost disappointed that Filipo's account confirmed the captain's, except for the length of the search. Filipo's time estimates were hazy; he didn't wear a watch. He wondered if time was still marked by the eight-bells system on modern fishing vessels.

'I thank you very much for your cooperation and your time, Filipo. You've helped us a great deal. We'll need to speak to you again. An officer will phone you when we need you. Is that alright?'

'Yes, I want to help Jimmy's family, sir. I will talk to you here at the station. Not on the ship.'

32

Horseman and Kau were both late for training. Once again the stalwart volunteers from Traffic got the session underway. Unless there was a catastrophic road accident, traffic constables' hours were pretty regular.

'No dinner for you, Joe, no dinner for you, Apolosi,' Pita, the team clown, yelled. 'You're both late!' This was his way of expressing his pleasure that they both turned up, however late.

A practice game was in full swing. 'About three-quarters of them are wearing boots, Apo. Tevita really started something.'

'*Io*, sir. Just think, two weeks ago some of them attacked him for showing off.'

'Ah, the fickleness of fashion. You'd better take your place on the line.'

It was a humid afternoon. At the end of training, the boys sprayed water over each other. They put their heads under the taps to cool off and drink at the same time. Dr Pillai made sure each had a good drink of water before they tucked into their chicken, greens and rice.

Afterwards, Tevita beckoned him aside. 'Joe, Joe, I been watching *Joy-13* for you. Down at wharf.'

He was taken aback. 'Why? I asked you not to do that, Tevita.'

Tevita's mouth turned down. He looked reproachful. 'You say to keep my eyes open. I want to help you, Joe.'

Horseman remembered he'd said something vague to lessen the boy's disappointment. He should have known better. '*Io*, I know you do. But you could get into trouble from security. How did you get through the gates?'

Tevita chuckled. 'Ah, that my secret, Joe. But Joe, I tell you those police you got down there, they don't know what to do.'

'Why's that, Tevita?'

'Talk to each other, Joe. Don't pay attention. But main thing—they stay too close to boat. Can watch only one side next to wharf. Monday night, first time I go there, I see a boat leave other side of *Joy-13*. Many people, Joe. They don't go on wharf. They get off other side in boat and go west. Row with paddles, Joe. I see. Then boat come back again and take more away.'

'Really? The officers didn't report this.'

'No Joe, because they all on the wharf, can't see other side of boat! I scout all around, front and back. When I good way ahead of *Joy-13*, I can see what happening on other side.' Tevita sounded as if his patience was sorely tried.

'Can you tell me anything about these people?'

'Not much, Joe. Many ladies, Chinese.'

'*Vinaka*, Tevita. But some men around *Joy-13* could be bad. If they caught you spying, they could hurt you. I order you not to go there again.'

'Okay, Joe, but I done good, eh?' He beamed.

'You did very well, Tevita, but don't go there again. Keep safe now. *Moce mada.*' They shook hands.

'*Moce*, Joe.'

Tevita wouldn't concoct such a story out of thin air. There must be something to it. Unfortunately, he couldn't check with the surveillance team right now. He had a sad date with Jimmy's possessions at the SOCO lab.

*

Ash unpacked the Flying Fijians sports bag, examining each item before putting it on the table for Horseman to check and sort into piles for Jimmy's family and his Fisheries employers, or supervisors or whatever their correct legal title was. He inhaled a stale whiff of sweat laced with mould as he emptied a plastic bag onto the table. Jimmy's laundry bag. A T-shirt, shorts, underpants, two pairs of socks. He must have kept on top of his washing, then. The remaining few sets of clothes were clean and neatly folded. A new-fangled inflatable life jacket was encrusted with salt crystals. Would it have saved him from the shark? Probably not—he'd seen reports of surfers paddling their boards losing a foot or arm.

A zippered wallet with the Fiji Observer Program logo contained salty smelling stained notebooks, two plastic ring-binders holding filled-in templates, manuals, a pencil case and scattered bits of stationery. Laminated pictures of fish, glossaries of fishing terms in different languages interested him but he couldn't take time to examine them. There were also caps, sunglasses, an iPod and charger, CDs, and a small Bible—all of them worn and a bit salty.

'I've already checked out the computer bag,' Ash said, pushing a plastic box across to him. The mini-laptop looked robust, maybe a special model supplied by Fisheries. A compact digital camera. The bag was empty, the cables, chargers and batteries jumbled together.

'Anything of interest on the computer?'

It all seems to be work-related. There're email messages, but nothing personal there. The account is on the ship's server. Whoever administers that can see the emails, so that could be one reason Jimmy didn't use it much.'

'Or he might not like using computers much, or not be very good at it. That would put him in line with the majority of Fijians, I suspect.'

'True. You'll probably want to check the files yourself. The camera, too. Lots of fish and shipboard life. You may need someone from the industry to interpret a lot of them. I couldn't see the point of some of the shots. Not many include people.'

'The camera may have been issued by Fisheries too. I'll ask Jimmy's supervisor.'

'What's interesting is what's not there.'

'I think so too. No passport, wallet, no cash or bank cards…'
Horseman trailed off.

'No mobile phone, no personal photos. But would he take these
things to sea? He couldn't use them, could he?' Ash asked.

'He'd need his passport to fly to Majuro and to re-enter Fiji, even
if the ship called at no other port.'

Ash smacked his head. 'Of course, how stupid of me.'

'You do alright for a SOCO,' Horseman teased. 'I'll check if
Jimmy left anything in Fisheries' care. I'll check with his friend who
reported him missing, too. Thanks for everything, Ash. What a sad
case this one is, eh?'

Together they repacked the bag. Horseman put everything likely
to belong to Fisheries in the box, put the bag on top and walked out.
He was certain he'd find Singh still at the station updating the case
file, as the paperwork for the case had ballooned days ago. He didn't
want to keep her late, but he'd like to toss ideas around with her
before the case review meeting tomorrow.

*

Horseman returned to the station to find a memo from the super,
anchored to his desk by his tea mug. He had to admit this was not
so easily overlooked as an email. Maybe Jimmy was like the super,
who was perfectly capable of corresponding by email but only
resorted to that medium when forced.

The super's news was like a pinprick to his balloon. Captain
Shen's solicitor had applied for bail, pending a challenge to the
jurisdiction of the Fiji Police Force over any crimes or
misdemeanours alleged to have occurred on the fishing vessel *Joy-
13*, registered in the People's Republic of China. Consequently,
Captain Shen had been released at six o'clock. He picked up the
telephone. The super answered.

'Joe? Thought I'd be hearing from you. Don't bother apologising.
There wasn't any choice. The captain has his rights too, you know.'

'Sir, I did check on our maritime jurisdiction and it's as I remembered. Fiji police have the power to investigate accidents and crimes committed on board foreign vessels within our territorial seas.'

'That's one of the matters under dispute. But not the only one. Shen claims that the fishing observer fell overboard beyond the twelve-nautical-mile limit.'

'How can he prove that? No one knows what time he went overboard. He can't have been much beyond the limit, by my reckoning.'

'Have you consulted a map?'

'No sir, I had no time. But even a marine chart isn't much use. We know where Jimmy's head was fished up, but that was at least twelve hours after he entered the sea. And tiger sharks roam over very large areas. Even the ship's log can't establish the location when we don't know the time. But I bet Shen's not offering us the ship's log anyway.'

'No, he's not.'

'Sir, I had to arrest the captain to declare the *Joy-13* a crime scene so we can get the log and other records. The SOCOs must search the vessel for any potential evidence relating to Jimmy Inia. What with the delay in approving the search warrants…'

'*Io*, the magistrate got in touch after you left this afternoon. He had second thoughts over the jurisdictional questions and decided to double-check the law himself. The warrants wait in the queue until then.'

'How—?'

'We all have to sing the same hymn, Joe.'

'Of course, sir. I understand there are grey areas—'

'Murky waters indeed. So, tomorrow morning, I'll meet with the magistrate and listen to the expert legal opinion.'

'Sir, my only interest is to find the truth about how Jimmy died. If you could have seen his head…'

'I'm not accusing you of being over-zealous, Joe. I understand where you're coming from. I'll be in touch as soon as my meeting with the magistrate is over.'

'I planned to have a case review meeting around half past nine. Should I go ahead with that?'

'Certainly, I'm not asking you to stop investigating. Speed it up if you can. But for now, no arrests of *Joy-13* crew and no crime scene. Surveillance, yes. SOCOs, no.'

'*Vinaka* sir. Got that. *Moce mada.*'

There was no sign of Singh so he sent a text alerting her to the magistrate's concerns and the meetings tomorrow. Then he walked down to Princess Wharf for a spot check on the surveillance watch.

33

Alon Diego Santo was at the station at eight o'clock on Friday morning, when Horseman arrived.

'Good morning, Mr Santo. I'm very glad you're here. First, let's get you fingerprinted since you packed Jimmy's bag. Then we'll talk. Would you like a cup of tea or coffee?'

'Thank you, coffee please.' Horseman passed Santo's request on to a constable at reception while another led Santo along the corridor to be fingerprinted.

By the time that was done, the constable had delivered the coffee tray, complete with biscuits.

'I appreciate your cooperation, Mr Santo. We interviewed most of the crew yesterday, as you probably know. Why are many of them reluctant to talk to us?'

Santo shrugged. 'Strange country, they don't know the language or how the police work here.'

Horseman nodded. 'Maybe. Some of them even denied that there was a fishing observer on board at all. That's odd, isn't it?'

'Sure, everyone knew about Jimmy and his job. He was a friendly guy. Even if he couldn't talk to most of them he'd always smile and greet them in their own languages.'

'One or two men complained about the conditions on board. About not being paid adequately and overcrowded conditions. Is that resentment rife?'

'Longlining is a tough life. But conditions on *Joy-13* are pretty good compared with other vessels. I'm an engineer, so my pay is better. The captain and all crew get a percentage of the catch proceeds, like a bonus. We depend on that. But *Joy-13* is only four years old, first-class engines that are a pleasure to work on.'

Horseman didn't say any more. He didn't want to divulge that it was Filipo, Santo's compatriot, who had complained.

'When did you last see Jimmy?'

'On Friday, maybe four in the afternoon. The crew had finished a haul. The conveyor belt taking the cleaned tuna to the cool hold kept stopping so I went along there to see what was the problem. A hook had jammed the works so I fixed it and made my way up to the bridge. I passed Jimmy on the stairs. He had his camera around his neck and his plastic case under his arm.'

'His plastic case—what's that?'

'Oh, he used to call it his toolbox.' Santo smiled fondly. 'His fishing observer kit—all his forms and things. Tough and waterproof.'

'Where was he headed?'

'It's hard for me to say. It was on the central stairs so he could have been headed anywhere.'

'He was going down and you were going up, I assume?'

'Yes, that's right.'

'Was Jimmy wearing his life jacket?'

'Oh, now let me think.' Santo screwed up his eyes as if to focus better on the past.

'These new inflatables are so thin you don't notice them.' He opened his eyes again.

'Sorry, I can't be sure.'

'Did he usually wear it?'

'Oh yes, when he was on deck, his PLB, too. Sorry, that's a GPS emergency beacon, He was a stickler for safety devices. I guess that goes with being an observer. It's all about abiding by the rules, isn't it?'

'I suppose so. Jimmy's role as an observer would conflict with the captain and crew, wouldn't it? The captain's goal is a profitable trip. The observer's role is recording the catch data. Doesn't that mean he records illegal things, too? Like banned species. Or dumping dead fish overboard, de-finning sharks and dumping the carcases overboard.'

Santo smiled. 'Oh, you know about longlining.'

'Not much. I'm just starting to find out. Did the captain commit these sorts of breaches on *Joy-13*?'

'I'm the engineer. I can't tell you.'

'You're too modest, Mr Santo. As you've served on the ship for three years, and you're second in command, I think you know what was going on.'

'Sorry, sir, I'm on the bridge or in the engine room when they're hauling.'

'You were Jimmy's friend. Did he talk to you about his work, any worries he had about the practices on board?'

'We did enjoy talking occasionally, but he wasn't a chatty man. Never gossiped. He didn't really share his opinions.'

'How did he get on with the captain?'

Santo shrugged again. 'Okay. They couldn't talk much. Occasionally I saw them together on deck or on the bridge. Jimmy would show the captain photos on his camera or something in his notebook. I don't know more than that.'

'What do you think of the observer's role?'

'I've only been on board with an observer once before. It's quite unusual. They have their job, to give the scientists information about fish stocks.'

'They must be outsiders, though.'

'I guess so. They are with us for just one trip. Sometimes they're in the way. Most of the crew ignore them as language is often a problem.'

'Thank you very much, Mr Santo. I may need to speak to you again.'

Santo nodded. 'I'm always willing to help, Inspector.'

*

'Troops, let's go back to last Sunday week. Twelve days ago, but seems like an age, doesn't it? A fisherman found a human head inside a shark. We didn't even know if the head belonged to a man or a woman. Through persistent digging, science and a bit of luck, we've identified the Fijian man, Semesi Inia, aka Jimmy, a fishing observer on the longliner *Joy-13*. You've all contributed to that discovery. Well done.'

The officers acknowledged his thanks with nods, smiles and murmurs.

'*Joy-13*'s captain made a statement yesterday, admitting that crew reported Jimmy missing exactly two weeks ago on Friday 8th September. As Jimmy was his own boss, it's feasible that he wasn't missed for some hours, as Captain Shen claims. Two of the crew confirm that the captain turned the vessel around and searched for some time—the accounts differ as to how long. Then the captain wrote Jimmy off as lost overboard by accident, presumed drowned.

'The captain faces criminal charges for failing to report a fatal accident at sea. However, Shen's solicitor has challenged the jurisdiction of the Fiji police and other authorities. The result of this is that the captain was released yesterday afternoon. Later today the super will be able to clarify the situation.'

'But sir—' everyone protested at the same time.

He held up his hand, patting the air. 'I know, I feel the same. But nothing has changed yet. We've got to drive this investigation as fast as we can, get to the answer before slow-moving bureaucracy can stop us.'

There were thumps on the table and smiles, '*Io*, sir.'

'I've double-checked maritime law too. What I remembered is correct. Crime trumps everything. If the police have reason to suspect a crime has been committed on board a ship in territorial waters, we must not discriminate because the vessel is foreign. We can and must investigate the crime, including searching the vessel and all its contents, just as if it was a shed at the end of the wharf. The catch is, Captain Shen now claims Jimmy fell overboard beyond the 12-mile limit. He can't demonstrate that unless he produces his log and unless he really does know the precise time Jimmy entered the water.'

'What if he did go overboard beyond the 12-mile limit, sir?' Kau asked.

'Then the jurisdiction belongs to China as the flag state—that's the country where *Joy-13* is registered. In practice, the flag state is often on the other side of the world and can't investigate a crime. They're happy to hand over the enquiry to the vessel's nearest port state, which in this case is Fiji, of course. But it's up to the flag state. China could decide to investigate and prosecute the case just to exonerate Shen. Not good for justice, I'm afraid.'

'Have you come across a case like this before, sir?' Musudroka asked, serious now.

'*Io*, the most relevant was when the master of a vessel outside the territorial limit radioed us about a knifing in a brawl. The injured man required urgent hospital treatment. We expedited port clearance for Lautoka, had an ambulance waiting and investigated both the brawl and assault. I've got a feeling our Jona case won't be so simple.'

There was silence as the team absorbed the fallout from Horseman's law lesson. As there were no more questions, he decided that was enough law for now.

'Sergeant Singh, can you do the honours with the whiteboard, please?'

Singh had already put up the photos of Jimmy's ravaged head and the passport shot she'd retrieved from Immigration. She added a photo of Captain Shen.

Singh addressed the team. 'We must find out how Jimmy died. Was it by accident or was he murdered? If he was murdered, was he pushed overboard to take his chances with the sharks or was he killed on the ship, then thrown overboard? Ideas, please?'

'The captain's statement may be correct though,' Kau said. 'Two crewmen confirmed the sequence of events in our interviews yesterday.'

'Three, including Santo, the engineer I spoke to this morning,' Horseman added.

Musudroka came in. 'But why didn't he report the accident? That's his duty. I reckon he's hiding something.'

'Pressure to fill his hold, he says. That's bad, but I can believe it,' Horseman added.

Singh wrote *How did Jimmy die?* below the pictures, then divided the board into two columns: headed *Accident* in red and *Murder* in blue. She wrote the points supporting each header beneath. She said, 'Under *Murder*, I'll add *no life jacket*. Two of the crew stated that Jimmy always wore his life jacket on deck.'

Musudroka piped up. 'What about the weather? One seaman told us it was fine and calm.'

'Check that with the Weather Bureau, Musudroka,' Horseman said.

Kau said, 'We don't know when he went overboard, alive or dead. It could have been anywhere from half past three in the afternoon to seven o'clock at night.'

Singh added, 'Exactly. It's a real shame those search warrants are held up. We need the ship's log but there's no way the captain's going to give that up without a warrant.'

As Singh wrote the points raised on the board, the blue *Murder* column lengthened. Horseman asked her to summarise.

'Looking at our list, it's clear there's doubt about the accident theory. We need to pinpoint where and when Jimmy went overboard as closely as we can. We need to solve the problem of the life jacket and why the captain didn't report a MOB. It may be because Jimmy was murdered. Remember the vessel was at sea for six more days before docking in Suva.'

Horseman spoke up now. 'Another problem has been surveillance of *Joy-13*. I've been told that officers take up positions where the far side of the vessel is hidden from them. I went down last night to take a look and that seemed to be so. By standing close to the ship, you can't see its opposite side. Musudroka? Kau? What are your observations?'

The two young DCs glanced at each other, surprised. 'Could be, I guess, sir. We were careful not to miss anyone entering or exiting the boat. I would walk to the bow and stern—check it out! I know those terms now!'

'Enough, man, get on with it!' Horseman normally tolerated Musudroka's high jinks, but not now.

'Sorry, sir. You're right, I didn't walk far enough away to get a view of the side of the ship facing the water—the port side, that is.'

'Right, here's the plan. One, we increase surveillance from now. The super will allocate more uniforms. Monitor crew movements and take names and contact details of all visitors. We may not have the right to insist but act as if we have. This is a serious duty, not a joke. Musudroka and Kau, speak to the crew coming and going, chat to them, be pally. Find out where they go in their time off—bars, nightclubs, cafés, even brothels. Ask them for their recommendations. In your time off, go to their drinking spots. Most don't speak English but you're resourceful. We'll meet again tomorrow. I expect you two to do the rounds of their hangouts on Saturday night.'

'*Io*, sir!' Musudroka gave him the thumbs up. The lad was irrepressible. Probably just as well.

'Second, Sergeant Singh, you can allocate the roster for surveillance and keep in touch with them by radio. First, I'll file an official request to Interpol for information on Captain Shen. He could have history. Then I'll handle the interviews with the remaining crew members. I have no clue as to how long this legal meeting will take or what the outcome will be. But I need to be here when the super returns or calls me.'

34

Nothing new came from the interviews and three crewmen still hadn't turned up. Nothing yet from the super. Time to call Singh.

'*Bula*, Susie. Are you still at the wharf?'

'Yes, I've reworked the guards' routine to fifteen-minute intervals to avoid boredom and keep them on their toes. They've got to check off their duties every interval, note events and sign off, then swap to a different position. It isn't foolproof, but these guys aren't bad. They didn't have enough structure and they got bored.'

'Sounds great. I ordered *Joy-13* watched and guarded on the spur of the moment, without much guidance for the uniforms or detectives. You've put it right now. Had lunch yet?'

'Heavens, no. I'm observing them go through their paces for a full interval. Ten minutes to go. If they don't do the right thing after that, they never will.'

'I reckon they'll shape up with you as drill sergeant.'

'They'd better!'

'I haven't heard from the super yet so I'm stuck here until I do. If you can talk for a few minutes more, I want to run something past you.'

'Sure, go ahead.'

'I haven't explained why I suspected the guards' lines of sight were restricted. It was yesterday afternoon at Shiners training. Tevita told me he was at the wharf and spotted a boat leaving from the seaward side, full of women.'

'What was Tevita doing on the wharf? How did he get in?'

'Good question. Now I've confirmed what he said about the surveillance gaps, I'm inclined to follow up on a boatload of women being moved ashore.'

She gasped. 'People smuggling? Prostitution?'

'*Io*. Makes more sense than fishing violations, doesn't it? As a motive for murder, I mean.'

'Sure does. I wonder how and when they were taken on board? The women couldn't have been hidden from the crew.' Singh spoke slowly, thinking the new scenario through.

'It fits in with Filipo's story of having to move into Jimmy's cabin. "A reshuffle," he said.'

'The captain must have sworn the crew to secrecy. Or promised a bonus, or threatened them with dismissal if they breathed a word. That explains their fear—some even denied there was a fishing observer on board. They were so petrified they played dumb. It all makes sense.' He heard her rising excitement.

Horseman added, 'But Jimmy can't have been part of the plan. The captain wouldn't have had much notice about the fishing observer placement on his vessel.'

Singh didn't answer right away. 'I see. Jimmy's placement threw a spanner in the works. But why did the captain still go ahead with the people smuggling operation?'

Horseman had thought about this. 'I think maybe it was beyond his control. A higher level. Organised crime. Maybe a triad gang running the people smuggling, quite separate from the vessel's legitimate presence here—a longliner licensed for Fiji waters. Good cover. Because she's a licensed vessel, *Joy-13* escapes the checks and inspections that an unlicensed vessel in transit would not. Shaddock and TTF help *Joy-13*'s credibility too.'

'There must be something in it. Where do we go from here, sir?'

'I'm reluctant, but I'm going to talk to Tevita. He might know more about where the boat went. I was so worried that he was in danger last night that I didn't encourage him to elaborate. But I can't see any other way. He could well know more.'

'Pity he's not on the surveillance team.' Horseman could hear the smile in her voice.

'Yep, he's had those skills since he was small: melting into crowds or shadows, alert to sounds, excellent vision. But it's depressing—he's had to be good at surveillance to survive.'

The super came into the room and waved at Horseman, pointed to his own office.

'The super's back, Susie. I'll keep you up to date. See you later.'

*

Superintendent Navala slumped into his chair, put his elbows on his desk and rubbed his face with his hands. The big man looked haggard. Not for the first time, Horseman wondered what work-life would be like when the super retired at the end of the year. And work-life was eighty, perhaps ninety per cent of his entire life now. The super was his first mentor, the man who had sought out a naïve university student and suggested a career as a detective. Lured him with the unbeaten record of police rugby teams. He had worked under other supers but none he respected more than Navala.

'Cup of tea, sir?' he offered.

'*Vinaka*, Joe, but not at the moment. It's not tea I need. That magistrate is the most cautious individual I've ever come across; in fact, he's scared of making a decision. Unfortunately, the Law of the Sea is not clear-cut when a crime is committed on a foreign vessel beyond the 12-mile limit. The nearest port state has a right, especially when a victim is a citizen of the port state. But the vessel's flag state has a right too. Which country ends up leading the investigation is usually negotiated between them, often through diplomatic channels. The expert advised China may view our investigation as a threat to her flag state jurisdiction. The best Fiji can aim for is to agree to share responsibility with China and divide various tasks between us.'

He had to protest. 'What? We didn't know our victim had

anything to do with *Joy-13* until a few days ago. That was just a coincidence. We haven't set out to deprive China of her rights!'

'Everyone knows we haven't, Joe, the Chinese ambassador included.' The super looked stern. 'However, he isn't going to let it go. Fiji's legal claims to jurisdiction mean nothing against the might of China. They know it, we know it.'

'Sir, it's quite possible *Joy-13* was within the 12-mile limit when Jimmy went over the side. If so, none of this debate is necessary. We can't know one way or the other without the ship's log and navigation data. By refusing to give it to us, Shen just looks more guilty.'

'I agree, Joe, but there it is. The Chinese ambassador is meeting with the Commissioner and the Foreign Secretary tomorrow morning. The Commish has asked me to be there to provide details of the investigation. He'll stress our willingness to complete the investigative work, which a Chinese team would not be able to do, practically speaking. He'll also offer to share our findings and information.'

The Commissioner might well prefer to lose than to compromise. Horseman could understand that. He kept these thoughts to himself.

The super gave him a tired smile. 'I'll call you with the outcome, Joe. I'll go straight home after the meeting. It's Saturday tomorrow—hasn't anyone remembered that? *Moce mada.*'

35

'I can't believe it—this is all mad,' Singh said after Horseman had relayed the super's news.

'Well, we don't have to stop investigating while others decide the fate of our case, do we? I'm going to send Interpol Toby Shaddock's details now. All that time he spent in Taiwan, he may have brushed up against the law. I'll call my rugby mate in Interpol's Hong Kong office too. He might be able to move my official requests to the head of the queue.'

'I've not been able to get an ID on the mysterious visitor we ran into on Thursday. He said his name was Mao Li, gave a hotel address. Neither checks out,' Singh said.

'I knew his details would prove false. I think of him as Mr X. Isn't he the only *Joy-13* visitor not identified?'

'Yes, everyone else checks out.'

'I'll ask Toby Shaddock about him. If he *is* a bona fide supplier to the ship, TTF probably arranged their deal, whatever that is. Let's drop in without warning. Take him by surprise.'

She grinned. 'I'm all for that, sir.'

'Had any luck with the crewmen who still haven't turned up for interview?'

'Yes, I spoke to Mr Santo. I'm going myself to collect them from the ship at eleven.'

'You won't have time to visit Shaddock then. Leave that to me.'

'Sure.' He could see she was disappointed.

'Show the crew the headshots, too. Might encourage honesty if we show them Santo first—I don't see why they wouldn't be willing to name their engineer. Follow Santo with Captain Shen, and finally Mr X. They might just let his name slip out, or his role.'

'Can't hurt to try. We've got blow-ups of passport photos for Santo and Captain Shen. I'll get Kelera to crop Tani's photo of Mr X down to a headshot so it looks similar.'

'Do that but I won't wait for it. Won't wait for a car either. I'll grab a cab and take the print of Tani's shot over to Shaddock now. We need to step up our pace. There's a chance the Commissioner will shut down the case. He'll do his best to save it but if he can't, we may only have hours.'

She opened her orange file and passed him the A-4 print. 'As you've often told me, we can only take one step at a time.'

He smiled. 'True. I'm right, aren't I? *Vinaka* for reminding me, Singh.'

*

With fishing vessels entering and departing every day of the week, port agents would be unlikely to quarantine weekends, just like the police. He ought to call first, but he told himself he wanted to surprise Shaddock. Really, he was so restless he just couldn't stay at the station.

A young receptionist escorted him to Shaddock's office. 'Tea or coffee?' he asked with a smile.

'Coffee, please. Black, no sugar.' Horseman hoped the quality would be better than at the station, where he always had tea.

'Me too, *vinaka*, Teri,' Shaddock said.

Teri nodded eagerly and departed.

'One of our cadets, a promising boy. We put them all on reception a few days a week, whatever their department. Best way to get a working overview of the business. Terrifies them at first, but they get to enjoy it soon enough.'

Horseman approved. 'Great idea. Even in the police, the

probationers want to specialise too soon.'

'With the old messenger system, trainees were familiar with every office and workshop, met every employee face to face, from the CEO to the cleaners. That was invaluable for a lad. We're trying to replicate that.' Shaddock's attitude was friendlier today.

Teri returned with a tray and set out their coffee. Horseman had guessed right—TTF did serve quality to their visitors.

'Really interesting, Mr Shaddock. I don't want to take up too much of your time. Have you lodged *Joy-13*'s forms and so on with the port authority yet?'

'*Io*, this very morning. They should be available to you now.'

'*Vinaka*. I'm still a bit mystified about how the system works in practice. I learned the other day that it's quite normal for foreign vessels not to be inspected by Customs. In fact, only twenty-five per cent of vessels are inspected.'

'*Io*, the growth in recent years has been too great. While there's still a random element, it makes sense for customs to concentrate their inspections on unknown vessels. TTF has considerable infrastructure here in Fiji and is trusted, so the vessels we handle aren't routinely inspected. Especially those like *Joy-13*, which are licensed to fish in Fiji's EEZ.'

Horseman still thought this practice simply invited crime, but he merely smiled and nodded. He didn't trust TTF enough to be sure company employees had no knowledge of *Joy-13*'s suspected people smuggling. He handed the A-4 print of Mr X to Shaddock.

'We'd like to speak to this man who's been on board *Joy-13*. He said he was visiting the ship on business. I wondered if he was connected with TTF.'

Shaddock glanced at the print and replied immediately. 'Oh, no he isn't.'

'But you do recognise him.'

Shaddock paused a moment. 'Yes, I see no reason why I shouldn't tell you. He's higher up the line in *Joy-13* owner's outfit. He seems to do roving inspections for the owners. He joins vessels at transhipment points, from the carriers, partway through a voyage. He'll leave the vessel and transfer to another at a port or another transhipment point.'

The explosive ring tone made them both jump. Horseman glanced at his phone before silencing it. The super. Great timing. 'So sorry, I had it on max when I was on the street and forgot to turn it off.'

Shaddock chuckled. 'No problem. That's quite a ring!'

'So, there are all sorts of inspections going on here. Interesting. Do you have a name for this man?'

Shaddock smiled. 'Oh, didn't I say? Wu Yee, goes by Charles with foreigners, I believe.'

Horseman scribbled the name down. 'D'you know him?'

'Not really. I've met him. I have a basic understanding of his role from the company's captains.'

Horseman pulled out his lists.

'He's not on your crew list for *Joy-13* and he didn't put in an entry card for Immigration.'

Shaddock shrugged. 'Maybe he didn't arrive on *Joy-13*. He could have flown into Nadi or Suva to board the ship here. Or he could be boarding another ship. The company doesn't inform TTF about his movements.'

Of course not. The company had every reason to keep them secret.

'*Vinaka vakalevu*. Of course, that makes sense. I'm on a steep learning curve with the fishing industry, and grateful for your help.'

'No problem. I guess we are a world unto ourselves.'

'As are the police, so I understand. *Vinaka* again.'

*

He snatched the phone from his pocket the moment he got to the foyer.

'Sir? I was talking to Shaddock at TTF. Sorry.'

'Fine, fine. The news isn't good, I'm afraid. But it could be worse.'

'What is it, sir? I'll be at the station in ten minutes, but if you could give me the gist now...'

'*Io*, Joe. The Chinese will send a team to conduct their own investigation. We'll be informed when they will arrive. Our cooperation will be appreciated. The Chinese detectives will conduct a search of *Joy-13*, so there is no need to pursue the search warrants we've applied for. Non-negotiable. The Commish has tried, but that's that.'

'I take it the ambassador claimed China's flag state jurisdiction was total?'

'*Io*, in a nutshell. As the representative of a totalitarian state, I guess that's his *modus operandi*.' The super sounded calm but grim.

Although he knew this was on the cards, his heart thudded against his ribcage. 'How could it be worse?'

'There was no mention of the Fiji police closing our Jona case. The ambassador probably just forgot that. Our Commish is so annoyed at hosting Chinese police in Suva that you can bet he'll support anything you want to do.'

'Apart from board *Joy-13*.'

'Apart from that. His hands are tied. The Chinese regard *Joy-13* as Chinese soil. No entry except by invitation.'

'Okay, so it's business as usual?'

'*Io*, Joe, business as usual. Telephone me if you need anything more.'

'*Vinaka*, sir. See you on Monday.'

36

It was to be Pizza Perfecta tonight, so Singh decided on her newish jeans and a yellow check shirt. She fumbled the buttons, looked down and saw her fingers trembling. What was this? Surely she was no longer anxious about meeting Brij? That had passed after the first two dates. She'd enjoyed their meals together since then, even looked forward to them. But this evening she felt different. For one thing, she was getting ready absurdly early instead of running late. This was partly due to the interviews finishing early. Two crewmen identified the engineer and the captain from their photos, but none of the three admitted knowing Mr X. It would have been good if one of them had confirmed the name Shaddock had given the boss. Still, Shaddock's story was plausible and she would get Immigration to check Charles Wu Yee's movements first thing on Monday.

She brushed her hair out and debated whether to put on her orange sneakers or gold sandals. As she had time to fill she'd walk from the police barracks down the hill and the full length of Victoria Parade to the pizza place near the cinemas. Orange sneakers, then.

Walking did help her marshal her thoughts. She tried to stay positive about the case, but the truth was she was out of her depth in the maze of jurisdictional debate that the boss had explained to her this afternoon. Her pride in her competence had no foundation, she realised. Away from these tiny islands, mere specks in the vast Pacific Ocean, she floundered. A mere twelve nautical miles offshore, the police force which she served with unswerving loyalty was powerless, unless it suited a foreign country to make use of their services. She needed to study more law.

Her indignation about the lawless high seas distracted her from delving deeper into her feelings about Brij. As she passed through Ratu Sukuna Park, dusk fell. The shrieking of the Indian mynahs in the fig trees blasted thought from her mind.

But a block away from her destination her stomach fluttered. Deep breaths did not calm her. Could she be falling in love? The romance novels she'd read as a teenager were her only evidence for this diagnosis, not any experience. She reached for the door. Lucky the doorman inside swept it open, for her hand trembled.

She was glad Brij wasn't there—it was her turn to be the first to arrive. But a pang of fear caught her breath—what if he had tired of her? She dismissed the idea as nonsense, she was ten minutes early. She willed herself to study the menu, then the blackboard specials. She resolved to choose two pizzas for them both—new pizzas she'd never tried before.

When he sailed in, smart in designer jeans and bright *bula* shirt, relief flooded her.

'What's made you look so happy, Susie?'

She felt her cheeks blush. 'You. I thought maybe you weren't coming.' Instantly she regretted blurting without thinking first.

Brij looked at his watch and smiled at her. 'I'm seven minutes early,' he protested, amused.

'You've always been the first to arrive. It's a new experience for me to be so early, I guess.'

Brij lifted his arched brows. 'What's happened? You're always so cool, calm and collected.'

'I don't know—nothing really. I've spent my time wisely, though. I'd like to try something new. How about Positano—that's tiger prawns, fresh sliced tomato, ricotta, chilli and fresh mint?'

'Mm, sophisticated you! I'll give it a go. Can I choose the other?'

'Only if it's Pumpkin Gorgonzola.'

'Not sure if I'm up for that.'

'It comes with pine nuts, garlic, caramelised onion and sage.'

'No, Susie. I'll have to put my foot down. Let me see. I'm a man of plain tastes, as you know.' He scrutinised the menu. 'Salsiccia: Italian sausage, bocconcini and fresh basil. Willing to share that?'

'You bet. The two make a good balance.'

'Like us, I'm thinking more and more.'

She felt the heat rise in her cheeks. Almost written off as too old to marry, yet she couldn't control her blushes any better than a fourteen-year-old.

'Don't be embarrassed, Susie. Don't ignore the elephant in the room. Admit it, we hit it off, don't we? I admire everything about you, even your reticence about personal relationships. No, really, I like that too. You're beautiful, clever and kind. What's not to like? Now, it's entirely understandable if you don't feel the same way…'

'No, Brij, I do. Like you, I mean. I've been so looking forward to our date. It's just that we've only known each other two weeks, so… I mean, we're both pleasant company for a good meal in a restaurant, but living together our whole lives…' The heat rose again.

He reached his hand across the table. Singh was clenching hers on her knees.

'Don't look scared, Susie. I'm pretty sure our parents didn't even see each other before their marriages. Not that I recommend that. Far from it. Imagine how scared they must have been.'

'Especially our mothers. They were just young girls.'

'Our fathers not much older. I bet they were equally terrified. But we don't need to be. We're friends, aren't we?'

She felt herself relax and grinned. 'Sure, but it's not the same as…'

He waved his hand from side to side. 'Please, don't quote Hollywood and Bollywood at me. *Ma* says movies are responsible for most unhappy marriages. She says love grows as long as there's kindness on both sides and a spirit of give-and-take. We surely meet those two conditions, don't we?'

Singh sighed. 'Yes, we do. But Brij, this isn't a proposal, is it?'

Brij laughed out loud. 'Don't look so alarmed. No, it isn't, but it sounds like I'm getting close, doesn't it? I surprise myself as well as you.'

She laughed with him as the waiter put their pizzas and beers on the table. The cheesy garlic aroma blended with the sharp sausage to make her salivate, but her stomach was now calm. They turned their attention to the food, eating and drinking in companionable silence.

Brij spoke up first. 'How was your day at work? Tense, I guess, judging from your mood when I got here.'

'Yes, it was. Frustrating. The case is getting mixed up in diplomatic problems.'

'The Jona case? Oh yes, what are they?'

'Brij, did you know that the force's jurisdiction over crimes at sea against Fiji citizens isn't clear? It can be disputed by the country a vessel is registered with.'

'Well, sort of, not that it's my area. What's happened?'

His eyes, so relaxed a moment before, were now alert. It would be easy to confide everything, use him as a sounding board, clarify her confusion. But no, she shouldn't have mentioned anything. She had no idea who his friends were. He possibly knew journalists. Kicking herself furiously, she hoped she hadn't gone too far. Brij was far from stupid, and there were bound to be Jona rumours flying around legal circles. She'd said enough for him to pass on useful information to the media or to their opponents. If he wanted to. She tried to hide her alarm.

She smiled. 'You know I can't talk about ongoing cases, just like you. It's just a hypothetical legal principle I've never brushed up against before. I was surprised. Interesting, though, don't you think?'

Their conversation flagged as they polished off the last of the pizza. 'Susie, I'm amazed at how you remain so slim when you have such a, shall we say, robust appetite.'

'Look who's talking! I was most ladylike and let you have the lion's share. You know, my long hours the past two weeks are catching up with me. I feel so dozy after the pizza I'd better take a cab straight home to bed.'

'I understand. I feel the same way. But let me drive you.'

'I won't say no. You're right. I probably ate too much.' She'd said too much, which was much, much worse.

37

Musudroka and Kau raced up the stairs to the CID floor. Horseman was amused they couldn't wait to report on their night roaming the city's seedier bars and so-called clubs.

'Sir, I've just seen Santo at church. Outside the Catholic cathedral, sir.'

'Start at the beginning, Tani. Sit down, both of you and tell me about last night.'

They frowned at each other but did as he commanded. Horseman was aware old school officers thought he was too lax with the young detectives, letting them get away with light-hearted banter that could be seen as lacking in respect. He didn't see any purpose in being strict for the sake of tradition and didn't want to dampen their enthusiasm or initiative. But they had to learn to start their reports at the beginning.

'Sir, we had a drink in each of the bars on the list we agreed on with you. We ordered coke or juice as you said, though that's actually hard to come by. Barmen got suspicious, so we ended up getting beers just to avoid being thrown out.'

'But we never finished them, sir,' earnest Kau assured him.

'Good idea.'

Musudroka continued. 'We came across some of the *Joy-13* crew, but not as many as I expected to. Some were getting plastered. On the whole, they didn't want to drink with us.'

'What was your impression, Kau?'

'Same, sir. The language barrier makes it hard, but it was more than that. We were friendly, offered to take them to other places we knew, but they weren't interested. We gave up around two in the morning. By that time the few still drinking were under the table, but just as tight-lipped as if the captain was watching them. They seem an unhappy lot. I guess they miss home.'

'Well done. You followed instructions, you persisted, you drew appropriate conclusions as far as I can tell. A negative result is not a failure. We've crossed off a potential source of information.' Both DCs brightened at his praise.

'Those places are dire, sir. Worse than I thought. Dirty, smelly, toilets stank—the drinks were only a bit less expensive than in a decent bar. Why do they go there?' Musudroka asked.

'Well, there were drugs, I reckon, although they knew who we were, so they kept that hidden. Prostitutes hanging around,' Kau reminded him. 'They were out of it, on drugs or drunk, or both.'

'Fijian girls, were they?' Horseman asked.

'Mostly Asian-looking, now you ask.'

'Yep, must be what the Asian seamen want,' Kau said with a shrug.

'Were they talking to any *Joy-13* crew? As if they knew them, I mean.'

Musudroka pondered for a bit. 'Hard to say. Not one of those guys impressed me as a conversationalist. The girls probably found them as hard-going as we did.' He laughed.

'Right, Detective Constables. Now you can tell me what happened this morning to get you so excited.'

'At last!' Musudroka said.

'Musudroka, try that again.'

'Sorry, sir. I went to nine o'clock mass at the cathedral. I was early so I hung about with others waiting for the eight o'clock congregation to come out. I saw Santo, the engineer. He wasn't in any of the places we went to last night, by the way. But he was agitated, fidgety, pacing up and down. I wondered if he'd been on drugs last night. So, I went up to him and said *bula*, said I was going to mass too. He stared at me, all anxious, started muttering. All I could make out was "confess, gotta confess" a few times he said that. Then about how he can't go to mass until he's confessed. Though his speech wasn't real clear, sir.'

'Interesting, Tani. What then?'

'I was shocked, sir. I reckoned he was admitting he had something to do with Jimmy Inia's death. So, I was real sympathetic, explained that he could come to the station with me and we'd see you and he could confess. I said you'd be understanding, sir, and wouldn't hurt him.'

'You handled that shock well. And then?'

'Santo got upset, annoyed too. He said he meant confessing his sin to a priest, nothing to do with the police. My wrong assumption, sir. I told him that he'd find a priest if he went to the office behind the church. Then he stalked off, like he couldn't get away from me fast enough.'

'What do you think that means?'

'I don't know. He told me I got it wrong.'

Kau said, 'One thing it means is that he's a Catholic and it's important to him to go to mass. I suppose on the longliners he can't get to church for months at a time. He must miss church.'

'Good thinking, Kau. that gives us insight into Santo's character.'

'Maybe I didn't misunderstand him,' Musudroka protested. 'Maybe he was just covering up when I offered to take him to the station. We don't know for sure.'

'Correct, Tani. We know nothing for sure. Much as I hate to pry into anyone's religious life, we'll have to try to find out what sin he feels burdened with. Getting drunk, taking drugs, visiting a brothel—it could be any of those. You're the only Catholic among us, Tani, what do you think?'

'Catholics don't consider getting drunk a sin, sir. Drugs or prostitutes, definitely.'

Horseman got up from his desk. 'And it could be something he did on *Joy-13*, too. In which case, we have to find out. I'll go and look around the cathedral. You two, get yourselves a cup of tea, get your notebooks and diaries up to date and write your reports. You've done well.'

On his way out, he smiled at the usual Sunday morning gaggle of hungover men fronting the public counter. The night before was now a blur in their memories. They clung to the slight chance that their wallets, phones, or bank cards had been found by honest citizens who had lost no time in handing them in. They would hang around the station for hours rather than tell their wives they had lost their lifeline. Or admit it to themselves.

The desk sergeant waved him over as he flipped up the counter exit and passed through. '*Bula*, Inspector Horseman! You might want to take a look at this.'

Horseman went up to the public side of the counter. *Bula*, sergeant. 'What have you got?'

'Taxi driver just handed this in.' He showed a scuffed passport. 'Honest guy, eh. Left in his cab, of course. He thinks the passengers could have been crew off the Chinese fishing boats. It's a Philippines passport.'

Horseman flicked the passport open. Filipo Moreno, the senior deckhand, he recalled. 'You're alert for a Sunday morning, sergeant. I've got to rush off now, but please bag it and send it upstairs. Just leave it on my desk.'

'*Io*, sir. Glad to be of help.'

*

Santo was nowhere to be seen near the cathedral or any of the few cafés or holes-in-the-wall in the vicinity. Horseman rang his mobile again and again in vain.

By the time he'd eaten the roti he bought from a street vendor and returned to the station, Musudroka and Kau had disappeared, leaving their completed reports on his desk. He looked up Filipo's number but got a message that the mobile was turned off.

He was at an impasse. He should be working on several lines of enquiry but he couldn't take the next step on any of them until he got responses from others. Familiar, but exasperating all the same.

He hadn't yet had a response from his official Interpol request, and his rugby mate in their Hong Kong office was still silent. But he could now send Interpol the name for Mr X, identified by Shaddock as Charles Wu Yee. He submitted another official request, adding Yee's name to his photo, and shot off an email alerting his Hong Kong mate. Naturally, it would be fruitless to ask Immigration to check anything on a Sunday. That must wait until tomorrow. Yee may well have entered Fiji by air, as Shaddock suggested. He'd ask Immigration to check back for two weeks.

He made tea, brought it back to his desk and examined Filipo Moreno's passport. Nothing out of order that he could see. Filipo was probably sleeping off the excesses of Saturday night.

The diligent sergeant had included in the evidence bag the form he'd filled in with the taxi driver's information. That was something, he could talk to the driver. He was even more pleased to discover that he was acquainted with the driver: Livai Yayawa, formerly a corporal in the Fiji Infantry Regiment, a veteran of United Nations peace-keeping missions in Kosovo and Lebanon. Filipo was lucky to have dropped his passport in Livai's cab. He called Livai.

'Eh, *bula vinaka*, Josefa Horseman, star of Hong Kong sevens! I'm sorry but I'm driving a passenger to Nausori airport. He's running a bit late, so I can't pick you up right now.'

'*Vinaka*, that's okay, Livai. I don't want to be responsible for you talking on the phone while you're driving. Can I ring you back in half an hour?'

'*Io*, Josefa. When I'm at the airport I'll call you. Maybe in twenty minutes.'

He made another mug of tea and flipped through the case file while he waited. Perhaps he would find something that needed following up. He wondered when the Chinese detective team would arrive. Surely it would not be for another few days. It occurred to him that the Chinese did not need to read this entire file. Much of it, leading to the identification of Jimmy Inia, was irrelevant to the cause of his death and *Joy-13*. A useful task would be to mark the pages that should be passed on to the Chinese. It would be a much slimmer file. He went to Singh's desk, borrowed a lime-green highlighter and set to work.

The taxi driver called back when he was half-way through the file.

'*Vinaka*, Livai, this is good of you.'

'My pleasure, Josefa. How can I help?'

'It's the passport you handed in this morning. The sergeant tells me you were sure which passenger dropped the passport.'

'*Io*, I always tell my passengers to check for their belongings, especially between the backrest and the seat. It's a nuisance if I have to drop into the police station with lost property every other day. So, I remind everyone before they get out. But these passengers didn't understand me. They spoke a foreign language to each other.'

Horseman remembered Livai's detailed reports. There was no hurrying him, and he prided himself on being accurate. 'Would you recognise any of them again?'

'Maybe. I saw two Asian men clearly, not sure if they were Chinese, Japanese, Thai or something else. About one o'clock last night, or this morning, to be precise.'

'Where did you pick them up?'

'*Oi lei*, Josefa, outside bad place in Flagstaff. Its official title is *massage parlour*, but it's really a brothel, if you'll excuse the term.'

Horseman smiled. 'I will, I'm a policeman. Let me note down the address.'

Livai dictated the address. Horseman was surprised he hadn't heard of the place.

'The sergeant mentioned you had three passengers.'

'*Io*, indeed. The third man was in a stupor—drunk or drugs or ill, I don't know. But he was slumped between the other two, they were holding him upright. I didn't really see his face properly, his head was hanging down on his chest. If his passport had fallen out of his pocket, he wouldn't have known anything about it.'

'Where did you take them?'

'Near the wharf entrance gates. That's the reason I told the sergeant that I thought they might be seamen. But how would I know where to find them?'

'You couldn't possibly, Livai. You're a model citizen. You've done everything you should and more. *Vinaka vakalevu.*'

'Happy to be of service, Josefa Horseman. I hope we run into each other again soon.'

'*Io*, Livai. So do I. *Moce mada.*'

He checked the *Joy-13* surveillance roster. The report for Sunday morning wasn't filed yet. He'd chase the officers up tomorrow.

He tried both Filipo and Santo again. Again, no answer.

He'd exhausted all the possibilities he could think of to inch the case along. Better to do something useful now: go home and take Tina for a long romp along the edge of the bay.

38

Singh was already at her desk when he arrived at eight o'clock. She looked up with a spontaneous smile. 'Good morning, sir! How did you go yesterday?'

'Lost most, but won one. I've got a lot to tell you.'

'I've been looking through the file. What are these strange lime green blobs on some of the pages?' Her tone was severe, but she was grinning.

'My colour coding, Detective Sergeant. Imitation is the sincerest form of flattery, isn't it? We don't know when the Chinese investigators will show up, so I made a start at deciding which parts of the file would be useful to them. The painful steps we took to identify the unknown remains won't be of interest, for example.'

'How thoughtful, reducing their reading burden.'

'Yes, I thought so too. I'm about halfway. You may have time to skim through and add your own suggestions later. I've got a lot to tell you before we plan today. Let's do that over coffee at Arabica. I need a kick start.'

*

They left Arabica with plans in their notebooks: Horseman's an untidy series of phrases and dashes; Singh's numbered, dotted and highlighted. Kau would come off surveillance mid-morning when Musudroka took over: he couldn't delegate jobs to the lower ranks today.

The first step in his quest for Filipo Moreno was Princess Wharf. The gate security men told him they hadn't been on duty on Saturday night. He would have to check with the office to find out who was working when Livai's taxi dropped the seamen in the early hours.

'Don't you log everyone in and out?' Horseman asked, hearing the impatience in his voice and regretting it.

'*Io*, sir. Between you and me, I wouldn't rely on that happening a hundred per cent on the weekends.'

'Who is likely to be missed?'

'Sometimes lady visitors to the boats, sir. If you know who I mean. But only guests of bona fide crew, you can be sure of that.'

'Well, that's all right then, isn't it? Man, what has become of this wharf? Used to be all by the book.'

The guard looked reproachful. 'Just trying to help you, sir. I've watched you play, you see.'

Horseman softened. '*Vinaka*, it's good to have the heads-up.'

At the office, the sleepy-looking security guard looked perplexed at his request.

Again, Horseman couldn't hide his impatience. 'It's hardly ancient history, man. I'm only talking about Saturday night, you know. Well, Sunday morning actually. Between one and two o'clock.'

The reluctant guard leafed back several pages in the file and extracted two sheets. 'Take your pick, Inspector.' He handed them over.

'*Oi lei!* What's this—thirty or forty people entering at that time?'

The guard nodded.

Horseman ran his eye down the list. He recognised half-a-dozen names from *Joy-13*, but there was no Filipo Moreno. If he'd been dead drunk, maybe his name was missed. But why? Maybe just general slackness. Or maybe the trio didn't go through the gate after getting out of Livai's taxi. He spied a photocopier in one corner. A good idea to get a copy anyway.

'Could I take a photocopy of these pages, please?'

The guard hauled himself from his chair. 'I've got to do it,' he said, taking the papers from his hand and lumbering four steps to the copier. What use would he be in a chase?

But when he was done, the guard handed over the copy with a half-smile.

'*Vinaka vakalevu*, that's a great help to me.' Horseman wanted to make up for his impatience earlier.

His third call was to the port authority itself. He waited in the public section of the POSA offices beneath the control tower. Before long, Manoa Naulu, the shift supervisor he had spoken to on his visit a week ago, beckoned him in. Horseman settled in an armchair in Naulu's office and accepted tea.

'How can I help you today, Inspector?'

'Once again, I need to check on *Joy-13*'s entry documents, Mr Naulu. Mr Shaddock, the ship's agent, told me he'd already lodged them with POSA and I could access them through you.'

'He did, did he? Understandable, I guess. Let me check.' He swivelled to his computer and clicked his mouse for a while, frowning at the screen. Horseman liked computers, but he couldn't help thinking how much quicker it would be to retrieve a physical file.

'What did you want exactly?' Naulu asked.

Horseman smiled. 'I'm not sure what you've got. What would be most useful to me is the actual ship's log, or an itinerary, listing the vessel's route each day. What would you call that?'

Naulu shook his head slowly. 'Most of the information is related to fishing. I regret we don't have such a document. This isn't a travel agency, you know.' He chuckled at his joke. Horseman joined in, but he felt more like crying in frustration.

39

Singh decided to call the Immigration section manager who'd been so cooperative with the *Joy-13* crew entry cards. The data entry clerks either took pleasure in making life difficult for the police or were so lazy they only performed on direct orders from their supervisor. She couldn't relate to that attitude at all.

'You see, Mr Shaddock of TTF said he knows Mr Yee has previously arrived in Suva by air and departed by fishing vessel or vice versa. Although there's no entry record for him arriving on *Joy-13* on 15th September, we want to be quite sure before we conclude he entered Fiji illegally.'

'Of course, Detective Sergeant Singh, of course. Even when boat crew are flying in and sailing out, they still must show evidence of return air bookings in order to qualify for a visa. They still need a visa even if they're only spending a few days in Fiji.'

'I see. I don't know how long he's been in Fiji this time, so I can't tell you the time period to check for Yee's entries and departures. I'd be grateful if I could rely on your experience.'

'No problem. Instead of searching for a date or time period, simply request a name search. The only complications could be that there are multiple Chinese visitors with the same names and you don't have his passport number. However, our search will soon reveal that and you can then identify him from his passport photo. Make sense?'

Perfect sense. A rare commodity. 'That's exactly what I need. Is there a form to submit?'

'Technically, but no need to worry. Just shoot me an email stating the name.'

'Any indication how long this will take?' she asked.

'I'll give this to one of the best. There are other urgent requests ahead of yours, however. I can't promise this morning, but definitely before five o'clock this afternoon.'

'Wonderful, sir. I'll send the email right now.'

Afterwards, she recorded his details in her own alphabetical index of useful contacts under 'I' for Immigration. She noted her email request on the running sheet.

*

Singh had mixed feelings, or rather attitudes, towards prostitution. Much like her parents, she would be horrified to discover a friend or family member had turned to this occupation, but for different reasons. Not for fear of shame enveloping her as an associate of the outcast, but because she could not imagine a more abhorrent or humiliating labour. These days, with ten years of police experience, she knew it to be ruinous to body and soul. Whose health would not be broken by such savage invasion, assault and enslavement by the evilest of men? Day after day of obedience to sadistic profiteers and pathetic customers.

On the other hand, she accepted that the oldest profession was a fact of any society bigger than a village. She felt no antipathy towards individual prostitutes. She accepted that some girls and women would always be persuaded or forced into it, or even choose it as the best option for them in desperate times, as Salome seemed to have done. Salome must be almost unique if she was indeed an independent operator who made a comfortable living, as Horseman claimed. She wondered if that was really the case. He was so chivalrous in his approach to women he could easily be deluded. One of his nice qualities as a man, but a blind spot for a police officer.

She sighed and dialled Vice—the last area she'd want to work in herself. She'd prefer Drugs or even PR to Vice.

'Inspector Elaisa? DS Singh, Suva Central. DI Horseman's team.'

'*Bula*, DS Singh. What can I do for you?' His voice was gruff and nasal like he had both a head cold and a sore throat. Maybe it was just his voice.

'Three foreign fishermen of interest to us left premises in Flagstaff in the early hours of Sunday morning. Their taxi driver said it was a massage parlour and brothel in Waqa Street. I want to check with you for any information about it before I approach the occupants of the address myself.'

'Well, I'm very glad you've done that, Sergeant. Please don't approach anyone there.'

'May I ask why not, sir?'

'You may ask, but I can't give you much of an answer.'

She heard a hoarse choking sound that may have been a chuckle. 'I'll appreciate whatever you can tell me, sir. I can promise it won't go beyond DI Horseman and myself.'

'All I can tell you is that address is part of a wider ongoing vice investigation. Our officers are keeping a low profile. The proprietors are likely to shut down the premises the moment they detect any police interest.'

'I understand, sir. Can you confirm that the address operates as a brothel, then? We don't automatically accept the taxi driver's opinion.'

'No, I cannot. I'd just say that we often find taxi drivers to be useful sources of information.'

'*Vinaka*, sir. You seemed to imply that this address is part of a chain or network run by the same operators. Could that be the case?'

'I implied no such thing, Sergeant. That was your take on what I said. Please explain to DI Horseman that any further enquiry of his into this address could wreck our long-term investigation. I know he wouldn't knowingly do that.'

'No, sir. I'll pass on the message.'

'I'll send him an email, too.'

Two wins in one morning didn't often happen. It was time for a lunch break. She'd pop into Tappoo's and browse for a new top. She wondered if Brij had ever gone to a brothel. She dismissed the question. She didn't want to know the answer.

40

Salome sat beside Horseman on a bench facing the bay in Ratu Sukuna Park. 'How are you, Salome?'

'It's difficult adjusting to a new future, Joe. I thought Jimmy and me had it all worked out. Well, we did. Now he's gone, and my future with him.' She dabbed at her eyes with a handkerchief.

'You will rebuild your life, Salome. You told me you have plans. Good plans.'

'My plans depended on Jimmy. Very much so. He managed to save a good sum to set us up before too long. I didn't want to admit it to you before, but I can't go on much longer. Things are changing, more dangerous now.'

'Tell me about it.'

'Gangsters are moving in. Foreigners—especially Chinese. As you know, I work for myself and I operate in a clean manner. I've never taken drugs or committed any crime, even though some of my customers probably have done so. The Chinese bosses won't tolerate independents like me. I've had threats. I used to feel protected in my place next to Holy Trinity. I believe the bishop understands that. But these new thugs moving in have no respect for churches or any religion. You're right, Joe. The time has come to move out of this filthy business.'

'Do you know if Jimmy left a will?'

She was taken aback. 'What? I don't know. Sometimes he talked about the dangers at sea, but not often. I could hardly ask him about that!' She smiled at the very idea.

'I'll look into it for you, with Fisheries. They arranged Jimmy's assignments.'

'*Vinaka*, Joe. I'm grateful.'

'It would really help if you could tell me more about these foreign operators. They're probably in Fiji without permission. I could help get rid of them if I knew more.'

She glanced around. 'They bribe and threaten, Joe. They've got protection from some police, some other government people.'

'I hate to think that, Salome.'

'I'm right, Joe. Believe me.'

He'd respected his colleague Elaisa's request to stay out of an ongoing op, but was that just a smokescreen? He hated to think so. How could he find out?

'Asian girls seem to appear out of nowhere, filling the Chinese brothels. The girls aren't all Chinese, some from the Philippines, I think. Other places—I don't know. How do they come here?'

'Good question. I don't know either. But it's not hard to come to Fiji as a tourist and just stay on.'

Salome again looked around, anxious. 'Have you got a notebook, Joe? I'll write some addresses for you. You might be able to do something.'

Horseman handed her his notebook and biro, open at a fresh page. '*Vinaka*, Salome. Any names you've heard would be useful, too. It doesn't matter if you're not sure. Leave the investigating to us.'

He didn't ask more questions while she was thinking and writing. By the way she clenched the biro, he could see this task was a struggle for her, taxing her writing skills and her courage both. When she finished, she painstakingly read through what she had written and handed Horseman his notebook.

'*Vinaka vakalevu*, Salome. You've done a good thing here.'

'I hope so, Joe. When I see the streets flooded with these young Asian girls—it's not right, Joe. Talk about the walking dead! There's something badly wrong with them. But you must keep my name out of it.'

'Absolutely. You can trust me.' He pulled out his phone and showed her Yee's photo. 'Do you recognise this man?'

Salome angled the phone close to her face. 'It's not very clear, but I don't think so.'

He wondered if she was short-sighted or dazzled by the reflection off his phone. He glanced around, no one was near. He fished the print-out from his notebook and unfolded it. 'Is this clearer?'

She shook her head. 'I don't know who he is. What about Jimmy's things I gave you, Joe? Can I get them back now?'

'I'm sorry. The Forensics officers haven't finished with them yet. Jimmy's parents also asked about his possessions. Unless he left a written will, I'm afraid his immediate family have the legal claim.'

'*Io*, I might have known. I would just request one or two keepsakes, you know, Joe.'

'Let me check if he left a will first. I'll write out their details for you. But at the moment, Forensics are keeping them safe.' This time, Salome waited in silence while Horseman jotted down the details, tore off the page and handed it silently to Salome. She made unwise choices when she was a desperate teenager, yet grew into a woman of dignity in an iniquitous world. He stood and looked around. He should have been more careful. What she had just done was a killing offence in Suva's new, vicious underbelly.

He tried calling both Santo and Filipo again. Nothing.

41

Musudroka brought back the surveillance notes from *Joy-13* after he handed over to Kau. He made copies for his two superiors and plugged in his camera to Horseman's computer.

'Let me just run through these shots, sir.' He took charge of Horseman's mouse. 'You spoke to Yee at close quarters on deck. Maybe we didn't recognise him among all these faces coming and going.' He clicked through the shots the surveillance team had taken of *Joy-13*'s crew and visitors coming and going.

Horseman looked at each one with care. 'No, apart from that first blurry shot you took before we started proper surveillance, he's not here. I'd say he's left the country or we've scared him away from the docks at least.'

Singh checked her phone again and sighed. 'But now Shaddock's identified him by name, we'll have a result from Immigration this afternoon. I was hoping it would come through before this meeting.'

'If Shaddock gave us a false name, knowingly or not, Immigration may be having problems matching him. The guy's got *criminal gang* stamped all over him. Who knows how many passports and aliases he has?' Horseman's frustration was increasing. He tried to rein it in.

'Tani, you're best placed to find Santo and Filipo. Are you sure neither of them is on board?'

'Can't be sure, sir. Filipo wasn't seen coming or going today at all. Maybe he's on board. Santo was checked coming off this morning, but hasn't returned.'

'And you've got someone checking the port side, now?'

Musudroka looked rueful. '*Io*, sir.'

'Santo or Filipo, whoever you come across first, persuade him to come back here with you. Sergeant Singh and I will find Yee if he's still in Fiji.'

'What about Shiners training, sir?'

'If you haven't found Santo or Filipo by half past four, hotfoot it to training. I'm going to be on time today myself.'

*

Horseman was true to his word—about turning up at training on time. That was because he had not located Yee, if that was his real name. He could tell from Musudroka's face that Santo and Filipo hadn't shown up either.

'No luck yet,' Horseman said. 'Same for you, Tani?'

'*Io*, sir. If only we could barge in with a warrant and search that ship!'

'I know how you feel, but we can't. What we can do in the next hour is give these boys the best training session they've ever had. Right or right?'

'Right, let's go.' grinned Musudroka, slapping a high five.

The squad responded to the intensified focus of their coaches. Horseman's frequent late arrival to training could have affected the motivation of the boys. That surprised him. Even so, his unreliability couldn't be helped—if the super thought for one minute that he put the Shiners before a case, well, that would be the end of the Shiners.

It was half an hour before he noticed that every boy was wearing rugby boots. He hoped they'd bought them at Bargain City and the other second-hand warehouses. If there was a surge in reports of stolen rugby boots the squad wouldn't last long either.

The boys showed extra vigour and determination in their final exercise, the practice game. Dr Pillai approached him during their meal, this evening a sausage sizzle.

'The boys had that extra strength this afternoon—spirit as well as muscle and know-how. Don't you agree, Joe?'

'I do, Doctor. Your nutritious food is having an effect.'

Dr Pillai wagged his head. 'Partly, perhaps. However, the main factor is you showed your total commitment this afternoon. They respond in kind instinctively.'

Horseman nodded. He didn't want to admit the boys' dependence. He didn't want to be their hero. But he would always listen to the wise and kind doctor.

'I just can't give the commitment they need and deserve. I think I'll have to concentrate on getting a reliable roster going with volunteers from Traffic. The current case is difficult and frustrating and that's hardly unusual.'

Dr Pillai cocked an eyebrow. 'You do well, Joe. Did you notice they all have boots this afternoon?'

'Yes, I should say something to them.'

'I think so. Most of them will have either pinched feet, blisters or they'll trip over in oversized boots. But they're proud of their achievement and that will do them good.'

So, when everyone was eating, Horseman spoke from his heart to his rough squad. 'Shiners, I'm sorry that I'm hardly ever on time to training these days. You deserve a coach that can give you a hundred per cent of his effort. But know that I do the best I can. If I'm not here with you when I should be, it's not because I'm sleeping or having fun, it's because I'm doing the job that pays my bills. I'm proud to say that my job is also important. The police help keep Fiji a good place by catching criminals who hurt innocent people. You understand that and forgive me when I'm late, or even when I can't come at all. I want to say *vinaka vakalevu* to you for understanding, and *vinaka vakalevu* to my police colleagues and Dr Pillai, who are all committed to making the Shiners a team to be feared. Let's thank them with three cheers.' Three lusty cheers exceeded the safe decibel level.

'You performed with an extra spark this afternoon, Shiners.

That's not because of anything I and the other coaches did. That's because you did something for yourselves. You've all managed to buy your own rugby boots, even if some aren't the right size.'

Hoots of laughter greeted this remark. A few boys leaped up and mimed limping about.

'I want to congratulate you on helping yourselves, Shiners. If you want a word of wisdom from your coach, which you probably don't—'

Shrieks of protest erupted. He noticed Tevita pull his boots off, sling them around his neck and slip away without a word to anyone. Where did the boy need to be?

'What I want to tell you is that what you get by your own efforts will always give you greater satisfaction than a gift. So well done Shiners. Congratulations!'

One boy threw his boots high in the air. Suddenly it was raining boots. Dr Pillai reacted at the upturned faces.

'Oh no, look down! Cover your eyes!'

He looked at Horseman and they shared a laugh while the Shiners hurled their boots at each other. It was just the type of high jinks Tevita would love. Normally.

42

The super loomed in his doorway as Horseman came up the stairs. The big man ushered him into his office.

'*Yadra*, Joe. Sit down, sit down. I'm the bearer of bad news. The Deputy Commissioner called me just now. A team of detectives has flown in from China. You and I are summoned to meet them up at HQ at eleven. The big boss thinks the best we can expect is to be consulted.'

He'd half-expected this, but not so soon. His racing heart and prickling palms told him he hadn't truly taken this possibility seriously after all.

'And the worst?'

'To be excluded from their enquiries. As if that weren't bad enough, there's a suggestion that my team has overstepped our jurisdiction and offended our ally, the People's Republic of China.'

'In the person of Captain Shen, I assume,' Horseman said.

The super lifted his eyebrows in assent.

'What line do you want to take, sir?'

'The Deputy Commissioner now wants to see what he can achieve by being very friendly and cooperative.'

'I can do that, sir.'

'*Io*, Joe, you can. I've also known you to speak your mind. You may not be asked to speak at all. Even if you are, do not do so unless I give you the nod. I may choose to speak for you instead. Please remember that. Your role is to be a resource of case knowledge for us.'

'*Io*, I can remember that. In fact, it's a role I prefer. I know when

I'm out of my league. Sir, Singh and I have been working through the case files, marking pages that would be important to share with the Chinese detectives. We worked from the standpoint that only the evidence relating directly to Jimmy Inia's fall from *Joy-13* would be relevant to their enquiry. Just looking for your direction on that. We're about halfway through the process.'

The super gazed out the louvres, then up at the whirring fans.

'Tricky, isn't it? The boundaries between these incidents and even the fishing license violations aren't clear. In fact, they overlap. Was poor wretched Jimmy tossed overboard for recording illegal fishing practices or people smuggling, if that's what it is? Or something different altogether? We don't know yet. But given time, we will.'

'How selective should we be with the file, sir?'

'It wouldn't be a good idea to wheel a supermarket trolley full of case file boxes into the meeting. No need to show them how good we are at our job. So, I'd say you're on the right track. *Io*, stick to the MOB aspect and the captain's undisputed failure to report that. If we're talking about volume, I'd estimate that one box file would be enough. Let them ask for more details if they want to. However, I suspect their investigation will be a sham, just a ploy to exonerate their own citizens.'

'*Vinaka* for clarifying, sir. If we're meeting at eleven, we'll need to put the file together extra fast. Could we borrow a constable from another team just for the photocopying and filing?'

'*Io*, I'll send you someone right away.'

'If you do call on me in the meeting, do you want me to give a full debrief of the file?'

'I think not, Joe. Just the—what do they call it now? *Io*, the executive summary. Such a delightful term. If the DC or I ask supplementary questions, answer them briefly. If the Chinese ask questions, the DC will answer, unless he directs the question specifically to you or me.'

'Got it, sir. I'd better get this file slimmed-down first.'

*

By the time Horseman had to leave, the combined efforts of all three had produced a neat, chronological and presentable file. When they got to the Commissioner's conference suite, a secretary whisked the file from him and returned it moments later bound in two sky-blue binders, with the Fiji Police shield on the front.

'*Vinaka*, impressive,' he smiled.

Both the Commissioner and his deputy were gracious hosts to the Chinese delegation, serving lime-coconut drinks and dried banana nibbles in the foyer. When the unsmiling guests entered the conference room, they ignored the soaring beams with intricate sinnet bindings, the tapa-cloth hangings, the flower arrangements. They sat where the welcoming secretary indicated and placed their portfolios in front of them. They waited without a flicker while Fijian caterers in blue-and-white *bula* shirts served tea.

Horseman put the two fancy file binders on the empty chair beside him and glanced surreptitiously at his counterpart *SIO*, Chief Inspector Jun Han. When they were introduced, Han had merely bowed curtly. Horseman had tried to make pleasant conversation, but Han was clearly not interested. Unless he was being clever, trying to unnerve him.

After another formal welcome from the Commissioner, the Deputy Commissioner spoke.

'We are pleased to welcome Chief Inspector Han and his team. We are impressed that the People's Republic of China accepts its responsibility to investigate and prosecute crimes committed on ships who sail under her flag, in this case, *FV Joy-13*. For more than two weeks Superintendent Navala's team has investigated the identity of human remains found in the sea. Against all the odds, they identified that they belonged to Semesi Inia, who was placed as a fishing observer on *Joy-13* under the terms of the WCPFC, of which both China and Fiji are founding members. We are pleased to fully cooperate with Chief Inspector Han's team, sharing our resources and pooling our skills. Again, welcome.'

Polite applause followed. The First Secretary of the Chinese Embassy stood to reply.

'Thank you for your hospitality, Commissioner. As I said at our last meeting, the investigation into any alleged incident on *Joy-13* is China's duty. Inspector Han and his team have arrived with all haste and are ready to start now.'

The Deputy Commissioner was a little put out by the brevity of the First Secretary, Horseman could tell.

'Would Chief Inspector Han care to ask any questions about our CID investigation?'

Han also stood to speak. The Deputy Commissioner waved him down. 'Do sit, Chief Inspector. We do things *bula*-style here in Fiji, you know.' His bass chuckle rumbled.

Han remained inscrutable but did sit after a brief hesitation. 'I have no questions yet. I would prefer to read the case file first, and I may have questions for the Senior Investigator later.'

Although Han's English was grammatically correct, his pronunciation made him difficult to understand. The Deputy Commissioner slowed his speech in response, pronouncing each word separately.

'Certainly, very sensible procedure, Chief Inspector Han. Shall we set a time for our next meeting after you've had a chance to digest the files?'

Han did not consult anyone before he answered. 'No, that won't be necessary.'

The Deputy Commissioner addressed Navala. 'Are your contact details in the file, Superintendent?'

'Yes, sir. Chief Inspector Han is welcome to call me at any time.' He nodded to Horseman, who handed him the ceremonial files. Navala got to his feet, walked around the table to Han, bowed slightly and offered the sky-blue folders.

Han stood to accept them. 'Thank you, Superintendent. Goodbye.' Then the other three Chinese stood, all four bowed stiffly and walked out without a backwards glance. One of the caterers closed the double doors.

The Fijians looked at each other. 'We'll be generous and put it down to jet lag, eh?' the Deputy Commissioner boomed. 'Just an anecdote from the cross-cultural interface, eh?'

The Commissioner was mildly irritated. 'I'd laugh if it weren't so serious. I can't read this situation, and I'm no stranger to inter-governmental negotiations, as you know. They haven't asked us to stop surveillance on *Joy-13*, which was the first request I expected. They haven't asked us for anything.'

'Except the files,' Navala reminded them.

'*Io*, except the files. Selected files, I assume?'

'*Io*, sir.'

The Commissioner nodded. 'So we wait. I don't have a good feeling about this one, gentlemen. Let's hope I'm wrong.'

*

'What's behind this?' Horseman asked the super on the way back. 'Here I was, expecting to be accused of overstepping my authority, maybe even banned from the investigation, and—nothing. Why weren't we asked to stop watching *Joy-13*?'

'Well, well. I suppose they know the wharf isn't Chinese territory—yet.'

Was the big man joking? Horseman looked at his face but detected no trace of humour.

'Okay, but the other day the First Secretary protested about that—claimed we'd no right to investigate anything connected to the MOB incident.'

'He certainly made his point, didn't he? Perhaps that's all he wanted. As the Deputy Commissioner says, now we wait.'

'The possible people smuggling is unrelated. I'll pursue that. I'm expecting intelligence from Interpol any moment about Shen and Yee. Shaddock told me Yee was a sort of roving inspector for *Joy-13*'s owners. It fits so neatly, almost too neatly. Yee is likely to be the people smuggler, which means the vessel's owners are the ultimate criminals.'

'Who would have thought fishing was such a stinking business?' The super betrayed no hint of a smile.

'Ha, ha, sir. You know, when I was shown over *Joy-13* last week, I didn't catch a fishy smell anywhere. I was really surprised.'

'Well, well, it's not the fish that stink.'

'*Io*, sir. Finding Santo and Filipo is even more urgent now. They could be in danger. Not everyone around the wharf can be trusted, so I haven't widened our search. What do you think?'

'I agree. Keep going but keep it quiet for now. Smuggling entails lots of people being paid to turn a blind eye if nothing more. Can't afford to telegraph our suspicions, or whatever people do these days. Post it on Facebook, isn't it?'

'Good analogy, sir. I'll keep in touch.'

43

At last! The call he'd been waiting for: his rugby mate from the Interpol office in Hong Kong.

'*Bula*, Joe. See, I remember my one word of Fijian. It took me a while, but I've now got hold of what you need. Can't be a hundred per cent that we've got the same man but it's ninety-eight per cent certain, I reckon. Best I can do.'

'*Vinaka vakalevu*, Dave. That's thanks very much.'

'Right—I remember now. Can you give me your best fax number please?'

Horseman gave the number. 'Can you email it?'

'Sorry, security problem. Are you near your fax?'

'Yes, stepping across now.'

He heard the warble of the fax handshake and the chug of the printer. 'It's coming through.'

'Cover plus one page. I'll wait till you tell me it's through. Are you coming up for the Sevens?'

'Man, I'd love to. You'll have to arrange a temporary job for me to justify it. I desperately need Interpol training, so see what you can do,' he joked. 'All through now, Dave.'

'Good, can't chat now. See you, Joe.'

The report was worth waiting for. Horseman recognised the pudgy face and broad nose, the penetrating stare. The triad gangster's official name Yo Wu Yee was almost the same as the one Shaddock knew him by—Charles Wu Yee. He came from South

China from a family of seafaring petty criminals. He was the first in his family to complete high school, then entered a college to study business. But he began associating with gangs and dropped out to make more money as a full-time triad, learning on the job. His gang ran small shark-fishing boats and processed the fins. After a while they progressed to piracy, hijacking fins from competitors, then recruiting their victims until the triad dominated the shark-fin trade.

Yee moved up through the ranks. Clever, ruthless, a collector of antique jade scholar's objects. Rumour spread he used legitimate licensed tuna longliners to transport drugs all over the South Pacific. Some drugs stayed in the islands to develop the local market, ensuring a supply of future workers. Most continued their journey to the lucrative markets of Australia and New Zealand. So far, solid evidence had eluded several police forces.

Horseman supposed Yee used the same model for prostitutes.

Singh hurried in, wished him a cheerful good morning and deposited her backpack on a chair. Horseman wondered why she never put it on her desk. Tidiness? She opened her umbrella, propping it underneath her desk to dry. He hadn't noticed it was raining.

He waited until she'd organised her belongings. 'The Interpol brief on Yee came in. He fits the frame for people smuggling, although Interpol doesn't mention that. Maybe that's something we'll be able to help them with. Take a look.'

'Thanks.' She sat at his desk. He picked up his tea mug and she nodded, frowning.

When he returned with their tea, she was still frowning. 'So is the roving company inspector really a roving pirate, of the worst kind?'

'Could be running his own business on the side with or without the blessing of the fleet owners. Or the owners are triads and he's a middle ranker, organising the smuggling for a number of vessels.'

'Both *Joy-13* and the brothels are barred to us. We can ask questions about the owners of *Joy-13* though. Toby Shaddock would know. He gave up Yee's identity. Do you think he's on our side?' Singh asked.

'I couldn't be certain. He's committed to his clients. But he's Fijian—that should count for something, shouldn't it?'

Singh persisted. 'The owners' identity isn't commercial-in-confidence, is it?'

'I hope you're right. Only one way to find out. I'll give him a call now. The intelligence on Yee puts the captain in a different light, too. He could be scared of Yee.'

'Yes, we thought the crew were terrified of Captain Shen, but that may not be the case at all. It could be Yee they're afraid of.' She was bubbling with excitement. 'Oh, I forgot to tell you. I'm seeing Marisa at Fisheries to ask about Jimmy's will and so on. I wanted to do that this morning, but she couldn't see me until this afternoon.'

'She's probably in meetings all morning.'

'I couldn't stand it, could you?'

Horseman smiled at her shudder. 'No.'

'Could I take back the Fisheries property? You know, his reports, the safety gear and so on? She might feel grateful and less defensive.'

'I doubt it. No, we need to hang onto that. We need evidence of murder, and you never know, some might be relevant.'

'Okay, then I'll apologise profusely for holding onto their property.'

Horseman thought some more. 'Ask Marisa whether the camera and computer belong to Fisheries or Jimmy. The data Jimmy collected belongs to them and they'll want that in due course. Don't say anything about murder though. As far as Fisheries is concerned, we're still investigating a mysterious accident.'

'Understood.'

'Where are Musudroka and Kau?'

She didn't consult her notebook. 'Kau's on surveillance at the wharf. Tani was on last night, so he's off duty now.'

'The longer they're missing, the more I'm worried about Santo and Filipo.'

'I'll try them again, check the surveillance logs too.'

He felt like talking to Shaddock straight away and was a bit put out when TTF reception told him that wasn't possible and gave him an afternoon appointment.

He needed evidence of *Joy-13*'s whereabouts at the time of Jimmy's murder. Surely Shaddock or the POSA staff had access to this data but he didn't trust either of them enough. His lack of expertise left him vulnerable to deception and they all knew it.

Suddenly, an idea struck him. There was another resource he hadn't considered—the Fiji Navy. He'd met Lieutenant Timoci Vodo at an inter-service meeting not long ago. He could trust a naval officer. He found Lt Vodo's business card in his top drawer and called. The navy couldn't be too busy repelling invaders, because the lieutenant invited Horseman to Walu Bay HQ this morning.

He paused at Singh's desk, looking through the louvres at the rain while she talked on the phone. When she finished, he asked, 'Any news?'

'No, neither Santo nor Filipo were seen getting on or off *Joy-13* in the last twenty-four hours. I'm still getting a phone-turned-off message when I call them.'

'How would you like to come with me to Navy HQ for a lesson in navigation? It's no good if I'm the only one who understands the instruments they use.'

'Great, sir! Oh, I don't have to go on a boat, do I?'

'I don't know. It depends where they keep their instruments. But I'm almost positive the boat will be stationary and well tied-up.'

She smiled, grabbed her umbrella and closed it. She took a small waterproof bag from her backpack and stuffed her notebook and pencil case inside. 'Ready?' she asked.

44

The naval base was just west of the Suva wharves, on the opposite side of the inlet of Walu Bay. Two grey, workmanlike vessels lay alongside the wharf.

A man about their own age was waiting on the veranda of the two-storey building behind the wharves. He came down the steps to shake hands.

'*Bula vinaka*, Detective Inspector. I'm pleased to meet you again.'

'*Vinaka vakalevu*, Lieutenant. It's a pleasure, especially as I've come begging.'

'I'm glad to help. I'm sure "improving inter-service relations" must be in a mission statement somewhere. Pleased to meet you too, Detective Sergeant Singh.'

'*Vinaka*. What are these ships?'

'You're looking at our pride and joy, and two-thirds of our fleet. These are Pacific class patrol boats, designed and built in Australia for Pacific island countries' needs. A most welcome gift. We have another based in Lautoka.'

'How are they used?' Singh asked.

'Search and rescue, surveillance patrols, and everyone's dream job, intercepting foreign vessels engaged in illegal fishing.'

Horseman couldn't think of anything diplomatic to say—just three small boats.

Lt Vodo seemed to read his mind. 'Clearly, not enough to patrol Fiji's EEZ of 1,290,000 square kilometres. However, the modern instruments you want to know about turn a hopeless situation into something very different. Come inside and I'll show you.'

A dozen men hunched over arrays of blinking screens in the surveillance room. They wore headphones and navy work uniforms. Lt Vodo stopped at one station. The man stood and saluted.

'Carry on please, sailor. These police officers want to see the plotters. We'll look over your shoulders,' Lt Vodo said.

The sailor nodded and sat down again.

Lt Vodo continued. 'This one is a ship plotter. All ships over 300 tons must carry an Automatic Identification System. The AIS broadcasts the ship's identity, position, course, speed and destination so that other ships know where they are. Whether you're at sea or in an office like us, you can see a map of all the ships sailing in the area. Zoom out, please.'

Horseman and Singh leaned in and saw little coloured boat shapes pointing in different directions.

'Fishing vessels are coded pink,' Lt Vodo said.

When the sailor hovered over a pink ship, the screen displayed its name, vessel type and company line.

'Switch to Ship mode now, please.'

The name of the ship they'd just seen on the map popped up, together with its destination, ETA, latitude, longitude, course, speed and vessel dimensions.

'Worth its weight in gold to you, I imagine,' Horseman said.

Lt Vodo grinned. '*Io*, that's why we're at work in here and not aimlessly patrolling. When we spot something suspicious, or a ship in distress, we can contact them by radio and find out what's going on.'

'And if the ship doesn't respond to your radio call?'

'Then we'll go say *bula* and assess what we find.'

'Suppose it's a clear case of illegal fishing, what happens next?'

'We need to board to be sure what they're up to. We secure their logbooks, GPS plotters and fish so they can't ditch evidence overboard. After that, we escort them to port and hand over to

Fisheries inspectors. The vessel owners are prosecuted and cop a heavy fine.'

'Do they pay it?' asked Singh.

Lt Vodo laughed. 'That I don't know, Sergeant. I hope so.'

'If they're foreigners fishing illegally, why would they care about a fine? What can any authority hold over them?'

Lt Vodo looked unhappy. 'I suppose you've got a point. The Australians are harsher—they often confiscate the illegal vessels.'

Singh nodded in approval. 'Good on them. That's a sanction even a pirate might want to avoid. Why don't we do that?'

'That's not my province, Sergeant. Fiji is a partner in several regional fisheries management treaties and of course has ratified the Law of the Sea Convention.'

'I bet Australia's joined up to all of those too. Anyway, sorry, it's not your fault. I'm just learning about all this and it makes me mad to think pirates can avoid all these laws. I wouldn't pay the fine if I was a pirate and could just sail away.'

Horseman looked at Lt Vodo and laughed out loud. 'You'd be a tough pirate, Singh. Please don't consider a change of career. You do much better as a tough detective.' She looked delighted.

'What range does the ship plotter have?' Horseman asked.

'Up to twenty nautical miles at sea level. Our patrol boats have these, of course.'

'Do longliners have them?'

'It depends. The big industrial longliners certainly do. But vessels under 300 tons aren't required to even have AIS transponders, so we can't see what most of them are up to. That's where VMS comes in.'

VMS was an acronym Horseman recognised. 'I think the assistant harbourmaster mentioned that. Words of one syllable please.'

'*Io*, POSA has access. VMS, that's Vessel Monitoring System, is compulsory for fishing vessels over twelve metres. Vessels can't turn it off because its purpose is to increase compliance with fishing regulations. Satellites transmit vessels' positions to receiving stations on land every two hours.'

'Who gets that data?'

'The port and fisheries authorities. We have our own receiving station here.'

'You what? Do you mean you can find out *Joy-13*'s route on Friday 8th September?'

'I can.' Lt Vodo looked puzzled. 'I thought you'd get it from Fisheries.'

Astonished, Horseman looked at Singh then jotted in his notebook.

'Fisheries didn't tell me about VMS. I guess it's not their fault— I didn't know what questions to ask.'

'Give me all the details before you go and I'll request the data for you—it's called a VMS track, by the way.'

'Wonderful. Our case hinges on this VMS track.'

'I'm sorry, but it'll go in a queue. But you should have what you need within twenty-four hours.'

'*Vinaka vakalevu*, Lieutenant.'

'Timo, please.'

'Call me Joe.' He was aware he was grinning like an idiot. But he was also beating himself up because his ignorance had needlessly held up the case.

'Have you any more questions?'

'What's the difference between the AIS ship plotter you showed us and a chart plotter?'

'Over here.'

Lt Vodo led them to a workbench against a wall. He pulled up stools and they sat in front of a small box with a screen at the front and control switches beside it, like a little old-fashioned television set.

'Every fishing boat that works beyond the territorial limit would have one of these. GPS has revolutionised safety at sea. They're getting less expensive all the time, too. It receives GPS satellite signals and overlays the information on a map, so the skipper knows his precise position any moment he cares to look.'

Horseman thought of Fireti Kaba, who fished up Jimmy Inia's head. He'd mentioned his GPS.

'Who sees this information?'

'Only the vessel's skipper or crew. Routes can be saved and fed into automatic pilots.'

'So, the chart plotter records where a vessel has been?'

'Sure, we seize them for evidence when we intercept an illegal vessel.'

'Good, I'm getting the picture now. How does this all fit in with the Port's surveillance?'

Lt Vodo looked surprised. 'Oh, they have their own ship plotting equipment with all the bells and whistles. Have you been to their control tower?'

'*Io*, I have, but I didn't understand what I was seeing. When I asked for information on *Joy-13*'s voyage, the assistant harbourmaster said he didn't have it. I guess I didn't know the correct jargon.'

'Sounds like he was fobbing you off. Of course he would've known what you wanted.' Lt Vodo looked perturbed.

Horseman was relieved to have his suspicions supported by the naval officer.

'Timo, do you have any handbooks for these instruments we could refer to?'

'Sure, I'll email some things to you. No trouble. And I'll fill in the form to access the VMS track. Sit here and give me the details.' He selected an online form on a computer and together they filled it in.

'We won't take up any more of your time. *Vinaka vakalevu*, Timo.'

'I'm pleased to help. Any question at all. Call me anytime. *Moce*.'

As they went down the steps the rain became a deluge.

45

Marisa, the coordinator of FOP, greeted Singh with a wary smile. She was right to be wary, for on their last visit she'd as good as admitted that she knew little about where her observers were and how they fared. Singh agreed with the boss's view that FOP's care of its employees—well, contractors, was not good enough.

'I'm here this time on behalf of Jimmy Inia's parents, Marisa. I was the one who broke the news to them, just as soon as we found out the recovered body parts were Jimmy's. I'll never forget that afternoon. You'll understand how at first they couldn't bring themselves to believe the evidence. When they did, they entrusted me to return Jimmy's few possessions to them. I promised them I would do that personally. I'm sure you've spoken to Jimmy's parents since.'

Marisa's face froze but her eyes filled with tears. Singh hoped they were tears of shame.

'No? Well, when you do, you can check their instructions to me.' She couldn't help rubbing Marisa's face in her mess.

'We have retrieved some of Jimmy's possessions, but some personal items are missing, including his wallet, bank cards and mobile phone. I realised that he couldn't use any of these things on board *Joy-13* unless the ship called at a port during the voyage. I wondered if observers left items like this with FOP for safekeeping when they're away.'

'Not routinely, but it's possible, I guess.' Marisa was guarded, her first priority to protect herself from blame, from the responsibility she was paid well to take.

'I would appreciate you checking that.'

Marisa stared as if mesmerised, then snapped back to the moment. 'Yes, I'll do that now.' She swivelled to her side table and made a muttered phone call. She turned back to Singh. 'Jimmy's placement officer is following up your request now.'

'As the work of observers is so risky, I wondered if you require them to file legal wills?'

Again, Marisa stared for a few beats, before a wide smile cracked her face. 'Yes! I should have thought—why didn't I? I know that perfectly well. We do! Honestly, Jimmy's death, when we learned that his head and hand—well. It was such a shock to us all here. Traumatising, actually. I pray for his family.'

What a shame Marisa was too traumatised to do her job, to respect Jimmy's parents. Singh had no sympathy for any FOP staff.

'His family need his will to carry out his wishes. Does the coroner need it for the inquest?'

'I don't know. I will look into that. This has never happened to us before, so there's not quite an agreed procedure in place…'

'I assume there is an insurance policy to compensate employees, sorry, contractors, who die at work?'

'Well, certainly for employees, I'm not certain about fishing observers.'

'What about his salary or whatever you call it here, his other entitlements, expenses and so forth. Have they been paid?'

'You'll really need to speak to Human Resources about all of that.'

'I'm a police officer. I'm asking you as Jimmy's program coordinator, to give me any possessions of his, a certified copy of his will, and information about the money he's entitled to and when it will be paid. I don't want to be rude, but you have known he's been dead for ten days. Surely I don't need a search warrant to get a government department to cooperate with the police and the parents of their dead employee?'

Marisa seemed to pull herself together at this. 'Of course. Would you like to come back in say, around two hours?'

'No, I have another appointment later. I'll wait here, thank you.'

'Um, certainly. Would you take a seat at the coffee table? I'll organise refreshments.' She made another muffled phone call and darted from the room.

Singh surprised herself by the sincerity of her annoyance. Usually she harassed interviewees purely as a tactic to get results. Rarely did she feel angry with them. But she felt angry today.

However, the afternoon tea tray of juice, coffee, and buttered scones mellowed her. She needed this break and resolved to be more pleasant to Marisa, who seemed to be out of her depth rather than lazy or uncaring.

Marisa returned and introduced Siale, the Human Resources Manager.

He looked concerned, as if he was a doctor. 'Sergeant Singh, Jimmy's death has affected us all. You more than most. I understand that you retrieved his remains.'

He shook his head in sorrow. He had a soothing manner—clearly forewarned about Singh.

He opened a large envelope with the Fisheries logo. 'Here is the copy of Jimmy's will for you, also his bank account numbers and the debit card he authorised us to use while he was on an observer assignment. Only on his specific instructions, you understand.'

He pulled out other papers, laying them in front of Singh. 'This is a list of his payments owing from us, and his entitlements following his death while on duty, which will be paid into his account soon. We are holding none of his possessions other than the debit card.'

Singh was grateful for Siale's quiet competence. 'I will call Jimmy's parents and give them this information. I promised them I would. However, it would be kind if you—'

'Don't worry. I'll make sure one of us here, probably Marisa or me, visits his parents and explains everything to them. We will also express our appreciation for Jimmy's work. You can rely on that.'

'Thank you, Siale. That will help them, I know.'

She shook hands with them both. Marisa's eyes brimmed with tears again. Maybe the woman *was* traumatised. They both looked very concerned. Perhaps they were right and everyone connected with Jimmy was traumatised. Even herself. Had she been wrong to dismiss the idea of trauma as self-indulgent? But she didn't have time to think about that, nor was it her way. She must visit the Australia and New Zealand Banking Group.

46

Horseman waited for Singh at Arabica. The loftiness of the old spice warehouse, the century-old hardwood columns—all this reassured him that some good things lasted. He could focus better on the alarming developments in the case. He hoped Singh had turned up something.

But her half-smile when she came in didn't promise good news.

'Your phone call was enigmatic, Singh. I'm on tenterhooks.'

'I couldn't speak freely at the bank. But you first, sir. Was Shaddock any use?'

'You should have seen his face when I told him Yee was a ranking triad. Genuine shock. And he was pleased he'd been useful. Without his help, we still mightn't know that bastard's name. I couldn't trust him completely but I reckon he's basically law-abiding. He'll always be torn between his loyalty to Fiji and his foreign clients. That's unavoidable. But he promised to try to locate Santo and Filipo. Not that he expects to succeed. Said he hadn't seen them since he visited *Joy-13* last Thursday to give us a tour.'

'Heavens, was that a week ago?'

He nodded, inhaling the aroma from the coffee ovens. 'Does that smell do you good, too?'

Singh rolled her eyes. The waiter brought her long latte and his second espresso. Singh added sugar and stirred with care.

A few moments later the waiter returned with plates and a basket lined with a white cloth. 'My mother's just dropped these in, fresh from the oven. Rock cakes.' He opened the cloth with a flourish. The cakes were golden brown and erupting with sultanas.

'*Vinaka vakalevu*, your mother knows what I need.' He took one and bit into it. 'Mm, nothing beats good home baking.'

'*Vinaka.* I had afternoon tea at Fisheries, but I've got to sample these,' Singh said.

Horseman said, 'I'm guardedly optimistic the VMS track we've ordered from the navy will close the case. Our only chance is to pin the location of *Joy-13* during those hours when Jimmy must have been killed.'

Singh's face lengthened. 'Then the VMS track is the only way.'

'*Io*, barring a confession, but we're not going to get that. I wonder what the Chinese team are doing, if anything.'

Singh shrugged. After a few moments she said, 'You eat your cake up. My afternoon was more enlightening than yours, but not in a good way.'

He popped a piece of cake into his mouth and gestured for her to continue.

'First up was the FOP. I think Marisa now realises Jimmy and the other fishing observers haven't been well protected. Siale from their personnel section came in and explained Jimmy's entitlements following his death on duty. He assured me that he or Marisa will go to see Jimmy's parents and express their appreciation for his work. I hope so. He gave me Jimmy's bank details and a copy of his will, which is interesting. He left one-third of his estate to Salome and two-thirds to his parents.'

'I'm glad Salome will get something. Her plan to start a sewing business won't be easy without Jimmy's support.'

'She'll get rather more than something, sir. I've just been to the ANZ bank manager who was keen to help. Take a look at these statement printouts.' She dived into her backpack and fished out a plastic sleeve.

He stared at her when he saw the bottom line—a little under one hundred and forty thousand dollars.

'So, with his insurance pay-out, neither Salome nor his parents need to go without. Take your time to go through the five years of statements, sir. The earliest page is at the back, starting with three hundred and twenty-one dollars. It's easy to see when the corruption started—three years ago. You'll notice the FOP payments identified. Then the cash deposits start—different amounts, irregular but steadily increasing in size. I got a shock. I mean, we know nothing about him really, but because of how he died—' She clapped her hand over her mouth.

'*Oi lei!* I know. Odd isn't it.' He reached out and patted her arm. 'His terrifying death cast us as his avengers. Once I found out about fishing observers and the risks they take, I've looked on him like a soldier who sacrifices his life for the good of his country. What a turnaround! A hero's feet of clay exposed in ANZ bank statements. Give me a minute or two, please.'

He never regretted his two years of university accountancy studies. He'd found the subject deeply unsatisfying, but the ability to understand financial data was useful to a detective. As he expected, he agreed with Singh's conclusion.

'Do you think there could be another explanation?' He could tell she was anxious for him to find one.

He threw his hands up. 'Anything's possible, but no. For now, we'll assume he was accepting corrupt payments in cash and depositing them over the counter when he got back to Fiji.'

'I remember he gave his parents money when he visited—fat envelopes, his mother said.'

'Did he? It all fits. Salome told me how well-paid fishing observers are.'

'How did it start? Did a captain offer him a bribe to overlook some breach of regulations and it got to be a habit?'

'It would be good to know, but it's not necessary.'

She shrugged. 'He could have been threatened. Maybe he had little choice.'

'I can believe that happening once or twice. But these payments are consistent. They're irregular because his assignments could be anything from a few days to more than a month. But there are so many over the last two years it looks like they became routine.'

'You mean he started demanding them? Like blackmail?' Singh asked.

'Probably. That's what it looks like to me.'

'Then why was he killed on *Joy-13* if he was happy to be paid off for the last three years?' Singh asked.

'Good question.'

Singh frowned. 'Was there something he wasn't prepared to overlook?'

'Possibly the people smuggling,' he replied. 'When are we going to hear from Tani? Kau will be coming off surveillance in an hour but he'll need to rest. It's up to you and me, Singh. First, how about you tell Jimmy's parents about his will? They know you and would be glad to hear the news from you.'

'Yes, I'll do that. Thanks, sir.'

'I'm going to call Salome. I think she deserves her good news sooner rather than later.'

'Right, sir.'

Horseman puzzled over Singh's attitude to Salome. As a woman, wouldn't she be sympathetic to her sad story and her desire to leave her vicious milieu for good? She didn't seem to be—she was neutral bordering on frosty.

Salome picked up his call. '*Bula vinaka*, Joe. Have you got any news for me?' She sounded fearful.

'*Io*, Salome. I'd prefer to talk to you in person. Can you suggest a convenient place to meet me? I can come straight away if you're free.'

'That would be good, Joe. I would like to talk to you, too. I'm in the Carnegie Library now. Could you come here?'

'Sure. See you in fifteen minutes.'

47

The rain had vanished and the atmosphere was steamier. It only took Horseman ten minutes to get to the grand old library building on Victoria Parade. It was packed out with school children doing homework. He spotted Salome in a nook between a row of shelves and the side wall, furnished with two chairs and a tiny desk. He shook hands briefly and sat at the table.

Salome spoke softly. 'I think it will be safe here. We can whisper. The school kids rushed in just after you phoned. I forgot about the time. It was quiet before.'

'It's fine, Salome. A good idea. But tell me what's happened. Are you worried you're not safe?'

'*Io*, Joe. A few times now, I've noticed a Chinese man watching me. Not secretly. He appears ahead of me, stands and stares, sneering and making obscene gestures. It's awful. I daren't walk past. After a minute he walks off and disappears. And, twice now, I've seen a Fijian boy with him.'

'Do you know who the Chinese man is?'

'No, but he looks hard as nails. Rough. A fighter. My guess would be he's in a gang running a protection racket. I think he's trying to scare me off.'

Horseman tried to look cheerful. 'I'll look into this, Salome. But I've come to bring you some better news. Jimmy left a will. Fisheries require all the fishing observers to do this. Sergeant Singh got a copy this afternoon. Jimmy must have been an excellent saver, his bank account balance is more than healthy. An insurance sum and his other entitlements from Fisheries will be paid into his account before too long. The good news is that he left one-third of his property to you and the remainder to his parents. You will inherit many thousands of dollars. You'll have to wait a while for it, maybe months, because there'll be an inquest into his death.'

Salome's mouth opened. She shut it again and looked away. 'I didn't know this, Joe. I just wanted some keepsakes of him, that's all.'

'It's clear Jimmy wanted to look after you if his life ended. That means he agreed with your plans and wanted you to carry them out. Please, Salome, I urge you, live on your own savings until you receive his legacy. Give up your work now and forever, right this minute. Stay in your cousin's garden flat and go out as little as possible. I believe you are in danger from evil men who see your independence as a bad example for their slave girls. They've come to Fiji to control prostitution and they'll stop at nothing. You can't win against them. It's time for you to retire. Your daughter needs you alive.'

'I know you're right, but—'

'I mean it, Salome. You must make do without Jimmy, but you will have his money before long to set up your sewing business. Your daughter cannot do without you.'

All the vitality drained from the thirty-year-old prostitute's face. A yellowish bruise on her cheekbone was obvious. She looked grey and beaten. No longer in denial, no longer pretending. '*Io*, Joe, you're right. I will do as you say.'

'I'll see you into a cab now.'

He called taxi driver Livai Yayawa on his mobile, walking along the row of shelves as he did so. 'Livai, there's a lady with me who's suffered a bereavement. Can you come to the Carnegie Library and take her home please?'

'*Io*, Josefa. For you, ten minutes, traffic permitting.'

'I'll give you the address when you arrive. Please accompany her into her flat behind the house and make sure she locks the door. An

Asian man has been harassing her. She's upset. Please take no notice
if she asks you to drop her somewhere else. I know I can rely on
you. I'll pay you in advance. Please call when you pull up outside the
library and I'll escort her out.'

'*Vinaka*, Josefa, I'm a veteran of the Fiji Infantry Regiment. You
can rely on me.'

When the taxi arrived, Horseman put Salome into the back seat
and said goodbye. She gasped as he closed the door. He glanced
around and met the scowling stare of an Asian tough, two metres
away on the footpath. Salome was right to be afraid. The man
smirked and stepped aside, allowing him to see Tevita trembling
behind him.

No time to think. He hurled himself at the man in a flying tackle,
swept him off his feet, pinned him to the ground. The tough
struggled, flailing, kicking, wild. Horseman punched him hard on the
jaw, rolled him over, pulled his cuffs from his pocket and snapped
them on. A traffic cop came running across the road. 'Guard him,
officer. I'll radio for a vehicle to pick him up.'

That job done, he looked around for Tevita. He'd gone. 'Did you
see the boy with my prisoner? Did you see where he went?'

'*Io*, he's a bad lot that one, sir. Used to be a shoe-shine boy, rough
but nice enough. The last week I've seen him hanging around with
that Chinese pimp. What's he doing here? He should be deported.'

'Where did the boy go?'

'Ran round the back of the library. He'll be hiding, I'd say.'

'*Vinaka*, man. Stay until the vehicle comes.'

'*Io*, sir.'

'I should have remembered you traffic cops know exactly what's
happening on the streets. *Vinaka.*'

A pimp, eh. It had felt so good punching the bastard—for
Salome, for Fiji, but mostly for Tevita. When the pimp moved to
expose Tevita to Horseman, he saw first bravado, then fear on the
kid's face. Where were his huge smiles and happy shouts of
welcome? Evil was corroding him already.

A small door at the back of the building was slightly ajar. Horseman lowered himself to the ground, opened the door and stuck his head into the crawl-space beneath the ground floor.

He tried not to sound angry. 'Tevita, you're in here, I know. Please come out so we can talk.'

Silence.

'Tevita, your Chinese friend is on his way to the lockup. He can't hurt you. Please come out.' He waited a full minute.

'Tevita, you do realise you're sacked from the Shiners, don't you? For working with a very bad criminal. Come out and tell me all about it and maybe I can let you join the team again. No one will know what you did except us.'

After a bit he heard a scraping in the dry dirt. Tevita crawled out. Tears gouged shiny tracks down his dusty face. He sat beside Horseman, copying his posture, leaning his back on the warm stone wall and stretching his legs in front of him. The boy's deeply scarred arms and legs softened Horseman's anger. With a childhood marked by violence and neglect, the kid had no one good to guide him.

'What happened, Tevita?'

The boy sniffed and wiped his face on his T-shirt. 'Joe, when I tell you about boat leaving *Joy-13*, you angry with me. I tell you I see ladies in boat but you no believe me. You say not to go near wharf or *Joy-13*.'

'That's because it's dangerous. I don't want you to get hurt trying to help me. That's not right at all.'

'You angry, so I didn't tell you all that happen, Joe.'

'Tell me now, Tevita. I'm listening.'

'Small boat head west, paddle slow, so I follow. It goes up Walu Creek, way, way up. Creek is shallow, but rubber boat can go okay. Ladies and one man get out and crew paddles boat back down creek. People walk to road and get in van. Van driver, he see me and tell me to come. He is more angry than you, Joe. He make me get in van and we drive to house.'

'Was he the same man you were with now? The one I punched

and handcuffed? The one who is now in the lockup?'

'*Io*, Joe. Same man! Mr Lee!'

'When we get to house, all ladies go inside. That house is their new home in Fiji. Mr Lee, he hit me but not so bad. He ask me what I do, if I go to school, if I work, can I speak English. Then he says he needs strong boy like me who can speak Fijian and English. Help him look after ladies. Men customers come to, you know, with ladies, pay big money. I can be guard, he show me other things. He say if I work well, I can have free turn with ladies, too.' He grinned, nudging Horseman, who shivered.

'You've been working with Lee one week now? Has he paid you?'

'Not yet, Joe. But I have bed in house, just mattress. But okay. I get free food there. Ladies are kind. I teach them Fijian words, English words too. Mr Lee don't hit me anymore. When we go to town, Mr Lee buy me food, too. He give me this T-shirt!' He wiped his face on the second-hand garment again, brightening. Tevita had experienced such misery in his short life that the gift of an old T-shirt was a cause for celebration.

'Tevita, if you want to belong to the Shiners team again, you must come with me now. We'll get a cab to this house, you will get your bag and I'll take you back to Pita's uncle's house. Can you still stay there?'

Tevita shrugged. 'I still got my shoe-shine box there and some things, all in bag. I dunno about bed.'

'I'll come in with you and talk to Pita's uncle. You can't stay in the ladies' house any longer, Tevita. They are very bad men there and those ladies are like slaves. They are no more to Mr Lee than your shoe-shine box: just tools to earn money. What they do is against the law and I don't want you there when the police come to check. You could end up in the lock-up too.'

'Okay, Joe. Can I play in Shiners now?'

'*Io*, if you do what I say. I asked you what grown-up work you wanted to do. Have you thought about that?'

'*Io*, but I can't decide. Maybe driver—bus driver, taxi driver?'

'You're not old enough yet, Tevita. I'll think of something.' Even if he gave up his brothel job to be in the Shiners, the boy would soon be recruited into some criminal life. Horseman suspected Tevita had no choice about the brothel job, but the boy cooperated because it provided him with a home.

'We'll go now. Come along.' Tevita willingly followed him back to the street. They were in the cab, Tevita giving directions, when Horseman's phone buzzed.

It was Singh. 'I heard you had a punch-up in Victoria Parade.'

'That's a vicious rumour. I subdued my prisoner who resisted arrest.'

'Glad to hear it. Who's the prisoner?'

'Probably one of the triads running brothels here. The women of *Joy-13* were taken to his house. I'm heading there now.'

'Sir, you need backup.'

He wasn't going to wait but wanted to reassure her. 'I won't go in. Tevita's been staying there, but he's going to collect his things and come with me.'

'Can't wait to compare notes. Musudroka rang. He's with Santo. Santo wants to tell his story, but he's scared. Can he stay in the lockup until he can fly back to the Philippines?'

'What about Filipo?'

'Santo says he hasn't seen Filipo for days.'

'We'll work something out for Santo. Get him in quick. Ask the super for advice. Keep me posted. I expect to be back within an hour, but it's dicey at the moment.'

'Good luck, sir!' He'd need that.

48

Horseman tapped on the interview room door and went in. Singh and Musudroka sat opposite a worried Santo.

'Excuse me for interrupting, officers. I'm very glad to see you here, Mr Santo. We've been worried. Please continue, Detective Sergeant.'

'Were you in the taxi with Filipo Moreno in the early hours of last Sunday morning, when he left his passport behind?' Singh asked.

'No, I wasn't with him that night and I haven't seen him since. I didn't know he lost his passport.' Santo sounded certain.

Singh persisted. 'As second-in-command, you must have some idea of his whereabouts.'

Santo shook his head. 'I've checked his cabin, asked around, called his mobile—no result. I'm anxious about him.'

'Is this the first time that Yee has brought women on board from a carrier on the high seas?'

'No. Several times before. But not every trip. Only sometimes.'

'I'll ask you to write a statement with details afterwards. Can you estimate the dates and how many women came on board each time?'

Santo thought for some moments, then nodded. 'Roughly, yes.'

'Did you witness Jimmy Inia fall overboard?' Singh continued.

'No, I didn't.'

'When did you find out about it?'

'I found out Jimmy was missing when Filipo alerted me. I got the crew to search the ship. Later, Captain Shen asked me to retrace our route to look for him.'

'Did you do that?' she asked.

'Of course, it was an order. I was very upset. Filipo told me Jimmy's life jacket and PLB were still in his cabin. Overboard in the dark, you don't have much chance without them. I didn't learn what really happened until Filipo told me hours later.'

'Did Filipo see Jimmy go over the side?' Horseman asked.

Santo nodded, fighting to control his welling tears.

'It was some time after they finished processing. Filipo and Jimmy were resting in their cabin. He said two crew came in, asked them to go up on deck with them. Yee was waiting. More crew closed in, grabbed Jimmy. He struggled but there were too many of them. Yee was quiet but scary. Filipo knows some Chinese, but not enough. But he knew Yee was giving orders. The crewmen tied chains around Jimmy's wrists. Yee shouted at them and they threw him in. Then Yee shot him with a pistol as he kicked in the water. Until he sank.' Santo crossed himself again.

Everyone was silent for what seemed like minutes.

'You have a clear picture in your head for someone who didn't see any of this.' Horseman was a bit suspicious.

'Sir, that's because Filipo showed me the secret pictures he took on his phone.'

Singh's jaw dropped. 'What? He's got photos?'

'I told him he was insane. He took them through a tear in his pocket, so they're not that clear.'

Hope surged through Horseman. Filipo and his phone would close the case if only they could find them. He could see Singh felt the same.

'Did Captain Shen know about Jimmy's murder?' Horseman asked.

Santo shook his head. 'I don't know. We may have backtracked just for the VMS.'

'I don't understand,' Singh said.

'The authorities can look at the ship's track on the VMS. They can check if the captain really searched for a man overboard or not.

If Shen knew what happened to Jimmy, he could still create that record just to get out of trouble, probably.'

'Why did Yee kill Jimmy?' Horseman asked.

'I don't know. Jimmy was quiet and careful. Did his job.'

'How do you get on with Captain Shen?'

'He's a strict skipper. Needs to be. But he's okay. He looks after the ship. He controls the fishing well. He knows his job.'

'Does he look after the crew well?' Singh asked.

'He doesn't respect the crew much. But *Joy-13* is a big new ship. Equipment is up to date. Crew accommodation is good compared to most longliners. Only crowded when prostitutes come on board. They make the crew nervous too.'

Horseman could imagine the charge the women brought to the atmosphere on board. A mutiny waiting to happen? He thought of Captain Bligh forced into an open boat with the loyal crew so the mutineers could return to the women of Tahiti. Bligh Passage in Fiji's waters memorialised his feat of navigation. No VMS in those days. Bligh sailed to Timor with the aid of a compass and sextant.

'Why did you come to tell us Filipo's story now?' Horseman asked.

'I met Tani here near the cathedral last Sunday, as you know. Later I saw a priest, Father Berenado. I told him everything. He urged me most strongly to have courage to tell the police. But it took me a few days to find my courage. I'm concerned about Filipo too.'

'Many thanks. You've done the right thing. We're doing our best to find Filipo.' Horseman offered his hand to Santo, who shook it fervently.

'Please, sir, I can't return to *Joy-13*. I just want to go home.'

'You can stay in the lockup tonight and we'll make arrangements tomorrow. Detective Constable Musudroka will help you write your statement now and we can check through it together in the morning. We may need to ask you further questions after that.'

*

'Singh, I've got to report to the super. Come with me, you need to hear.'

They met the super coming down the stairs. '*Bula*, sir. I want to brief you on developments this afternoon if you've got time.'

'I can see from your face this is serious, Joe. Let's go to my office. You come too, Susie.'

Horseman summarised his afternoon's discoveries. Despite the revelation that Filipo had photos of Jimmy's murder on his phone, he still wanted to pursue the lead on Yee's people-smuggling operations. He could do nothing about that without the super's ability to liaise with the secretive Vice squad.

'Joe, you see this as urgent. I see it as an emergency. This influx of Asian prostitutes and proliferation of brothels in Fiji's ports will soon reach the point of no return if we don't act. Your intelligence is valuable and timely.' He smiled his half-smile. 'It more than justifies the force you used to control that pimp this afternoon.'

'*Vinaka*, sir. That was my pleasure.'

'I will put this before Vice immediately. And I won't put up with being kept in the dark any longer about the Flagstaff place you reported the other day, the other addresses too. Santo's evidence sounds crucial. Pity he wasn't forced to watch the murder, then we'd have a credible witness rather than hearsay.'

'*Io*, sir. I told him he could stay in the lock-up tonight. He's scared. I said we'd keep him safe until he can fly back to Manila.'

'*Io*, we can protect Santo, the poor beggar. Those arrangements can wait until tomorrow. Now, speaking of *Joy-13*, when you waylaid me on the stairs I was on my way to see the Deputy Commissioner. The Chinese detectives have completed their investigation already.'

'What?'

'*Io*, you heard right. The ambassador told him this afternoon they were translating their report into English for us. No doubt it will be brief. However, he told the Deputy Commissioner they concluded that Jimmy Inia fell overboard by accident. Furthermore, Captain Shen's failure to report the accident was understandable due to pressure to maximise his catch before offloading in Suva. They really had no choice, did they? So, no surprises there.'

Horseman nodded. 'I've heard of show-trials in China. This is a show-investigation. Before you chase up Vice, sir, there's the matter of Tevita.'

'*Io*, we owe that rascal quite a bit, don't we?' Again, the half-smile.

'A boy like Tevita can get seduced by evil. Just a bit of stick and a bit of carrot—overnight! Give him a grubby mattress in a brothel and he's content enough. He's had no upbringing, he has no moral sense—' Horseman threw his hands up.

'Rugby isn't enough Joe. Good, but not all a child needs. It's his hero-worship of a decent man—you, that has saved him so far. Just by a whisker. However, he needs more attention than you've got to give him.'

Horseman nodded glumly. 'I want to help him train for a trade. This afternoon he told me he'd like to be a driver. I wondered—'

'Joe, your own children aren't born yet, you don't get it. Tevita hasn't a clue, he doesn't think beyond tomorrow, I bet. He just wants to please you and he'll say just about anything to do it. Lucky for us, he's been truthful recently.'

'Sir, he's bright enough, can live on his wits, he's curious. I wondered if the police garage could use a boy to wash vehicles, anything…'

He tried to keep the desperation from his voice but failed. Singh looked at him, concerned.

The super lifted his grizzled eyebrows. 'Not a bad idea, not a bad idea. After those leads he's given us, we should help him.'

'*Io*, sir. He's staying with the uncle of another Shiner. A kind man, but he's full up with hangers-on. He said he can only give Tevita two more nights or his wife will kill him—kill her husband that is, not Tevita.'

'We can't have that, can we? Your concern does you credit, Joe. I'll have a word with the garages at the barracks first thing tomorrow. I can possibly get him put on probation there, with a bunk in the apprentice quarters. I won't forget.'

Relief flooded through him. '*Vinaka vakalevu*, sir.'

'Let's not count chickens, eh? Forget Tevita for now. What I need most of all is an SIO who's focused on closing this case. Right now that means finding Filipo and his phone.'

'Agreed. We haven't found any trace yet. I'll get on to Toby Shaddock again.'

When Musudroka returned from helping Santo with his statement, Horseman showed him Jimmy's bank records and talked him through them.

Musudroka was silent, a horrified look on his face.

'Now we know,' said Horseman. 'Jimmy succumbed to fear, to greed and so to evil. He paid the ultimate price. Who can say they wouldn't take that first step, through fear?'

'You wouldn't, sir,' Musudroka was confident.

The young man's trust touched him. '*Vinaka*, Tani. I hope to God I wouldn't. I know you wouldn't either. And as for Detective Sergeant Singh, she wouldn't even be tempted.'

Singh leaned forward, intense. 'No, they're unscrupulous bastards. I might agree to turn a blind eye if I was frightened, but I would submit accurate reports all the same. How could the skipper know what was in my reports if I kept them secure?'

Horseman wondered if she could possibly be serious. '*Oi lei*! I'm glad you're on the side of the angels, Singh. But when Fisheries prosecuted the skipper for those violations, he just might suspect you hadn't kept your bargain, don't you think?'

She smiled. 'There's my criminal future down the drain!'

They all chuckled, despite the horrors they'd just heard about.

'You two go home now. Tani, you're on surveillance from four in the morning. Get some sleep. Filipo is our top priority now—make sure you ask the other crewmen about him. Call me with any news. We'll meet with Kau and the super in the morning.'

49

His phone blared. He jumped up, gasping. Two o'clock in the morning. He must change his ring tone to a less alarming one.

'Kau, sir. Sudden activity on *Joy-13*. Looks like they're getting ready to leave.'

'*Vinaka*, Kau. They're leaving Suva?'

'Can't be sure but that's what it looks like. The crewmen are securing the small boats on deck, closing the hatches. Everyone's busy.'

'Has a pilot gone on board yet?'

'I don't think so, sir. I've only seen crew returning.'

'Have any of them seen Filipo?'

'They say no, sir.'

'Keep watching, write down anything else that happens, just as you have been doing. Don't try to interfere, Kau. I'll alert the appropriate people. Keep in touch with further developments. Well done.'

'*Io*, sir.'

He called POSA. The watch supervisor sounded understandably sleepy. He argued that because *Joy-13*'s captain had not notified the port or requested a pilot, he could not possibly be preparing to depart.

'Your constable is misinterpreting the activity he's noticed. He's not a seaman.'

He hesitated to disturb the super but he needed to put him in the picture.

The super yawned. 'I'll let the DC know in the morning. You make your own decisions on this one, Joe. Don't hesitate to update me if you judge it necessary.'

Horseman hoped the super could get back to sleep.

Next he called Lt Vodo and explained the situation. 'Maybe you can work your dream job this morning, Timo. How about a hot pursuit of a foreign fishing vessel?'

'We can't pursue *Joy-13* until she's slipped port without clearance. Should be justified if that happens. I'll call Command to start the authorisation process. Keep me posted. The POSA supervisor will probably wake up and check on the vessel, anyway. It's unlikely we'll be needed.'

'Could there be a problem with authorisation?' Horseman asked.

'If *Joy-13* takes off, it should be good. This is what the navy's here for. In the meantime, I'll get myself and a crew down to the base and start getting good old *Kula* ready. If I wait for the green light, we won't start for another hour after that, so…'

'See you there.'

The last on his list was Wes at Fisheries.

At half past two in the morning, *Joy-13* slipped her berth without lights, without pilot, without port clearance. When Horseman and Wes got to Walu Bay, *Kula*'s engines growled as they warmed up. Under floodlights, Lt Vodo directed a bevy of sailors as they adjusted mooring lines, unlashed the gangway, carried boxes on board, hoisted signal flags. As more sailors hurried through the gate in ones and twos, Vodo gave Horseman the thumbs up—HQ had authorised a hot pursuit.

Vodo ran across to them, mobile to his ear, and shook hands while talking. A moment later, he ended the call. 'Still rustling up sailors. We can't leave short-handed. Got to allow for *Joy-13* resisting our boarding party. Come up to the bridge and stay there.'

'Keep out of the way, you mean?' Horseman joked.

Vodo grinned. 'Don't want to leave you behind and there's no time to look for you! Don't touch anything, that's all I ask. Wes, pleased to see a Fisheries officer. Been on a boarding party before?'

'No, this is my first.'

Vodo's grin faded. 'Well, if *Joy-13*'s hostile, it could be best if you stayed on *Kula*. I'll assess the risks when we see how they respond.'

Vodo dashed back to the deck. The bridge was a hive of activity. A sailor fiddled with the radar, another adjusted the chart plotter, a third tested the steering, another wrote in a logbook with a pencil.

Vodo caught Horseman's amused glance. '*Io*, a 2B pencil doesn't run out of battery charge at the crucial moment!'

The crew's excitement was palpable, yet each one was intent on his task. Just the same feel as waiting for the *Go* signal before a big police operation.

At half past three, RFNS *Kula* departed Walu Bay in hot pursuit, under the command of Lt Vodo and a crew of twenty keen men. They all knew their jobs yet still checked and rechecked their gear. Their ear-to-ear grins and hyped-up chatter were contagious. The grey patrol boat looked robust to him, but not built for speed. But what would he, a mere landlubber, know?

Nothing, it turned out. Once *Kula* left the harbour and negotiated the hazards in Suva Bay, she accelerated and sped off after *Joy-13*, her engines throbbing with reserve power. Both vessels now appeared on the AIS screen.

Lt Vodo was at the helm. 'Good getaway. I'll crank up the speed while the sea's calm. When we get beyond the barrier reef, conditions will be rougher.'

'Can we catch them up?' Wes asked.

'Of course! We're faster. How long it will take, ask me in half an hour. I'll have a reliable estimate of their average speed by then. They're doing twelve knots right now, but I doubt they'll keep that up. We're coming up to twenty. I'll get us all fed and watered. We'll need our energy.'

Fifteen minutes later a sailor came up to the bridge with a box of corned beef sandwiches and bananas. Horseman thought of the meals Dr Pillai provided for the Shiners. The charged atmosphere on *Kula* calmed while the sailors munched on the job.

Lt Vodo said, 'You can have a look around *Kula* now if you like—go down to the mess deck. The crew will be glad to meet you.'

Sailors sprawled on the fixed benches on the mess deck, eating steadily, some watching a New Zealand rugby game on television, some playing cards. They jumped up, pumped Horseman's hand and welcomed Wes too. A sailor poured them huge mugs of sweet tea. Rugby was the sole topic for the next hour until a voice from the bridge directed all hands to check their equipment.

Horseman's stomach protested at the patrol boat's pitching so he was glad to get out on deck. The *Kula*'s lights illumined a tiny patch of inky sea. He'd be more comfortable if he could see the rolling waves as well as feel them. Clouds masked the stars. He was glad of the bright white naval ensign, the union jack in the top corner.

Wes's face was pale. 'I can take the roughest water inside the reef. But this—there's no chop, but I feel sick as a dog.'

'Me too. You stay out here. I'm going up to the bridge, check how it's all going.'

Lt Vodo grinned a welcome. He was enjoying this mission. 'We'll close on them in another forty-five minutes. That means we have to prepare the boarding party, decide how we're going to do it.'

'Will this swell be a problem?'

'Won't be comfortable, but it's safe if it doesn't get higher. If the wind stays below fifteen knots, we'll be okay. Do you know if they're likely to stop on my command?'

'No, but it could depend on Yee, the people smuggler. If he's onboard, he may prevent Captain Shen obeying your orders. He's ruthless.'

'You'd better get tooled up, then. You're the only one who can identify the lead actors. Unless your injury—'

'What, you'll leave me out of the action because my knee's a bit sore? No way! Tool me up, Timo.'

He snapped on the utility belt. A sailor demonstrated the mini-VHF radio, the extendable truncheon, the pistol. Horseman tightened the holster strap around his thigh.

'Foreign fishing vessels usually comply when they see the game is up. But not always. If your people smuggler's on board, that takes the risk to another level. You said he shot the fishing observer?' Vodo asked.

'We have only one witness, so it's not certain.'

'We're still in Fiji's territorial waters, so there's no jurisdictional problem if you make an arrest. If they stop on my command we'll launch our RHIBs—they're inflatables—and board from them.'

'And if they don't stop?'

'Then it's Plan B.'

Horseman watched on the radar as *Kula* steadily closed the gap on *Joy-13*. Lt Vodo passed his binoculars. 'You can see their navigation lights now.' White lights bounced up and down through the lenses. More lights flared on *Kula* as groups of sailors ran to their positions, some getting into a RHIB suspended over the side deck.

'God help us,' Vodo said softly.

Horseman looked up in alarm, then realised the commander was praying before the action, not reacting to disaster.

'Radio operator, tune to Channel 16 VHF and order to stop,' Vodo shouted.

'Fishing vessel *Joy-13* on my port bow, this is Fijian Warship. You are required to stop. I will board you.'

Silence. He could now see *Joy-13*'s lights with his naked eyes. When the swell lifted the vessel he could see lit windows. No radio response.

The radio operator repeated the order every few minutes until *Kula* drew level.

'The signals sailor will flash the same message with the Morse light,' Lt Vodo explained.

The radio order repeated at deafening amplification. Blinding spotlights blasted *Joy-13*. The longliner's sole response was to veer away from *Kula*.

'Idiots! Can't they see we're moving faster than them?' Vodo was frustrated. Clearly, he did not want to escalate the action. After interminable seconds, he spoke into the VHF radio.

'Gunnery officer, a rifle shot across the bows!'

A sailor stepped up to *Kula*'s bows, bright in the floodlight, loaded and aimed his weapon.

The rifleman was a standing duck. '*Joy-13* can see him,' Horseman said.

'That's the idea. I hope the sight of our boy with his self-loading rifle might make them stop.'

On the shouted orders of the gunnery officer, the armed sailor loaded, aimed forward of *Joy-13*'s bow and fired into the water.

The order to stop blared out once more.

More shouts from the gunnery officer, followed by a burst of rapid fire into the water.

'Time for the heavy 50 cal machine gun. This will make the boys happy.' Vodo said gloomily. Ear-muffed sailors manipulated the gun, maintaining its aim ahead of *Joy-13*'s bow as she veered sharply to port.

'Engage!' The noise blasted Horseman's eardrums.

Vodo's voice was quiet but insistent. 'Now, radio operator.'

The radio warning blasted through the loud hailer again.

'Fishing vessel *Joy-13* on my port bow, this is Fijian Warship— you are required to stop. I will board you.'

Silence, save for the throb of the engines, the rhythmic slosh of the swell and the call of birds attracted to the lights.

'No choice now but Plan B,' Lt Vodo muttered.

50

Lt Vodo was determined. 'We're going to get this guy. What's he playing at? We're big, grey, flags flying, guns booming! A hundred metres away. Sea state's up a notch, too risky boarding from the RHIBs in the dark. Nothing for it but a graunch.'

Horseman knew he'd find out what a graunch was soon enough. Now was the wrong time to ask.

'Joe, all eight boarders will go simultaneously, under my second in command, Peni. He'll look after you.'

A huge man stepped up and pumped Horseman's hand. 'A massed tank charge works, Joe. This is the plan. Four to the bridge, four to the engine room, take control. Seize the logbooks, chart plotter for Fisheries evidence, secure the engine room to prevent sabotage.'

Lt Vodo turned to Wes. 'Stay here for now. When we have control of *Joy-13*, a sailor will escort you across and protect you while you carry out your search-and-seize.'

As the breeze stiffened, the swell increased. *Kula*'s crew worked with a new fervour. Orders cascaded from Lt Vodo down the line. A RHIB hit the sea, one boatman aboard. Crew tied it off at *Kula*'s stern. Sailors hefted bundles of ropes and steel. Others stood poised, muscles tensed.

Kula veered further to port, closing the gap to fifty metres, twenty metres. A collision course! *Joy-13* gunned her engines, tried to pull ahead, but the *Kula* matched her pace and direction. A grating crunch of steel on steel shook *Kula*. Horseman braced himself, hung on hard, both hands. Again and again, *Kula* forced *Joy-13* to port. As the ships slowed to a halt, the drawn-out bashing settled to a grinding screech that set his teeth on edge.

Grapples and ropes clanged on *Joy-13*'s deck. Peni grabbed Horseman's arm.

'Ready, Joe. Jump on three. One, two—'

They jumped over the smashed guard rails. Seven others hurtled across with them. Immediately, the screeching stopped as *Kula* eased away, rolling on the swell. Peni, with Horseman in tow, led three roaring sailors up to the bridge. Four others disappeared below.

Screaming, the five burst into the bridge. Two moved to bar the doorways.

'That's Captain Shen at the wheel,' Horseman informed Peni.

Peni boomed at the captain. 'This is Fiji Warship. I am taking control of FV *Joy-13*! Surrender the wheel, Captain Shen!'

The three crew on the bridge cowered behind the chart table, but the captain stood resolute, or perhaps petrified with fear. He looked at Horseman, who addressed him in a normal voice.

'Captain, the chase is over. Is Yee on board?'

The captain looked at him, nodded slightly. 'Hold,' he gasped.

Shen stepped away from the wheel. Peni took his place.

'Thank you. Logbooks, please!' Peni shouted.

Shen's mouth twisted slightly.

'Peni, I've got to get down to the holds to arrest Yee,' Horseman muttered.

Peni looked doubtful. 'Go, protect Inspector Horseman!' he yelled at a sailor.

'*Io*, sir!'

They hurried down companionways and along corridors to the cavernous fish holds.

A door was open, letting out a blast of freezing air. A crewman in a padded coat and gloves passed up a large white bundle through the hatch to the deck. The sailor roared. The crewman, another bundle in his arms, turned around. It was Filipo—alive. Horseman couldn't stop himself smiling, so great was his relief. He ran through the doorway.

'Filipo—stop there!'

Filipo was shocked too. He stood still, puffs of vapour billowing from his open mouth. Horseman closed the distance and muttered softly. 'Slip me your phone, man. Santo's told us what you've got.'

He grabbed the bundle in Filipo's arms. 'What's this, man?' he yelled.

Filipo said nothing but slipped his free hand into his jacket. He passed his phone underneath the white bundle to Horseman, as if he was wrestling the bundle away from him.

Horseman whispered. 'Your passport's at Suva police station.'

Filipo nodded, then shouted, 'You find out!' He hoisted the bundle up towards the hatch where it was seized by reaching hands.

Horseman raised his voice again. 'You go up to the bridge now, man. At once!' Filipo obeyed.

He extracted his radio. 'This is Inspector Horseman in *Joy-13*'s fish hold. Crewmen are passing unknown objects through hatch to deck. Please intercept. Repeat, please intercept. Alert Fisheries Officer Wes on *Kula*. Over.'

'Joe, this is Command. *Vinaka*. I'll get sailors to the holds right away. Please don't take any risks. Anything else? Over.'

'Command, I believe crew are dumping some illegal product. Please try to retrieve the white-wrapped bundles and alert Wes. Over.'

'Will do, Joe. Over.'

'Command, I believe Yee is on board *Joy-13*. We're searching for him. Over.'

'Joe, I repeat, take no risks. Good luck. Out.'

Horseman dashed out in search of a companionway up to the fish deck. Around a corner he found one, almost a ladder. He grabbed the handrails and climbed as fast as he could. Half-way up, something crashed into him. A body, he realised as they both fell to the floor below. Bulkier and heavier than any of the fishermen. Rolling on top of the body, he pulled out his truncheon and held it ready to strike. The man must have fallen heavily because he lay still. Horseman eased off and turned him over. Yee. Could he be unconscious? The floor was steel, he might have broken his neck in the fall. Horseman felt chill. Glad too.

Yee erupted like a volcano, raining blows. Horseman flicked the truncheon open, warding off many of the vicious kicks to his guts, his head, everywhere. Yee was not fit, he knew. If Horseman could hold out, the man would soon tire. Then Yee started pummelling his face like a punching bag. Waiting for him to tire was not an option. He swung the truncheon up hard. Yee's yelp told him he'd connected. He had no idea where. The punches stopped.

He hauled himself to his knees, managed to open one eye. Yee whimpered, curled up in a foetal position. Having been tricked once, Horseman straddled Yee, sat on him hard, got a cuff on one wrist, then wrenched the other arm from beneath him and dragged it behind his back. Snap. Done.

'Yo Wu Yee, you are wanted by the Fiji Police Force for questioning about murder and people smuggling. I am arresting you onboard FV *Joy-13* within Fiji's territorial waters and taking you back to Suva for questioning.'

He levered himself to a sitting position against a wall and pulled out his radio. The casing was cracked but the red light came on.

'This is Horseman. Assistance required. I've arrested Yee. I'm at the bottom of a companionway on *Joy-13* leading to the fish deck. Please assist when possible. Over.'

Commotion on the deck above suggested the dumpers of evidence were being dealt with.

'This is Command. Joe, are you in danger? Over.'

'*Bula*, Timo. Not anymore. Over.'

'Great job, Joe. Help is on the way. Out.'

*

He was aware of being lowered into a RHIB, then winched onto *Kula.*

'I'm Joni, medical sailor. You're going to be fine, Joe. What was the last game you played?'

'Where's Yee?'

'Don't worry. He's under lock and key on *Joy-13.* We wanted you back here on Fiji soil, eh. What was the last game you played?'

'For God's sake, man. Twenty-one months ago. Hong Kong Sevens.'

'Good, Joe. Now, this might hurt a bit…' As Joni pressed and probed his battle-weary body, asked him to wiggle his toe, bend elbows and knees, a scything pain in his ankle made his head swim.

'You'll live,' Joni pronounced. 'That's good, right? We'll get you inside now, find you a bunk.' He wanted to refuse but didn't have the strength.

As they carried him inside, the grey horizon expanded. Day was dawning.

*

The next thing he knew, he was on a bunk. A worried-looking Lt Vodo was standing beside him.

'Where's Wes?' Horseman asked.

'Wes had a good op too. He retrieved some of the boxes thrown overboard—shark fins, processed, packaged, all ready for market. Then he arrested Captain Shen under the Fisheries Act. Wes is staying on *Joy-13.* One or two of the boarding party can help him complete his inspection. Maybe even the fishermen will help.'

Joni came in with ice packs for Horseman's face, ankle and knee. His whole body was shrieking in protest now.

'You could do with some pain relief, Joe.'

Horseman was about to refuse when he heard himself say '*Vinaka.*'

He stared through the doorway as the needle pricked his skin. The sky was now a grey wash. Seabirds circling astern flashed white in the first rays of sunshine.

Lt Vodo said, 'We'll get the RHIBs back onboard quick smart, pick up speed and then it's plain sailing back to Walu Bay. Should be in time for a late breakfast.'

51

It was three o'clock in the afternoon before all the players took their places. Extra chairs were brought into the interview room. Horseman was pleased that Sam, the young Suva Grammar School teacher, was the interpreter once more. He had no skin in this game whatsoever, no reason to bias his translation.

The Chinese Embassy requested that a vice-consul accompany Captain Shen. The super reluctantly assented, on condition that she did not speak. Singh, although disappointed to miss the sea hunt, was eager to play her part in the kill now the big fish had been landed. A uniform stood guard by the door, another outside. They awaited Captain Shen's legal representative.

Horseman's face felt as bloated as Jimmy's decapitated head but at least he didn't have to look at it. When he'd examined his face in a mirror his eyes were mere slits in misshapen puffy flesh. He sympathised with the others in the room who had to pretend they noticed nothing strange about him.

After four long minutes, the uniform ushered the solicitor in. Mr Mishra was fortyish, slim and alert. He shook hands with Shen and nodded to the others. He looked shocked at Horseman's battered and bruised face, quickly averting his gaze.

Did Mr Mishra's eyelid twitch or did he wink at Singh? Maybe he knew her. Horseman glanced at Singh while the solicitor sat, took a file from his briefcase and placed it on the table. Her face reddened, then the colour drained.

He waited for her to turn on the recorder and make the routine announcements. 'Can we begin, DS Singh?'

After two seconds she rose and pushed her chair back. 'Please excuse me. I'm unable to continue this interview.'

She looked at him. 'Sorry, sir, please replace me.' She walked out.

'Excuse me a moment, please.' He pushed himself up, grabbed his crutch, found his balance and squeezed behind chairs and out the door. Singh was leaning against the wall.

'What's the matter, Singh? Do you need help?'

She looked like death warmed up, as his mother used to say. 'No. I know the solicitor. I can't continue. It's a conflict of interest.'

'But—'

'Sir, I can make that judgement for myself.' She turned away, but not before he saw her eyes fill with tears.

He sent the uniform to fetch either Musudroka or Kau, whoever was nearest, to replace Singh. He returned to the interview room and apologised. Ten seconds later a breathless Kau burst in, shrugging on an oversized borrowed jacket. Could it be the super's? Kau was quick to recover, took over the recorder and made the announcements in a business-like voice.

Through the interpreter, Captain Shen repeated his story that Jimmy Inia fell overboard by accident. His own failure to report this was due to the pressure to fill his holds on their final fishing days before entering port. The need for interpreting halved the pace of the interview, giving Horseman time to worry about Singh's wellbeing and wonder about her relationship with the man sitting opposite him.

Mishra now spoke up. 'As you have heard, Captain Shen does not wish to change the statement he tendered at his previous interview on board *Joy-13*. As you know, a Chinese team of detectives arrived on Tuesday morning to take over the investigation, in line with China's duty as *Joy-13*'s flag state. The detectives were grateful for the evidence you had already gathered. That investigation is now concluded, and as a courtesy, I wish to submit their report, together with an English translation, as evidence.' He handed a very slender plastic envelope to Horseman. It felt empty.

'Thank you, Mr Mishra. Superintendent Navala has already told me about the Chinese team's conclusions. However, I will be most interested to read the full report in translation. Now I will continue my questions to Captain Shen.'

Mishra lifted his eyebrows in mock surprise. 'I submit that the report I just handed you answers the charges laid against the captain. How can you ask any further questions? The matter is beyond the jurisdiction of the Fiji Police Force.'

'I won't dispute that right now. However, the happenings onboard *Joy-13* since she has been within Fiji's twelve-nautical-mile limit are within our jurisdiction, whether the vessel is sailing or in port.'

Mishra looked wary but nodded. 'Agreed.'

'Captain, who were the twelve women and one man who disembarked *Joy-13* in Suva on the evening of Monday 18th September? To help your memory, they disembarked under cover of darkness by tender on the port side, not by the gangway onto the wharf.'

Mishra did not hide his shock well. But the captain did. 'I know nothing of this.'

'Come, Captain, that's not true, is it? None of these people appear on your crew manifest, but we have since discovered that they all boarded *Joy-13* from a carrier on 24th August, on the high seas, during a transhipment of fish in one direction, supplies and women in the other. We have also discovered that the man's name is Yo Wu Yee, aka Charles, known in several jurisdictions as a ranking triad member who runs smuggling operations using legally licensed fishing vessels.'

The lengthy translations bugged him, but during this interval he enjoyed the succession of reactions washing over Mishra's face: surprise, dismay, panic.

The interpreter rendered the captain's growled reply as, 'This must be a mistake. I have no knowledge of what you describe.'

Kau had been trying to put two and two together, flipping through the file Singh had prepared for the interview. He snapped open the rings, and at Horseman's nod, placed the photo of Yee in front of the captain.

'I first met Mr Yee onboard *Joy-13*, on Thursday 21st September, when you invited us on board for a tour and to receive your statement. I am not mistaken. I had a conversation with him.'

The captain said nothing.

'It must have made life onboard difficult when Yee brought all those women on board. I can imagine how the crew reacted to moving out of their cabins to make room. Not to mention the bad effect on discipline. No wonder they say women bring bad luck to a ship. They've certainly brought bad luck to you, Captain Shen. People smuggling is a very serious charge, much more serious than shark-finning or submitting false documents, like the false manifest, to the port authority.'

Again, nothing.

'Maybe it wasn't people smuggling. How much choice did these women have about a career in tropical prostitution? Perhaps the charge will turn out to be human trafficking, which is even more serious.'

Mishra looked aghast. 'Detective Inspector, I would like to confer with my client. May I use the police interpreter?'

'By all means, go ahead. Let the constable know when you're ready to resume the interview.'

He took Kau upstairs to the CID room where he was relieved to find Singh at her desk, working on the case file. 'Can you get us some tea, Kau?'

Kau left.

'Susie, I won't tell you anything about the interview unless you tell me how you are.'

'I'm fine. I just had a shock when Shen's lawyer turned out to be Mr Mishra.'

'Why is that?'

'It's not relevant to the case, sir. It's private, in fact.'

'Mr Mishra is conferring with the captain—I don't know how long they'll take. I hope he'll persuade him to give us Yee to avoid the people smuggling charge.'

'When I've finished this, what do you want me to do?'

Kau came in with their tea mugs. 'Can you talk Kau through your interview file first? He's doing well, but he's not familiar with how you want the images presented.'

'Yes. We'll do that now.'

Horseman went to his own desk to check his messages, praying the one that might close the case would be waiting.

*

Singh powered along the footpath, crowded with children just let out of school. If she didn't stride out she'd start shaking again. She'd barely got through coaching Kau through the plan for the interview and the presentation of evidence, especially Filipo's photos. She and Horseman had worked it all out together. How she wished she could partner him in this all-important interview, right now.

She couldn't explain how she felt when Brij walked into the interview room, not even to herself. Her senses sharpened, her skin prickled. Her insides were still in turmoil, off-kilter, bounced around as if a giant hand had flipped her upside down and shaken her. Now she knew what it was to be betrayed, she could understand what a powerful motive it was for violence, even murder.

Brij had charmed her, no doubt about it. She'd been flattered by his interest in her work. How long had he been retained by TTF, or *Joy-13*'s fleet owners, or whoever he was paid by? Had his whole courtship, three weeks of it, been fake—just a ruse to get police intelligence?

But that couldn't be right, Jimmy's head wasn't fished up until after they met with the matchmaker at her parents' place. She must have attracted him at the beginning although she always wondered why. He might have been simply nosy. Or maybe his interest in her intensified when she let slip some details of the case, out of her own desire to appeal to him.

She liked him, he was an intelligent, amusing date, but she didn't know him in any real-life context. And she knew, from the moment he winked at her in the interview room, they had no future. She would never forgive him that wink.

His wink told her he would take risks lightly. He'd jeopardise his client's defence to show the others he knew her. He said he didn't take his work too seriously, but she'd not believed him. How could a lawyer give his clients less than his best?

She'd been wrong: his wink confirmed that his profession was a game to him. It was a game he wanted to win, but still a game. Neither of them could help the way they'd been made, but they could never be happily married. Her conclusion filled her with such regret that tears rolled down her cheeks.

Another thing she was certain of—she would never tell anyone the full story.

52

At four o'clock Mishra told the constable the interview could continue. He, the captain and the interpreter were already seated and drinking tea when Horseman and Kau walked in. Horseman's expected email had still not arrived, so he asked Tani to monitor his computer.

After the preliminaries, Mishra asked to speak. 'Captain Shen has reviewed recent events on *Joy-13* and asks me to read his statement, translated into English by police interpreter Mr Samuel McLeod.'

'Do you agree, Captain Shen?' The captain nodded.

'Continue, please, Mr Mishra.'

'I, Bo Hung Shen, master of FV *Joy-13*, declare the following to be a true and complete record of recent events on board during a voyage of four months' duration ending in Suva on Friday 15th September.

On 24th August, while engaged in offloading tuna catch onto a carrier on the high seas, I received a radio message from *Joy-13*'s owner that Mr Yo Wu Yee, also known as Charles, would board from the carrier together with twelve passengers who would disembark in Suva. I knew Mr Yee as an inspector for the company who had boarded a few times before to conduct a spot check of the ship, the catch and the progress of the voyage. I did not want to take passengers as a fishing vessel has crew accommodation only, but this was an order which I must obey.'

'Yee brought women passengers on board before, didn't he?' Horseman asked.

'No, this was the first time.'

'Really? I have a reliable witness to at least two other occasions, in January and May this year. On those occasions, the women secretly disembarked in Port Moresby and Noumea.'

Silence. There was a tap on the door. The constable entered and handed Horseman a folded print-out. Musudroka appeared just beyond the open doorway, both thumbs up.

'How did Yee get on with you and the crew?'

'I was scared of him. He didn't have much to do with the crew.'

'Why were you scared of Yee?'

The captain shrugged. 'He's very hard.'

'Did he threaten you?'

'Not exactly, but he didn't have to.'

'Because you knew he was part of a criminal gang, a triad known for ruthless enforcement of obedience. He would kill anyone who got in his way.'

Silence. 'I had no choice.'

'Was the fishing observer frightened of him?'

'No, he didn't understand. He talked to the women. He took photos.'

'Where are those photos now, Mr Shen? Jimmy Inia's phone and other items were not in his cabin on 21st September when I collected his packed bag.'

Mishra interrupted. 'This line of questioning must stop now, Detective Inspector. We have established that the enquiry into the death of Semesi Inia is closed and was beyond Fiji's jurisdiction.'

'Ah, yes. Remind me of the reason for Fiji's exclusion from the case?'

Mishra gave him a searching, wary look. 'Primarily because his fall occurred when FV *Joy-13*, a foreign-registered ship, was beyond Fiji's territorial waters, beyond the twelve-nautical-mile limit. Therefore, it was the duty of the vessel's flag state, China, to investigate.'

'Good, we share that understanding, Mr Mishra. But it was a

problem that *Joy-13*'s logbooks and chart plotter data were denied us, on the same grounds. The police had no way of verifying the vessel's position without that evidence. Is that not so?'

Mishra nodded. 'I suppose so.'

'You don't sound very sure. I share your uncertainty. What a complex world international fishing is and what a complex law governs it! I say this to excuse my ignorance that the Fiji government has the right to navigation data from an independent source: the Vessel Monitoring System or VMS. This data shows fishing vessels' position every two hours and their tracks are plotted.'

He unfolded the print-out and placed it on the table facing the captain and Mishra. The top half of the page was a printed report; the lower half showed a line of coloured dots on a map.

'I could have requested this data through our Fisheries Department or the Fiji Navy once we discovered Jimmy Inia had fallen from the *Joy-13*. But I didn't know this.

'See the coloured circles? They show *Joy-13*'s course. Each circle has a time-print. The black line on the map shows the boundary of Fiji's territorial sea, the twelve-nautical-mile limit.' He traced the line with the end of his pen.

'You can see *Joy-13* moved through Fiji's exclusive economic zone, the EEZ, then crossed into Fiji's territorial sea here at 1500 hours on Friday 8th September. The fishing observer fell overboard after 1500 hours.' He tapped the paper with his pen.

Mishra spoke up. 'Inspector, I will call a break here. My client and I need to examine this data carefully. I submit that the scale of this paper presentation does not permit this to the degree necessary.'

'I agree with you, Mr Mishra. I will have this chart blown up to A-3 size straight away. If you give me your email address I will forward you the original message just received from the navy so you can zoom it out even more. I would like to see this too. I suggest we also read the expert analysis of *Joy-13*'s track—that's the first page of this document. Shall we resume at six o'clock?'

Mishra replied immediately. 'In view of the critical nature of this evidence, I request time to consult an independent expert to interpret the data. A realistic time to resume would be ten o'clock tomorrow morning. I will request bail for my client.'

'That is your right. Unfortunately, you won't be able to confirm the VMS track with *Joy-13*'s logs because Captain Shen threw them in the sea this morning. Similarly, *Joy-13*'s chart plotter data has been erased for dates since 7th September. Very well, we'll resume tomorrow morning, ten o'clock.'

Good. He needed ice packs, he needed rest, he needed pain relief. Let Mishra waste his time applying for bail for a ship's master who had slipped out of port without clearance and defied orders from a Fiji warship.

53

Singh didn't feel calm enough to contact Brij until later that evening, alone in her room in the sergeants' barracks. She didn't want to say anything she'd later regret; she needed to be in control of herself if nothing else. Besides, Brij was otherwise occupied in an interview room at the station. When she did pick up the phone, her hand trembled. She put it down again. She would email instead. That way, she would not betray her emotion.

In the end, after editing again and again, she clicked *Send*. She hoped he'd be totally occupied preparing Shen's case and wouldn't even notice her message until morning.

Two minutes later her phone rang. There was no point in putting off this conversation.

'Susie? I've just read your email. What is this?'

'I tried to be clear, Brij. What don't you understand?'

'I don't understand any of it. I mean, I accept that I gave you a shock when I walked in this afternoon. I realise now I should have warned you that I'd be coming. But I've been flat out trying to get my head around this case since I got the call this morning.'

'What call?'

'From Toby Shaddock at TTF—the port agents for *Joy-13*. The navy's never run a hot pursuit on one of his clients. He didn't know what to do.'

'How long have you been employed by TTF?'

'Not me personally, Susie. TTF retains my firm on an ongoing basis so we can represent any of their clients at short notice. Usually for breaches of fishing regulations—nothing major. It just so happens I've only assisted on one or two cases for TTF, so I have the least expertise. Just by chance, I was the only one available today at no notice.'

Maybe Brij was not the big-shot lawyer she had assumed after all. Thinking back, he'd never told her or even implied that he was. Maybe she wanted him to be one.

'A quick call, Brij—just ten seconds. Then I could have excused myself in advance. I felt so humiliated when you winked at me.'

'Oh, come on, Susie—just a subtle wink! I didn't have time to warn you and I can see now I should have done. I apologise. But how could I know you would take it so seriously? Leaving the room like a drama queen. Professionals with private connections are bound to run into each other in a town the size of Suva. We just behave as if we don't know each other and get on with our jobs!'

'So, winking at me is behaving as if you don't know me!'

'Susie, have a heart. I messed up due to nerves. You, the case. For heaven's sake, I just winked!'

'Brij, I wanted to avoid this strife. I meant what I said in my email. I've thought about it for hours. I liked you. Very much. But today I found out we're fundamentally different in our approach to our work and life in general. To you it's a game, to me it's life or death.'

'That's okay, that's fun! Opposites attract, don't they? I'm sorry I didn't propose on Tuesday—I wanted to, just couldn't summon up the nerve. I know now is not the right time, but give me a chance, Susie. Let's meet again in a few days or a week. This case will be all wrapped up before then, by the way the great star DI Horseman is going. He's steamrolling it along, taking no prisoners.'

'You say that as if it's a fault. He's committed to justice.'

'Come on Susie, he's a has-been rugby player—captain, no less. This is a game for him too. He simply cares more about winning than I do.'

Brij paused. 'Susie, you should seriously ask yourself why you won't leave the force if you have babies. Is it because you don't want to leave your heroic DI Horseman? Unconsciously, of course. I mean, are you sure you even want to have real babies? Or is that self-deception, too?'

'Brij, stop this, please.'

'If your boss is so perfect, marry him and have his babies, why don't you?'

Singh gasped.

'Sorry, sorry, I didn't mean that. Let's meet in a few days. I'll call you.'

54

Horseman was at the station early to prepare for the suspended interview. After the naval technician had coached him, Horseman felt comfortable about presenting the VMS data, but his grasp wasn't strong enough to be questioned on it. He'd called the super who agreed that Lt Vodo could present the data and answer questions.

He hadn't seen the super since Wednesday afternoon after Tevita had led him to the brothel housing the women from *Joy-13*. It seemed like a week ago. Or more.

'Good morning, Joe. I'm behind you.' He was knocking on the door when he heard the super's jovial voice from the stairs.

'Good morning, sir. Have you got five minutes?'

'Indeed I have, Joe. My goodness, I heard you got yourself beaten up again, but look at your face! Someone's used it as a punching bag.'

'Good description, sir.'

'And that plastic boot thing. What have you done to your knee?'

'Knee's not too bad. Just a brace. No, I cracked my ankle this time, but it's all straightforward. These fracture walking boots are the latest thing. The crutch is just for a few days until I get my balance.'

'Come in, come in.' The super was puffed.

'Let's have the good news, first, eh? Your shoe-shine protégé may have found his niche. I twisted the arm of our garage manager and Tevita started with him yesterday. Best to keep him busy and away from evil influences. The two hit it off, and Tevita's mustard-keen. He's thrilled to bunk in with the apprentice boarders, too. The manager understands his situation. But it's up to the boy himself, now. It's not your fault if he doesn't stick at it, Joe. Not your fault.'

Horseman's anxiety went down a few notches. '*Vinaka*, sir. That's so good to hear. I didn't make training yesterday afternoon, so I was wondering.'

'Next is the not-so-good news. My colleague in Vice congratulates you on arresting Yee and appreciates the intelligence about him and the brothels. Vice will take over that case now and incorporate it into ongoing investigations. My colleague assures me a major operation will break soon, so long as the brothel sharks keep on thinking we Fijians are a dumb lot. Keeping *Joy-13* at the naval base for a few days should help delay the story leaking to the media.'

'We're still charging Yee with murder, though?'

'*Io*, Joe. He's under guard in hospital. You broke his arm rather badly, you know. He's having surgery today—realigning the bone and some pins, I understand.'

'Neat telescopic truncheons the navy has, sir.'

*

At ten o'clock the interview room was even more crowded than the previous day. First, there was Lt Vodo from the navy, who had set up a large monitor screen on a trolley wedged between the end of the table and the wall. He stood beside his laptop that teetered over a corner of the trolley. He looked his confident self, but the jiggling cordless mouse in his hand hinted at his nerves.

As Horseman predicted, Mishra brought his own specialist advisor, Dr Smirnov, a GPS expert from the University of the South Pacific. Surely this was unjustified—Captain Shen must possess the required skill in interpreting navigation data. But his lawyer would use any pretended disadvantage to claim the police had not proceeded correctly and their watertight case could be thrown out.

In the adjacent room, Musudroka, Singh and Superintendent

Navala were equipped with headphones listening via an extension.

Once Kau had made the announcements, Horseman began.

'We need to be accurate about the whereabouts of *Joy-13* on 8th September. I gave you the VMS data printout yesterday, together with the analysis by the naval expert. Today Lieutenant Timoci Vodo of the Royal Fiji Naval Squadron will present it more clearly and answer any questions.'

Lt Vodo clicked on the screen and cleared his throat. He zoomed in to show a trail of coloured circles. 'Each circle shows *Joy-13*'s position, which is transmitted at two-hourly intervals from the vessel's transponder via satellites to receiving stations owned by the Western and Central Pacific Fisheries Commission. Let's zoom in closer to look at the boundary between the EEZ and Fiji's territorial sea. You can see the vessel fishing in the EEZ here—the circles are close together where the vessel slows for some hours as the longline is set, then slows even more as she backtracks to haul in, a ten-hour process. Then the vessel moves off quickly again in a south-westerly direction, crossing the twelve-nautical-mile limit into Fiji waters here at 1530 hours.' He traced *Joy-13*'s course with the cursor.

'*Joy-13*'s speed is ten knots, so she's not fishing at this time. But here, between 1900 and 2100 hours on 8th September, we see the circles overlapping again. The GPS coordinates show *Joy-13* turned and backtracked slowly for two hours but remained within Fiji's territorial waters. This is a fishing pattern, but the time is much too short for longlining.'

'Captain Shen, this pattern matches your description of your search for fishing observer Jimmy Inia, doesn't it?' Horseman asked.

The captain stared at the screen for some moments before replying. Sam translated. 'Yes, but I think I was fishing for bait at this point, maybe.'

'The same day and time that Jimmy Inia fell overboard?'

'I don't quite remember. Maybe it was on Saturday 9th that Jimmy's accident happened. My logbook fell overboard during the navy patrol boat attack yesterday.'

'Dr Smirnov, could you comment on this data?'

'Yes, er, well I do not have much to say. Lieutenant Vodo, his interpretation was correct. There is nothing ambiguous about this VMS track at all.'

'Can you confirm that *Joy-13* was in Fiji's territorial sea at 1600 hours on 8th September?'

'Yes, there is no doubt of that.'

'Are there any more questions for our navigation data experts?'

Horseman paused. 'No? Then thank you very much, Dr Smirnov and Lt Vodo.'

The two experts left, leaving the screen displaying *Joy-13*'s course.

'Now we've established that *Joy-13*'s position on 8th September at 1600 hrs was within Fiji's territorial sea, do you agree that Fiji has the responsibility as the coastal state, to investigate the death of Semisi Inia, the fishing observer on board, conduct an inquest, and if appropriate prosecute those responsible for his death?'

'If that was when his death occurred, yes. But how can you establish a precise time of death?' Mishra seemed genuinely puzzled.

One by one, Kau laid in front of the captain and Mishra the sequence of images taken by Filipo.

'For the recording, Constable Kau is displaying photographs taken on a mobile phone on *Joy-13* over ten minutes from 1610 to 1620 on 8th September. The date and time of each photo is recorded.'

They stared in silence at the erratic shots. It looked like a fight. No faces could be seen, but there was one pair of dark brown, heavily muscled Fijian legs in denim shorts, and several shorter, lighter-skinned, wiry legs of crewmen. Then they saw the body of the Fijian bent over a ship's rail, rough fishermen's hands gripping his arms and legs. The next image showed the Fijian's hands secured behind his back with chains. The next, the Fijian body hitting the water on his back. Then a swirl of blood in the water. There were no more.

Horseman said, 'We've just witnessed the murder of the fishing observer, Jimmy Inia,'

The interview room was deathly silent, all eyes intent on the images on the table.

'These photos aren't sufficient to identify individuals,' Mishra protested with little conviction.

Horseman was unperturbed. 'The crewman who took them is willing to testify. However, what the shots demonstrate is the precise time Jimmy went overboard, which was 1620 on 8th September. This cheap old phone doesn't have a GPS chip so it can't tell us where the shots were taken. However, the VMS track of *Joy-13* shows her position at 1600 hours was within Fiji's twelve-mile limit. Indeed, the VMS track confirms the captain's statement that he did backtrack for a couple of hours later.'

'Captain Shen, why did you pretend to search for Jimmy when you knew he was dead?'

The captain's weather-beaten face was resolute. The next moment his ramrod spine collapsed in a slump. He looked from Sam the interpreter, to Mishra, then to Horseman, his eyes full of the helpless appeal of a child. Then he started speaking to Horseman in a rapid stream. Sam had to keep interrupting him to translate.

'I was scared of Yee. So were all the crew. We don't know anything about him, except the company sends him to inspect. But I know he isn't a fisherman—he is too smooth, his hands too soft, but his nature is hard and cruel. We all suspect he is a triad. We hate him but we keep quiet to avoid trouble. When Yee and the women transhipped from the carrier, that caused trouble among the men. But I did what Yee ordered.

'Jimmy didn't understand. I saw him talking to Yee on deck, quite serious. That morning. I never saw him again. I was on the bridge at this time, but I can't prove it because I dropped the log into the sea when the navy patrol boat chased us. Maybe the engineer's log can prove it. But Santo did not return to *Joy-13* before we left Suva on Wednesday.'

He trailed off, then recalled himself and spoke rapidly again.

'Yee forced a few of the crew to help him. They told me later.

They were very upset. He ordered the crewmen to tie his wrists in chains and throw him overboard. Then he shot him as he struggled in the water. Terrible! I don't know why. Maybe Jimmy threatened to report Yee to you police for smuggling the women. I don't know. Yee ordered us all to say nothing, or he would shoot us too. He told me to return to the EEZ and fish for another few days. That suited me because my holds were not full. You will see where we went if you look over the full VMS track. We are all innocent because we had no choice.'

While Sam translated, the captain covered his face with his hands. Soundless sobs convulsed his body.

'Your client needs a rest, Mr Mishra. I'll send in some refreshments. DC Kau and the interpreter will assist Captain Shen to make a full statement in Chinese and an English translation. We'll confer with the Public Prosecutor and resume at four o'clock to lay charges.'

Horseman gave silent thanks that Jimmy Inia was dead when that tiger shark opened wide its maw and tore off his head.

EPILOGUE

Friday 13th October

Horseman and Singh waited for Dr Young in the Holiday Inn bar. The pathologist had promised he'd get a cab straight from the airport. His direct Sydney-Suva flight should have landed an hour ago.

'Do you think Matt will have caught up with the news of the Vice raids this morning?'

'Bound to. Even if they didn't make the Sydney media, the Fiji newspapers would be handed out on the plane.'

'It's news I've been hanging out for. I'm still mad Vice left us completely in the dark even though you gave them Yee and several brothels on a plate!' Singh did righteous indignation well.

'The fewer in the loop the better with that sort of op, Susie. What a success! Criminal charges against several ringleaders and dozens of exploited Asian girls will be sent home within a few days.'

'I worry about what's waiting at home for them though.'

'Still, that Vice result was worth waiting for,' Horseman said.

'Of course I'm worth waiting for, guys!'

Dr Young squeezed past Horseman's chair. He stood grinning at both of them, hands on hips. Horseman hoisted himself upright with care and shook hands.

'*Bula vinaka*, Matt! Good to see you. How's Sydney? How're your kids?'

'Sydney's overcrowded, mate. The kids are fine, doing their uni exams now. I can feel them slipping away—it's a bit sad. They'll be back here for Christmas, though.'

Horseman made a mental note; he must find a home of his own before Christmas. When a waiter brought their drinks, he said, 'Let's go outside where it's quieter. Sunset, anyone?'

The waiter found them a quiet table near the sea wall. Dr Young raised his Fiji Bitter. 'Drink up, Susie. You're looking much too serious.'

'I'm just wondering what sort of life those young Asian girls are going back to,' she said.

'What, are they being deported?' Dr Young asked.

The others filled him in. Then they drank without speaking for a bit.

Dr Young broke the silence. 'Mates, let's look on the bright side. Joe, you should have been in a balaclava since Yee bashed you up, but I can just about tolerate the sight of your ugly mug now. When the colours even out you'll be as near to presentable as you'll ever get! You're out of the orthopaedic boot, you've chucked away the stick. Not quite jogging yet, but you'll make it. Here's to you!'

They laughed and raised their glasses.

'Shen and Yee are both locked up and awaiting trial, aren't they?' Dr Young asked.

Singh looked brighter. 'Yes. Shen's charged with shark-finning, other fishing violations and failing to report a death at sea. Yee's facing murder and human trafficking.'

'I'm worried Yee will give up information in return for a deal on his charges. I'll be mad as hell if he gets off,' Horseman said.

The pathologist gazed into his glass. 'Speaking of hell, do you know the Greek legend of Hydra? She guarded the underworld. She had many heads and acid breath. Whenever a hero chopped off a head, two more grew in its place. I hate to say it, but that legend is bloody relevant to all this organised crime.'

'Damn true. It's an invasion Fiji can't cope with,' Horseman said.

'Is the fishing boat still here?' Dr Young asked.

Singh pitched in. *Joy-13* was impounded while we looked into charges against the owners. So far, nothing's happened. The Chinese embassy protested and the vessel sailed away with a new captain and engineer supplied by TTF.'

'A great pity,' Horseman added. 'She should have been towed out beyond the barrier reef and sunk. That longliner would make a wonderful artificial reef for Fijian fishermen.'

Horseman stared at the lurid swirls of purple, orange and red above the glittering sea. 'You know what old Ratu Cakobau said in 1874 when he ceded Fiji to Britain? Something about if things didn't change, um, yes, I remember—"Fiji will become like a piece of driftwood in the sea, and be picked up by the first passer-by." Maybe his prediction is coming true.'

'I dunno, maybe not. Fiji's independent now and has you two and hordes more good guys striving for justice. I'm a simple doctor. I deal with one case at a time. I can't tackle all the ills of the world. But I have my small place in these bloody lovely islands and I do a useful job.'

Singh nodded vigorously. 'That's a much better way of looking at things, Matt.'

'Man, you're right,' Horseman said. 'But until Shen and Yee are convicted I won't feel optimistic.'

'Come on, mate. You two have solved the most baffling case I've ever come up against. You're brilliant, both of you!'

Horsman needed to put on a cheerful face or Matt wouldn't stop. He smiled. '*Vinaka vakalevu*. Let's have another beer.'

They watched the sun dive into the sea until the waiter set their drinks before them. '*Vinaka*. Fish and chips for three, please. Out here in the sea air.'

EXCLUSIVE BONUS – DELETED SCENES

Would you like to know what went into the recycling bin?

I ended up cutting quite a number of complete chapters from the final draft of this book. However, I do rather like these scenes so I've clipped them together in a bonus booklet for you. Now that you've finished reading the book, I hope you'll enjoy these extras too.

If you're not already a Fiji Fan Club member, you'll be given the chance to join when you visit the link below.

Get your bonus here:
https://dl.bookfunnel.com/gm85aoclbh

WELCOME GIFT FOR

FIJI FAN CLUB MEMBERS

I hope you enjoyed this book. Like other readers of my *Fiji Islands Mysteries* series, you may have especially enjoyed discovering Fiji. I was privileged to live and work in Fiji in the first decade of this century. Indeed, my motivation to embark on this mystery series was to share my love for these beautiful islands and their inhabitants.

When I published ***Death on Paradise Island***, I began a blog which has evolved to include Fijian food, customs, history, sport…whatever occurs to me. I was so delighted with readers' responses, I compiled the best into a slim illustrated volume. ***Finding Fiji*** is a short, subjective collection of snippets that enrich members' enjoyment of the novels.

Finding Fiji is exclusive to *Fiji Fan Club* members, so I invite you to join us today. Each month, I'll write to you with a post about Fiji and the latest crime fiction promos. You'll always be the first to know about my new releases too. As a welcome gift, I'll present you with *Finding Fiji*.

Get your free copy here:
www.bmallsopp.com

GLOSSARY AND GUIDE TO
FIJIAN PRONUNCIATION

bula - hello
moce - goodbye or goodnight
moce mada - see you later
io - yes
vakalevu - very much
vinaka - thank you

Acronyms
DI - detective inspector
DS - detective sergeant
DC - detective constable or deputy commissioner
MOB – man overboard
SOCO - scene of crime officer
FAD – fish aggregating device
FO - fishing observer
WCPFC - Western and Central Pacific Fisheries Commission

Spelling
The Fijian alphabet is based on English but it is phonetic, so each sound is always represented by only one letter, unlike English.

Vowels
a as in *father*
e as in *met*
i as in *Fiji*
o as in *or*
u as in *flu*

Consonants

Most consonants are pronounced roughly as in English, with the following important exceptions.

b = *mb* as in me*mb*er eg. **b**ula = **mb**u-la

d = *nd* as in te*nd*er eg. **d**ina = **nd**ina

g = *ng* as in si*ng*er eg. li**g**a = li-**ng**a

q = *ngg* as in stro*ng*er eg. ya**q**ona = ya-**ngg**ona

c = *th* as in mo*th*er eg. mo**c**e = mo-**th**ay

ENJOY THIS BOOK?
YOU CAN MAKE A BIG DIFFERENCE.

As an indie author, I don't have the financial muscle of a major world publisher behind me. What I do have is loyal readers who loved my first book and took the trouble to post reviews online. These reviews brought my book to the attention of other readers.

I would be most grateful if you could spend just five minutes posting a short review on Amazon, Goodreads or your favourite book review site.

ALSO BY B.M. ALLSOPP

Death of a Hero - how it all began: Fiji Islands Mysteries Prequel

Meet young Joe Horseman. How much will he risk to save his dead hero's honour?
When Horseman finds his rugby captain's corpse in the changing shed, he vows to help investigate. But the police refuse to pass him the ball.

Read more... https://books2read.com/u/3Geqnp

Death on Paradise Island: Fiji Islands Mysteries 1

An island paradise. A grisly murder. Can a detective put his rugby days behind him to tackle a killer case?
Joe Horseman knows he'll have to up his game when guests at an island resort witness a young maid's corpse wash ashore.

Read more... https://books2read.com/u/mBP50k

Death by Tradition: Fiji Islands Mysteries 2

Must DI Joe Horseman sacrifice his chance at love to catch a killer?
Only 5 more days... Horseman can't wait for his American girlfriend, to join him in Fiji. So, when a young activist is murdered in the remote highlands, Horseman sets a deadline to crack the case. But he knows nothing of the dangers looming through the mountain mist.

Read more... https://www.books2read.com/u/4XKwy1

ACKNOWLEDGEMENTS

Many people helped me create this book. I owe enduring thanks to Mr Waisea Vakamocea, retired senior officer of the Fiji Police Force, who patiently answered my many questions when I was writing my first *Fiji Islands Mystery*.

Death Beyond the Limit is the richer for the expertise of Francisco Blaha, Fisheries Consultant, and Commander Piers Chatterton RAN. I thank them for their generous help when I was out of my depth and also for reading my final draft and advising me of lingering errors of terminology and fact. I am entirely responsible for any mistakes in this book relating to commercial fishing and naval operations in the Pacific.

I am most grateful to the expert professionals who transformed my manuscript into a real book. Author and editor, Joseph Nassise, gave me perceptive advice. Polgarus Studios designed and formatted the text with flair and Maryna Zhukova of MaryDes once more created a stunning cover.

As for the volunteer advance readers of Horseman's Cavalry who eliminated so many errors and told me how much they enjoyed the story, I can't thank them enough.

Finally, I thank Peter Williamson for his advice through reading draft after draft, his enthusiasm for my writing and constant support.

Made in the USA
Middletown, DE
17 October 2020